Did you miss MOSAIC 2010 ?????

MOSAIC2010 presents a collection of short stories and poetry by members of The Brooksville Writers' Group. Established in 1998, The Brooksville Writers' Group includes members who reside in Hernando, Sumter, and Citrus County, as well as some from farther afield.

There is something in this first volume of MOSAIC for every taste, from reimagined ancient tales to stories based on current events, or science fiction and ghost stories. Some of the them are delightfully charming, suitable for children, while others are definitely adult in theme. A couple of the stories, for example, Becker's *Winter Visitor,* are parts of a longer work. The variety of stories in MOSAIC reflects the diversity of the writers in the group.

Although the first print run of MOSAIC 2010 is sold out, you can find copies on Amazon.com in a second printing of the paper book, and as an ebook for Kindle or from Barnes and Noble for their Nook.

MOSAIC
2014

A Second Collection of
Short Stories *and* Poems
by members of the
Brooksville Writers' Group
Brooksville, Florida

International Digital Book Publishing Industries

MOSAIC 2014

Additional copies of this book as well as MOSAIC 2010
are available from Amazon.com and
other select outlets.

ISBN 978-1-57550-046-1

Printed in the United States of America
Cover Art by Johanna M Bolton
First IDBPI Printing

The stories in MOSAIC 2014 are original works of fiction.
With a few noted exceptions, all the characters and events
portrayed in this book are fictional, and any resemblance to
real people and incidents is purely coincidental.

THE BROOKSVILLE WRITER'S GROUP

Established in 1998 by Don Kafrissen, The Brooksville Writers' Group currently includes 18 plus published, self-published, and almost published members who write in a variety of genres.

The group welcomes potential members who reside in Central Florida. It meets in Hernando Country on the first Wednesday of every month to read and discuss members' work and anything else. (The refreshments are excellent!). This year they plan to host the first of a number of workshops for writers and aspiring authors throughout the state.

The Brooksville Writers Group welcomes everyone from beginning writers to published authors. For more information visit http://idbpi.wordpress.com.

Members include:

Marlene A. Becker
Johanna M. Bolton
John Boyle
Judy G. Burford
Christine Cock
Mary Cooper
Jerry Cowling
Joan Donohue
C.J. Goldman
Michael Goldman
Don Kafrissen
Sam Kafrissen
Dennis Pupello
Mary H. Sheldon
Al Svoboda
Jill V. Svoboda
Linda Welker
Karen Ann Wilson

Author biographies begin on page 260.

ACKNOWLEDGEMENTS

- *Monty Python Had No Idea*! © 2014 by Marlene Becker
- *New Neighbors, The Sweetest of All* © 2014 by Johanna M. Bolton
- *Anime Girl, Highland Woman, Triangle* © 2014 by John Boyle
- *Dungeon of Despair, Jumbo, Richard's Revenge, War Dogs, The Yard Sale Mystery* © 2014 by Judy G. Burford
- *All Cut and Down, Cranes Rising, Morning Ride, Reincarnation of an Acorn, Water and Light* © 2014 by Christine Cock.
- *Chocolate, Love Slightly Skewed, Wheels, Writers' Delirium* © 2014 by Mary Cooper
- *A Date for Thanksgiving, The Hunt for Sam Bass's Gold, My Dear Friend, Unus Spatus Terribulus* © 2014 by Jerry Cowling
- *The Pig Did It* © 2014 by Joan Donohue
- *The Cossack & the Swede, Love Story, Winter Woods* © 2014 by C. J. Goldman
- *The Carousel, The Lily of the Mohawks* © 2014 by Michael Goldman
- *Amanda and the King's Horse, A Small Dream, To Tombouctou & Back, A Warrior's Story* © 2014 by Don Kafrissen
- *Mac* © 2014 by Sam Kafrissen
- *King Willy* © 2014 by Dennis Pupello
- *Don't Yell, Run!, IRS* © 2014 by Mary Sheldon
- *Esperanza's Sorrow, Sparrow on Whole Wheat* © 2014 by Jill V. Svoboda
- *Group 1* (Hermit Crab, The Real Thing, Fish Quick, Mosquito, River Run, March Sky, Winter Drought, Shore Birds, My Love is Hid), *Group 2* (What's Ahead, The Best of Both Worlds, For Goodness' Sake, Picture Perfect, Christmas Down South, New Day), *Group 3* (It All Happened Before, Tattoos and Skin, Smooth Jazz, Young Man's Tune, White Collar Crime), *Group 4* © 2014 by Al Svoboda (Earthquake, Communication, Incident)
- *A Mayor for Catfish, Run Smitty Run, Sadie's Palace* © 2014 by Linda Welker
- *Anniversary, Karma* © 2014 by Karen Ann Wilson

International Digital Book Publishing Industries

INDEX

All Cut and Down

I have heard trees whisper
    among themselves about the weight of vines;
how scratchings by delicate birds

tickle and their nests tangle
    within branches; of fierce, amputating winds
from which there is no shelter.

I have heard trees moan and tremble
    as they thrust deeper into earth; felt fluids
rise; been charmed by rain trickling down

needles: by burls, fronds, and dangling moss.
    I have seen trees breathe in light
Offer it back as shade

And   still   we   make   them   beg   for   mercy

Christine Cock

Amanda and the King's Horse

Don Kafrissen

Amanda was very good with horses. All the king's men and even some of his knights said so. She had thought that after her father had gone off to the crusades with the mad monk, she would be cashiered and sent back to her father's village, but she found that she had a knack for calming and even talking to the horses. She had a nice little room off the stables, a soft straw filled mattress and a small desk with which to keep her records. Yes, she could even read and write, which was more than could be said for some of the knights.

Old Moses had taught her when she was a small child and he'd been the king's seer. Between him, her father and Jocaro, the court jester, she'd had a pleasant upbringing. Her mother had died of consumption when she was only three and the three men had all been family to her. The cooks had taken a shine to her and even showed her some of their secrets for flavoring and took her with them when they went to the forests and fields searching for herbs.

She was seventeen now and many young men coveted her. Some for her position at court, some because she was petite and quite pretty and some because she might, just might be a witch and, at these times, that was a favorable thing. Many years ago, when the church was strong, witches had been shunned and even driven from the kingdom. However, when Alferic, the present king, had come to the throne, he'd encouraged everyone to believe what he or she wanted and the church, though still a presence, was afforded little power. The land was at peace, the crops were plentiful and the cattle and horses fat. King Alferic was brother and half brother to two neighboring kingdoms and the three brothers took a similar view of the world.

One fine spring day, Jacob, the king's youngest son, came to the stables. He stood at the door to her room and politely knocked against the frame. She was startled for a moment then smiled when she saw who it was.

"Oh, hello, Your Majesty, can I help you?"

"Amanda, I've told you many times to call me Jacob, haven't I?" he said with a crooked grin on his hairless face. Jacob was a year older than Amanda and they'd grown up together. All the time they were children, Amanda had called him Jacob, but her father had cautioned her that when he was officially admitted to court, she must start calling him "Your Majesty." Her other fathers agreed and she'd only called him by his first name when they were alone.

Jacob strolled in and sat on the edge of her bed. "What are you doing, girl?" he asked curiously, looking at the papers she was writing upon.

She shrugged and said, "Just some bookkeeping, Jacob. Look, I'll show you." She moved over on her stool so he could fit next to her. She liked the feel of her thigh touching his. They bent over the papers and she pulled the oil lamp closer. "See, this is how many ricks of hay we purchased last month. The next figure is the number of bushels of grain we took in and the last is the number of horses we have stabled here. I have keep notes on how many of each feeding every horse has eaten and how many miles each has been ridden the past month." She looked at him anxiously, "Do you understand what I'm trying to do?"

Jacob snorted, "Of course. You're trying to figure out how many miles per bushel and bale of hay each horse has consumed." He smiled, his face near hers, "I'm not stupid, you know."

She flushed and felt his arm around her waist, whether it was to keep both of them on the stool or more, she wondered. "That's right. And that way I can estimate the number of each we will need in the next month and each month to come!" She brightened. He was a very smart fellow, this youngest son of the king. And not bad looking either! She smiled inwardly. Not at all like his older brother, Samuel.

They discussed the purchasing of supplies for the coming winter for a few minutes, then he jumped to his feet as he heard footsteps approaching. She jumped up also and faced the door.

"Girl! Where are you, girl?" Her heart fell. It was Samuel. He always called her girl, never Amanda. He considered himself above the mere servants, not at all like his father or youngest son. The people in the castle were not waiting expectantly for the day when he'd take over his father's place as king.

Old Moses and Jocaro had tried training him in service to his people but he'd grown up being tutored by a Father Luttel, a corrupt friar of the church. All Samuel respected was power and demanded that his tenants grovel to him. Amanda was afraid of him and with good reason. He thought he could take his leisure with any girl in the kingdom and had with many. Amanda had managed to stay out of his way as much as possible, using her helper Frum, each time he demanded his horse. But lately she'd noticed him looking at her longer each time. She tried to look disheveled and even dirty whenever the fastidious young man had announced himself at the entrance to the stables, but this time she had brushed back her hair for Jacob and tied it in a bit of rawhide and hadn't had time to smear herself with dirt.

"Dammit, girl, I want my horse!" He stamped his foot and she heard him hit the doorway with his quirt several times.

She hurried out, trying to slump a little like Jocaro had taught her when they'd performed skits together. "Yes, Your Majesty, I'm coming." She came around the corner leading to the stalls and nearly bumped into him. "Oh, I'm sorry, Sire. Which horse would you like?" She hurried down the long stable row stopping at the stall with his favorite, a tall gelding that was rather skittish. She hoped that the smart horse would throw him right on his head. Once he'd brought the poor horse back with spur cuts on his flanks. It was strictly forbidden to wear spurs when not in battle but Samuel ignored many of his father's edicts and she was afraid of his wrath if she told on him.

He came after her and, grabbing her arm, spun her to face him. "Well, well," he smirked, looking at her up and down, "look who's growing up, the little stable brat. Hmmm, I may want to take sport with you one day soon, my little wench." He was about to say more when Samuel looked over her shoulder and said, "What do you want here, little brother?" This last said like they were foul words.

Amanda looked over her shoulder and tried to ask Jacob to be silent with her eyes. She knew he understood but at the same time he said quietly, "Let her go, Samuel. She has work to do for father."

Samuel started to argue, then thought better of it. He shoved her away at Jacob then snapped, "I wish to ride my father's horse, Warrior, today. Saddle him up, and make it fast."

Both Jacob and Amanda froze for a second. No one was allowed to take the huge warhorse out except the king. Amanda looked at Jacob beseechingly as if asking *"What do I do?"*

"I...," she was dry mouthed. "I am supposed to get the king's permission before he's to be exercised, sire." She spoke formally and with both feet together, bowed slightly at the waist, trying not to antagonize him.

He waved a hand negligently and said, "Yes, yes, I know, but I have his permission, so saddle him up and be quick about it, girl." Once again he grabbed her arm and roughly shoved her toward the deluxe stall and the huge beast.

"I'll just be a few minutes, sire. I have to talk to him and make him understand that you'll be riding him and not your father." She grabbed a halter and entered the stall, all the time murmuring softly to the great white beast. She held a hand out with a lump of coarse dark sugar in it. When the great head came down for it, she deftly slipped the bridal over the erect ears and the shiny bit between the powerful jaws. She leaned against the horse's head and whispered in his twitching ear. He nodded his head as if listening and understanding. She rubbed his muzzle and between his large eyes, never stopping her talking. After several minutes, Samuel called to her, telling her to get a move on. She lifted the long head and looked in the brown eye. Then she patted the muscular neck several more times, stroking the soft, well-combed mane.

Amanda led the great beast into the alleyway between the stalls and let the reins hang as she fastened the buckles. Then a quick toss of the blanket and she heaved the heavy war saddle onto his back. As she tied the cinch, she kneed him in the belly, preventing him from puffing out to keep the cinch loose. She almost regretted this last. Maybe Samuel would fall and crack that arrogant skull. She sighed and gathered up the reins, leading the great horse outside into the courtyard where Samuel waited with several friends. Frum

was there with three other horses he'd saddled for the others.
He didn't look too happy, and the others were making fun of
his limp and crossed eye.

Samuel had to climb a small two-step ladder to reach
the stirrups and saddle. He hated this as his father could grab
the pommel and swing himself up from the ground but he
was neither as tall nor as strong as the king. Jacob couldn't
resist a small smile. Samuel saw this and swung his quirt,
catching Jacob on the side of his face. The quirt left red
marks and Jacob brought his hand up against his cheek
muttering obscenities under his breath.

Amanda took the horse's head against her chest once
more and pulled it down where she could whisper into the
great ear once more.

Samuel shouted angrily, "Unhand him, witch! I'm
riding." He looked down at her and smirked once again, "I'll
deal with you later." He whacked the great horse with his
quirt and they were off at a gallop, hooves ringing on the
cobbles. His men noisily followed.

Amanda and Jacob stood looking after them for a long
time, their fingers unconsciously entwined.

It wasn't until much later after they'd gone to the
kitchen for a bowl of the cook's stew and a corner of bread
that the news reached them. One of Samuel's friends came
breathlessly into the kitchen gulping great breaths of air and
trying to tell them something. After he'd gotten his wind
back, he said that Samuel had been thrown while trying to
remount from a fallen tree. The horse had reared and come
down with a heavy hoof on his head and cracked it like an
egg. He said it had been a terrible accident and the horse had
run off, looking wild eyed. He supposed the white horse
would eventually come home, and it eventually did.

Jacob looked curiously and a little fearfully at Amanda
wondering just what she'd said to the poor horse. He
shrugged the thoughts away as nonsensical. He was now the
heir to the throne and would have to tell his father
immediately about Samuel's death. He was not entirely

despondent but would remember to show Amanda the proper respect in the future.

Amanda never told what she said to the king's horse, Warrior, that day, even after she and Jacob were married. She was a good girl, she was.

Well, most of the time.

The End

Anime Girl

John Boyle

Mr. Ishizawa told us welcome a new transfer student, a Miss Miyuki Muto who'd just returned from France and would need one of us to show her around our school. Saying Miss and France in the same sentence made all the guys in our homeroom sit up. I stared out of the window at a particularly interesting cloud.

The door opened and Miss Muto entered. An audible gasp burst from every guy in the room. I turned, bracing myself for another cute young thing who'd make sure the ugly guy with the fire-scarred face was so far below her league that my even looking at her would be a crime against nature.

But to say Miyuki was attractive was like saying the Pacific Ocean was large. Before us stood the real-life version of what lay hidden in the deepest recesses every anime artist when he threw another half-finished sketch into his overflowing wastebasket. Just to add to her out-of-this-world gorgeousness, she'd dyed her hair the kind of deep blue that came in a child's five-color paint set.

She did wear our school uniform, but I'll swear her skirt rode six or ten centimeters above the ones the other girls wore and those thigh-high black stockings drew every eye to the smooth whiteness of her upper thighs. Kento, the leader of the school's karate club, broke the silence by standing, performing an elaborate bow and welcoming Miyuki to his school.

Mr. Ishizawa told Miyuki to sit in one of the two vacant seats. She didn't walk toward the one next to the still standing Kento, but to the one next to me.

I tried to hide my despair as the prettiest girl in the school walked toward its ugliest guy. She smiled at everyone, the drooling guys with their eyes fixated on her chest and the envy-green girls who looked away until she'd passed them.

"Pleased to meet you Yori sensei," she said with a slight bow and took the seat next to me. "I'll try not to be a burden."

Oh god, she was one of those. It'd only happened once before, but once was enough. Some girls weren't satisfied with just letting a guy know they thought him homely. Some thought it funny to lead him on and get him to hint friendship might be possible before going into an ego-satisfying denouncement of his repulsiveness. I couldn't go through that again.

Homeroom ended and I escorted her to our first class. Yep, she hung onto my arm. Everyone, I mean everyone and possibly even the school ghost, stared at us. If this had been an anime, smoke would have come out of Kento's ears.

At lunchtime Miyuki wanted us to take our lunches and eat on the school building's roof.

"They keep the stairway to the roof locked," I explained. "Student's aren't allowed up there."

"But...but," she stammered. "Japanese students always go up onto their school's roof. It's important. It's where lifelong friendships are formed. It's where lovers confess their true feelings. Why would they keep such a place locked away?"

"Maybe some of the smaller schools still do that," I said. "But this is a big school on the seedy side of downtown Tokyo." I was tired and wanted this craziness over with, so I blurted it out. "You'll just have to make do with me confessing my undying love in some green-painted stairwell."

She looked at me, her huge blue eyes staring into mine. I braced myself for the coming slap. "No," she said. "We'll go to a beach with an amusement park and ride the Ferris wheel. When we're at the top and looking out over the water at a setting sun--that would be the right place."

"You've watched far too many anime episodes," I muttered.

She acted subdued for the rest of the afternoon. Perhaps my joke had upset her, but I think she'd begun noticing how all the other students pointed at her and whispered to one another.

Gym class was the last period and afterward I met her in the hallway.

"Someone stole my underwear when I was in the shower," she said as I approached. "The gym teacher just shook her head and walked away when I told her." I had to look. Yeah, the tight, damp material of her white blouse didn't hide anything. I removed my jacket and put it on her. When the final bell rang, me and my new shadow headed for the exit.

"I'll see you tomorrow." We stood beside the school's gate. "I have to catch a train and go to my job now. You can return my jacket in the morning."

Kento and four of his karate goons came up behind me. The bastard grabbed my belt and threw me into the school's gate. I lost my balance and slipped to the ground.

"Get lost looser," he snarled. "This French cutie wants to hang with us."

"You're being a bully," Miyuki shouted. "Girls don't like bullies." She slapped his hand when he went to reach for her shoulder. Karate boy yelped and rubbed his hand.

"Bitch," he yelled and two of his buddies lunged at Miyuki. They grabbed her jacket--my jacket--and tried to pull her toward them. She stood as immobile as a steel post driven a hundred feet into the ground. The old jacket ripped, and the karate boys ended up holding two pieces. They stared at her now visible chest until Miyuki ran over and stood between Kento and me.

"Leave us alone!" she shouted. "Go away or I'll hurt you."

"Someone's gonna get hurt," said Kento. "You'll come with us or I'll smash in the other side of your boyfriend's face."

Miyuki stood with her feet apart as an unexpected wind whipped her hair and skirt around. She held her hands to the side as if holding an invisible basketball. I swear she hovered a good ten centimeters above the sidewalk. Then, from every finger, miniature lightning bolts jumped.

"Yeouch!" she screamed. The lightning stopped and she dropped to the ground. Miyuki put some fingers into her mouth.

"Holy shit," said Kento. "She's not wearing panties. Damn, did you see what I saw! That was for real man."

"What's going on here?" Mr. Ishizawa strode over to us.

"The wind blew Yori over, Mr. Ishizawa," said Kento. "We were just coming over to see if he was hurt." Miyuki helped me to my feet, and after everyone assured Mr. Ishizawa we were all friends, we went our separate ways.

Miyuki followed me. "Are you really all right?" she asked.

"I'm all right. I just need to hustle to the train station so I can get to my job." I picked up the remnants of my school jacket. Torn so badly that I doubted my mother could fix it.

"Your coat is ruined," said Miyuki. "I have a

motorbike. I'll take you to that uniform store. Afterward, I'll take you to your job so you won't have to wait for a train."

I took one of her hands. Besides the burns on her palms, the tips of every finger appeared blown open. I sighed. "You can't steer a bike with hands like this. Let me call my boss and claim sickness, then I'll walk you over to the hospital. It's not far."

She looked at her hands. "Skin isn't very tough, is it? You can use my bike. Drop me at the hospital before going to your job."

I shook my head. "I can't drive a motorbike. I don't have a license."

"No problem, my bike has a license on the back. It's legal."

"Not a license plate. A license from the motor vehicle department proving you know how to drive. Didn't you know you needed one?"

We walked to the hospital. Before entering, Miyuki insisted she'd be fine and told me to go to my job. I didn't disagree, I needed to buy a new jacket with yens I didn't have.

I debated going to school the next morning. My mother couldn't fix the jacket and, with my wheelchair-bound little sister needing more medicine, all our available money wasn't enough for a new one. As I was eating a breakfast, Miyuki banged on the apartment door. She held a neatly wrapped package.

"I bought you a new jacket." As I stood wondering how to react, she pushed past me, slipped off her shoes and entered our apartment.

"Hello," she said as she bowed to my mother and sister. "I'm Miyuki, Yori's girlfriend. I came to take him to school." She turned to me and held out a little plastic card with her picture on it. "I have a license now." I looked at the license and learned she was certified to operate motorbikes, cars, trucks, buses and high-speed trains. I handed the license back.

Miyuki owned a huge American Harley-Davidson. I found it really erotic to hold her slim waist and glance down at those wind-exposed legs. I did my best not to notice the fender-benders in our wake. We were almost to the school before I realized that when we stopped, Miyuki didn't put her feet down. We just hung there, perfectly balanced, until traffic began moving again. When we arrived at the school I took one of her hands and pulled off the pink glove. Perfect, unscarred fingers.

"We need to talk," I said.

"Tonight," Miyuki replied.

My self-proclaimed girlfriend didn't hang around me during the day. With innocent foolishness, she approached many other girls and tried to strike up a conversation. Soon, I started to worry that all those put-downs and snubs would break her spirit.

As we left the school grounds she turned to me. "I'll pick you up after your job and we'll go to dinner."

Later that night, with a half-moon high in the sky, she stopped her bike in front of one of those fancy places near the Tokyo Tower. I explained how a dinner in such a place would cost more than I'd make all year. She handed me a credit card. It had my name on it.

We sat at a prime table alongside a window that gave us a view of the lights of downtown Tokyo. I ordered the cheapest thing on the over-elaborate menu. Miyuki ordered the most expensive. If that card were bogus, I'd be spending the night in jail.

"Are you an alien?" I ventured after the entrées arrived.

"I'm robot," Miyuki cut into her cooked-rare Kobe steak. "Wasn't built on Earth though, so you could call me an alien."

She didn't eat but kept talking. "It took me several thousand years to get to your planet and my ship traveled at close to the speed of light. It's easy for me to tap into your simple computers, so I asked Google where a robot might find a guy who'd fall in love with her. Japan came out on top of the list and after watching your television shows, I knew this was the place for me."

She put down her fork. "I wanted a cool boyfriend and a gang of friends who'd go with us to the beach and fairs and amusement parks and do all the fun things that high school kids do in Japan."

She looked down at her steak. "But nobody's any fun. The girls are all mean and you're the only guy in the whole school who'll look me in the eye--and not just at my body."

"You are exceedingly attractive, Miyuki," I said. "I think that intimidates other girls. And those shows--well, they're about the way Japanese kids wish their world was like. But really we're obsessed with getting into a university. Those who don't make the cut, well their job prospects are pretty miserable. After the car accident that killed my father and left my sister and I scarred, my mother, who only has a high school education, needed to look for a job. She was lucky to find a position cleaning hotel rooms. Without my after school work, we wouldn't eat most days and we couldn't afford the special medicines my little sister needs. I'm sorry, but you chose the wrong country."

"No," She grabbed my plate of vegetable pasta and handed me her steak. "This is the country with you in it. Eat the delicious steak. I'm a robot, so anything I decide tastes great--tastes great to me."

"Will the people who sent you here come looking for you?"

"It takes too long. I'm just one of many thousands of robots my builders sent to every star with the possibility of a planet. We robots have two computer systems. One for the trip and an AI program that's only awakened if the destination star has a planet with life on it. If it doesn't, the computer self-destructs the ship."

"What! It kills you?"

"More like never be born. Think how awful it'd be to orbit a lifeless planet for several thousand years with nothing to do and no way home."

"So you lucked out."

"More than you know. My ship malfunctioned and there was a fire. After it ran out of options, the basic computer woke me up. That was more than six hundred of your years ago. I saved the ship, but once we're awakened it can't be reversed. Sitting there with nothing to do was awful. Yori, I was so lonely."

Six hundred years and all the while expecting to be blown up. I put my hand out toward her and she grasped it with both of hers. "You're so beautiful Miyuki," I said. "You could have any man you wanted. Why ugly fire-scared me?"

"Remember, my makers didn't know what the life-forms I might encounter would look like. So I can change my appearance--and consciously alter the way I feel about appearances. The guys who built me weren't mean--they wanted me to be as happy as possible while monitoring the planet's development."

"So you're here to report on how we're doing?"

"No. Those guys learned everything you know thousands of years ago. They just checking to make sure that some other beings with a completely different way of thinking don't discover how to travel faster than light and rule the galaxy."

"So you're stuck here for a thousand years with no assignment?"

"Just like you I was damaged in a fire and my power source is low. Maybe I'll last a hundred years. Yori, my fellow fire survivor, I want to know a little happiness before I shut down. Please, can you love a robot?"

"Well, if you made your blue hair brown, you'd be the most perfect woman in Japan and no man could help but love you." I smiled.

She stood and pirouetted, letting her hair and skirt fly outward as her hair and body morphed into something more real, and for that reason, far more beautiful. A waiter dropped a soufflé. Two diners spilled their wineglasses, one choked on a piece of fish. The old guy at the table next to us clutched his chest.

We now attend a smaller school that still lets its students onto the roof. With Miyuki's more normal appearance we've made friends--I suppose our unlimited funds for neat things like fairs, amusement parks, and beach trips help make us popular too.

My little sister sees a specialist who assures us she'll walk again, and my mother gets a weekly paycheck from a fictitious conglomerate. Mom's coming out of the depression she was in since the accident and last weekend went out on a date. I think maybe she's a bit envious of how Miyuki walks around with a dreamy look on her face most mornings.

So yeah, a human can fall in love with a robot. No problem. Although I'll never be able to look at a toaster the same way again.

The End

Anniversary

I married you,
because you beat me at Scrabble
('quetzal' is a four-letter word)
and because you could iron.
Coquilles St. Jacques,
my only domestic skill,
was your excuse.
And because I said what I thought,
not what I thought you wanted to hear.
At least she's not boring,
you told those friends
who questioned your sanity.
When time tugs at
the lustier attributes,
there's always that, you said.
We loved communing with nature,
ours and Mother's,
got high in the Rockies,
floated with the fish along A1A.
We spent richer days
hopping the bars down under,
quenching aboriginal hungers
and thirsts with abandon.
How could you know
I'd go on a diet?
How could I know you wouldn't?
Now, after years
of lawn care and home improvement,
the backpacks are
camped out in the attic,
and cobwebs cover the SCUBA gear

like encrusting coral.
I can be found entertaining
my muse and dreaming of Pulitzers.
Your fantasies score nightly
on ESPN, while crosswords
fill in the spaces at halftime.
Still, the passion is there,
hidden like the sun at midnight.
We are an old pair of boots—
sturdy, comfortable,
the left in perfect harmony
with the right.
Over bran muffins and decaf,
we talk of retirement
and butterfly gardens,
our metamorphosis nearly complete.
And, while you listen to Chopin and poetry
in quiet resignation,
I silently pray that Duke will win
just one more time.

Karen Ann Wilson

The Carousel

Michael Goldman

It was on a bright starry night that the circus rolled into town. The weather had just turned cold, but that would not stop the circus. All the roustabouts went to work unloading truck after truck, huge canvas tents to be erected before dawn. Lights on tripods were set up over the whole area so the men could work as if it was daylight. The elephants were unloaded and put into their harnesses -- their help was needed to pull the giant canvas big top over the main pole. Next to be set up was the cook tent; food and plenty of hot coffee would be needed before this night was over. Work proceeded rapidly since the hands had performed this chore many times

Close to the big top some men erected an old carousel. It needed painting. The horses and coaches were dull and faded. The mirrors around the center column were all cracked and crusted with grime. Several of the old hands and performers gathered at the food tent, staring at the carousel. They had never seen it before. Someone commented that must be something the management had added to the show. But why? It was a mess and no one would want to ride it on something like that!

Still, an old man was tinkering with the mechanism. Once he finished that, he started painting the horses. The circus people stood, by the food tend, drinking coffee and talking about the new ride. Despite its shabby appearance, they agreed to go try it out once the worker finished restoring it.

Sadie the fat lady walked up to Don, the master of ceremonies and asked, "When do you think it will be finished?"

"At the rate that old man's moving I'd say it might be next year sometime," he replied sourly. "Who's the old chap anyway? I've never seen him before."

"Well, I was talking to Jake, the juggler, and he said the old man's a tramp that follows the circus around."

"Yeah," Jake added. "We don't think he knows a damn thing about fixing the carousel."

The old man had grey hair. He was tall and thin with a bushy mustache and crystal blue eyes.

The sword swallower, Steve walked up and joined the group watching. "Are you thinking what I'm thinking?"

Don and Sadie turned and laughed.

"I'll believe it when I see it." Sadie blurted out as she waddled off.

Dan the muscle man walked up and declared, "We're having a party tonight out back of the big top. Be obliged if you'd pass the word."

"Okay. Will do." Don replied as he flipped his cigarette away.

All the while, the old man just kept working on the carousel.

Mildred, the midget walked over and greeted the old man "Hello there old timer my name is Mildred what's yours?"

"Henry Carter, ma'am." He removed his hat and gave a low bow "Pleased to meet you."

"Same here" Mildred replied. "There's a party tonight out behind the big top. You can come if you want."

"Well, thank you, ma'am. I will try to attend." He gave another bow and replaced his hat as she moved away. Alone again, he returned to his work on the carousel.

People started to gather for the party. Leo the lion tamer started a fire in a big barrel. "Someone needs to bring more wood so we won't run out," he called. Tables were set up and food appeared. Someone rolled out a barrel of beer and started filling eager mugs. Soon the party was in full swing.

It was late when the old man finally made his appearance. Heads turned to look at him as he came into the firelight. "Hello everyone," he said making a polite bow.

Voices called greetings back and someone handed him a beer while offering him a seat. The old man smiled. "This is just the way it used to be," he remarked. "People are nice to each other and care about each other. I am honored to be here."

"Are you married, Mr. Carter?" Carol the bearded lady asked him.

"No. But I was once engaged to the most beautiful girl in the world. She was as sweet as she was beautiful." His face reflected his sadness. "I still miss her so." Tears glistened in his eyes.

"Oh, I'm sorry, Carol said. "What happened?"

He looked down and took a deep breath before he answered. "We were so in love and so young. Her father was against us getting married and so we ran away. I borrowed my friend's car and told her to meet me a couple blocks from her house. That was fifty years ago the fourteenth of February."

"Valentine's Day," Sadie commented.

"And she will be my valentine forever," he said. He drew a deep breath and continued his tale. "That night about two hours before I was to pick her up, a storm started brewing. The wind howled, the clouds darkened, and rain came in sheets. Thunder rolled across the sky and lighting lit up the night, but still she came. She loved me that much. When I got there I found her standing in the heavy downpour, drenched to the skin, shivering and cold. Anyway, we made it to the next town before her father caught up with us."

Sadie gasped.

"He forced her to go back home." Carter sighed at the memory. "I didn't it know then, but our paths were never to cross again."

"Oh, no," Carol commiserated.

"Why? What happened?" Leo demanded.

"I started working for the carnival and traveling around a lot so. I always planned -- I hoped to get back to her again, but some years later I heard she was killed in a car accident."

Everyone listening felt his sorrow and declared how sorry they were.

A silence fell, but this was a party and no one could be sad for too long. An Irishman named Clive was one of the clowns and felt it was his job to change the mood.

"Does anyone know who threw the overalls in Mrs. Murphy's Chowder?" he demanded, breaking the silence.

Laughter broke out. Other voices were raised, and over by the beer barrel, the fiddle player started an Irish jig. Clive and his little dog Lady moved into a clear space and started to dance. Lady was just a black and white mutt with a white tip on her tail, but she was sharp as a tack.

Eventually the fire in the barrel burned down to glowing embers and the party neared an end. Everyone was yawning and sleepy-eyed, drifting slowly away to their beds. The old man was the last to leave.

Morning came and the sun rose bright in a clear blue sky as the circus began to wake up. People wandered out of their caravans ready to face another day. They headed toward the food tent, intent on breakfast when they noticed something different about the old carousel. Such a beautiful thing it was, the horses looking almost alive as their eyes glinted in the morning sun, their tails dancing in the breeze.

The newly painted coaches were stunning with bright paint, and the center of the carousel wore sparkling new mirrors. The whole ride seemed to beckon a person to get on.

While they stood there, gazing in amazement at the transformed ride, music started and it began to revolve. Its lights blinked off and on, the horses rose and fell on their striped poles as the carousel came to life.

The Henry Carter stood at the controls with a grin on his wrinkled face and a twinkle in his eye.

"Come on, everyone," he called. "Come for a ride." His teeth flashed as he smiled. "No charge! The ride's free today because it's Valentine's Day!"

One by one, he ushered them onto the platform where they selected their mounts. "Just hold tight," he told them as he moved back to the controls.

Then carousel began moving faster and the music got louder as the horses went up and down, up and down. What fun they were all having. For some reason, the carousel made everyone feel happy.

But then the carousel began going even faster and some of the riders began to be frightened. And yet faster and faster it went. They could barely see the old man grinning at them as they flew by. The music got louder as the horses galloped around in their circle. The carousel was running away! But just when everyone began to fear they might be killed, the carousel slowed and came to a halt.

The dizzy riders stumbled off of the horses, moving quickly away. Silence fell over the area as they all gazed at the now silent machine.

And then they looked at each other. And then down at themselves.

What had happened to them?

As impossible as it seemed, they were all young again. Aching bodies were pain free, wrinkles and lines had disappeared. Gray hairs were miraculously gone. The carousel, it seemed, had spun them back in time.

"What? What happened?" everyone was mumbling in astonishment. Carol was weeping tears of joy as she gazed at her beautiful hands, the ugly age spots gone and her skin sleek over fine bones. Mildred was bouncing and skipping on joints that no longer gave her pain, a happy grin on her face.

They returned to the carousel, looking for Henry Carter -- what had he done to them? But Henry Carter was gone. They searched the grounds; however, the old man who restored the carousel was nowhere to be found.

Later that afternoon, Tom Larsen, the owner of the circus arrived in his shiny car. He didn't say anything as he stared at the younger versions of the men and women who had worked for him for years. He walked through the circus with his employees at his back, making his usual inspection and admiring their new ride. When Don told him that the old man who worked on the carousel was missing, he didn't seem too concerned. He just assigned the job to one of the other roustabouts.

"What if Mr. Carter comes back," Don wanted to know.

"Who?" Mr. Larsen asked. "What's his name?"

"Henry Carter," Leo told him.

The blood drained from Mr. Larsen's face "It couldn't be Henry Carter. It just can't be." He looked at the carousel again. "I thought this machine looked familiar," he said softly.

"But we all saw him. It was Henry Carter," Carol assured him.

"Henry Carter used to work for me a long time ago," Mr. Larsen told them. "And he worked on this very carousel. But," he added gazing at the young-looking faces of the people around him, "Henry Carter dropped dead on this very carousel, fifty years ago, on Valentine's Day."

The End

Chocolate

Your eyes,
Chocolate brown,
Staring into mine
Are all I see.
Your smooth white skin
Brushing against me,
Wondering how it would feel,
Steals all other imaginings
From my mind.

I met you once,
Twice,
Three times,
In a bland, professional way.
I haven't seen you since then,
Four or five months now.
I'll probably never see you again.
Except at night,
When I dream.
Then
Your eyes,
Chocolate brown,
Staring into mine,
Are all I see.

Mary Cooper

The Cossack & the Swede

C.J. Goldman

Dad went into town one day to get some things we needed. He was really late getting back and we all wondered why. This is the story he told us. He said he was in the general store when Mr. Boggs walked in. Mr. Boggs was an old friend he rarely got to see since his ranch was way the other side of town at the foot of the mountains.

"Well," Dad began, "Mr. Boggs offered to buy me a drink. I told him I needed to get back to the family, but he insisted, and, being an agreeable man, I had to agree."

We went down to the saloon and found seats at the bar. It was noisy, smoke filled, and dim. Me and Boggs started talking, and time passed quicker than I realized. I was looking around when I spotted this big hairy man at the end of the bar. He was hard to miss since he kept getting louder and louder, and started causing a ruckus.

"Who is that loud mouth?" I asked Mr. Boggs.

Boggs said "He's a Swede that works down at the new school construction. Best keep outa' his way. Man's a troublemaker."

Sure enough, while we watched the Swede stalked over to a table of gamblers and laid his hand on the shoulder this short little guy with horned eyebrows.

"I wanna buy ya a drink," the Swede slurred.

Mr. Boggs leaned into me and whispered, "That's Lyubka, the Cossack. He works at the livery. They say he's a deserter from the Russian army."

The Cossack leaned back and said with his thick accent, "Take your hand away, meester. Can't you see I'm in the meiddle of a game? I have no interest in drinking wit you now."

But the Swede was not listening. He closed his fingers on the other man's shoulder and dragged him off of his chair.

"What tha…" The Cossack spun and swung a fist, catching the Swede with an upper cut. It was a lucky punch and knocked the other man towards the bar.

The Swede regained his balance and staggered forward. He grabbed the Cossack by the collar and slung him across the room knocking over tables and chairs.

With blood in his eyes the Cossack pushed to his feet. He ran and jumped astride of the Swede, wrapping his legs around his waist. They both fell against the stairs. The Cossack, grabbed two hands full of the Swede's hair and pounded his head against the wooden runners.

With a howl of rage, the Swede shoved him off. The Cossack fell, knocking over the spittoon. The Swede grabbed a beer bottle and cracked it over the Cossack's head splitting a gash in his forehead. Blood ran into his eyes. Then he jumped on the smaller man and started pounding him with his fists.

Undaunted, the Cossack gave as good as he got. The two men fought, wallowing around in slimy tobacco juice, beer, and blood. Those of us standing at the bar had to jump right smart to stay out of their way, but we still got splattered with gore.

"Well, that's when I got up and scrambled to the swinging doors, trying to get out of the saloon," Dad told us. "But I just didn't make it in time."

"The Swede rolled free almost right on my feet," Dad said. "I was lucky he didn't pay no attention to me, but just got up, his eyes fixed on the Cossack."

With a crooked grin, and bloody foam on his lips, the Swede pulled a knife from his boot. But before he could do anything more, however, there was a loud crack. The Swede slumped to the floor with an expressions of surprise on his face.

"Through the smoke I could see he was gut shot," Dad told us solemnly. "Before we even realized what had happened, his eyes filled with tears, his skin turned pale and sweaty. We all watched as he clawed towards the door. His fingernails dug into the wood floor. He rolled onto his back, his shirt wet with blood. His whole body trembled and as he exhaled he gave a last cry.

"And that was all there was to it. When I was finally able to leave the saloon, I had to step over the Swede's corpse as it lay with its stone cold eyes fixed on a sign reading, 'EXIT'."

The End

Cranes Rising

They rise in silence, a darker grey
            than early mist, from an opening
in soft, hay-mown earth; grasses concealing,
            then quietly releasing, morning's

beauty. Swallowtails, skippers,
            wings delicate and damp, meadowlark
song, each floating note like light,
            bright bells

recalling us from our own slow-breathing,
            metallic fog; affirming all
that for which we grasp in our stuttering rise
            to the surface. It is necessary

to rant, to pray, to remain
            subjective. It is necessary to love
natural eloquence; this pair of cranes,
            feathered smoke ascending.

                                        Christine Cock

A Date for Thanksgiving

Jerry Cowling

You'll never believe what happened to my wife and me the first Thanksgiving after we got married. She was the mountains of southwestern Virginia and I was from the plains of Texas. I worked for a newspaper in Upper East Tennessee in Kingsport, a nice-sized city on the state line with Virginia, but we were both small town folk so we decided to buy a house in a village called Falls Branch just south of town.

We got the last house on this street that meandered into the foothills. Everyone else on the street was rather swarthy looking and talked funny. Now my wife had told me about this people who lived together way back in the mountains called Melungeons. No one knew where they came from, but they looked Portuguese or Turkish, and they spoke something that sounded like Old English.

"I don't think they're Melungeons," my wife said.

It was the weekend before Thanksgiving, and my wife had agreed to bake my mother's old recipe for walnut date bread. We were walking out of the store when I showed her the bag of dates.

"Oh, that's way too many," she said. "You'll have to give some of those away."

Just then one of our neighbors walked up. We hadn't spoken much.

"Would you like some dates?" I asked. There's no better way to make friends with the neighbors than to give them food.

He stopped, straightened his shoulders, looked at my hand and then at me.

"Dose dates?"

"Yeah."

"Youse givin' me dates?"

"Yeah."

"Where youse from?"

"Five Points."

It was named for a rock formation in downtown which was outside Lubbock

Our neighbor's eyes widened. "Youse from Five Points?"

"Yeah."

"Youse miss de family?"

"Oh sure."

"Youse good people. Come de our house for Thanksgiving dinner."

"Isn't that nice, honey? We're eating with the Melungeons."

"I don't think they're Melungeons," she whispered.

On Thanksgiving Day we walked across the street with our freshly baked walnut date bread. Al of the men in the neighborhood wore black pin-striped suits, black shirts and white ties. All the women wore dresses with plunging necklines revealing perky bosoms.

"I didn't know Melungeons believed in breast implants."

"I keep telling you," my wife said, "these people aren't Melungeons."

In the middle of dinner, which strangely had lots of pasta and lasagna and no turkey and dressing, the host turned to me, with his mouth full of ravioli, and said, "Hey, Five Points, what kinda bidness youse in?"

I didn't want to tell them I sat around all day editing news stories and writing headlines so I thought back to when I was on the police beat.

"Well, I've witnessed a lot of crime in my day."

All the men around the table laughed out loud, blowing bits of marinara sauce on the table cloth.

"Yeah, widnessin' dat crime can be dangerous."

Another man with a nasty scar across his check said, "Yeah, den youse uncle had to give youse protection."

"Yeah, Uncle Sam has given us all a lotta protection," the host added.

They laughed again, and more marinara sauce splattered everywhere.

"I didn't know Melungeons had such a good sense of humor," I whispered to my wife.

"Shut up," she hissed back.

"Whaddaya call us?" the guy with the scar said.

"I said Muh—"

"Shh," the host interrupted, putting his finger to his lips. "Don't use dat word around here."

"Why? You should be proud of your heritage," I exclaimed. At that moment I became aware of my wife's fingernails digging into my thigh. It hurt very much.

"Dat's what we tink," the host said, "but Uncle Sam makes de rules."

"Yeah, he pays all our bills," the man with the scar said.

"No offense to your Uncle Sam, but I think he's much too controlling."

My wife's nails broke the skin on my thigh, and I clamped my mouth shut to keep from screaming in pain.

"And exactly," my wife announced in a loud but firm voice, "what exactly did you think was my husband's intention in giving you a date?"

"Jeez, Mario," one of the wives spoke up. "She talks with a lotta big fancy words."

Mario, the guy with the scar, slapped her on the back of the head. "Keep youse pie hole shut."

I was beginning to think these Melungeons weren't as nice as my wife made them out to be.

"Liddle lady," the host said, "back in de old country, when youse give somebody a date it's like, hey, youse one of us."

"So you think we're one of you?" my wife said. Her voice was very tense which wasn't like her at all. She was usually very relaxed around strangers.

"Why, honey," I began to reassure her, "we're no Muh—"

"Youse not a Muh—"

"Oh, I'm a Muh," my wife said quickly. "He's not a Muh."

"You're a Muh?" I said. "That's great. I always wanted to be married to the Muh."

My wife stood and grabbed me by the hand. "Thank you very much for the Thanksgiving dinner. It was lovely, but we've got to go now."

For some reason my wife insisted we sell the house immediately and move to Lubbock. We never saw those nice Melungeons again.

The End

Don't Yell, Run!

Mary H. Sheldon

Sharon held her scream in her mouth as she stepped off
the curb. It almost gagged her with the mixture of venom and
fear, but she didn't dare to let out even the tiniest of noises.

Her morning started last night. You know, one of those
days with so many things to do that she had to make a list.
…actually a chart of what needed to be done. It was 11:48
when she finally pulled her feet off the floor and then sighed
as she remembered she hadn't taken the blood pressure pill
that was on the kitchen counter. She had put it there after
dinner so she would see it before going to bed. Well, that
didn't work, did it? She didn't put her feet in her slippers or
wrap her robe around her shoulders. "Who cares?" she
growled. The floor was cold. The air was cold. And the
kitchen was at least a half a mile away! The water from the
faucet was cold, Sharon complained to herself, as she
washed down the little Lisinopril tablet. She ran down the
hallway and would have done a dive into bed if she could
have, but she could only manage to sink to the edge of the

bed and collapse. "I can't have high blood pressure tomorrow ," she thought. The clock blinked, 11:55pm.

The phone rang at seven in the morning. Steve had gotten to Jimmy and Carolyn's yesterday morning and was calling again to say he would be out the door after breakfast to help Jimmy with the fences. Steve's older brother had "retired" to a forty-acre ranchette in Wyoming three years ago. Jimmy's days were filled with chores from morning to night. He says he has never worked so hard for so little pay. He'd been asking Carolyn for a raise, but she always was spending their money on hay for the four horses and for Ruthie, the milk cow! They both laughed and laughed.

Now, Steve was taking more of his vacation days to drive overnight and to spend three or four days out there helping with the projects that Jimmy said had to get done before winter. Sharon wondered what they would do all winter, if all the projects were finished!

Anyway, with Steve gone, Sharon was relishing her freedom and the morning was moving fast. She had made the piecrust dough and put it in the fridge by the time her friend, Roberta, dropped off a bushel of corn. Roberta had just picked it from her huge garden and the supple green husks were still drenched with the morning dew. Sharon was trading a bushel of apples for Roberta's corn and the two women loaded the apples into Roberta's little pickup truck. They had a quick cup of coffee and caught up on neighborhood news before Roberta left for a doctor's appointment.

It was close to two o'clock when Sharon looked at the mess in her kitchen and decided to take Homer for a walk before cleaning up. Homer, the Happy Dog, as he was known, had been pacing or sitting, staring at her since noon. "Do dogs know that when they raise one eyebrow they make you feel guilty?" she wondered, as she clipped on the red leash.

Maybe it was the sun catching some chrome or a movement that made her turn her head to the right and to look down Grafton Street. But she saw the white van moving slowly down the street. Then she saw the little boy with the yellow tee shirt. The van stopped and the driver got out.

Roberta's newsy words were suddenly like neon in her head; "Creepy guy in a white van in the neighborhood."

Alarms went off in every part of her body. She let go of Homer's leash. Calmly, she stepped off the curb into the street. No traffic. Good. The creepy guy had walked around the van and stood with his back to her and was talking with the boy when she started running. She worried she might run faster than her sneakers could go. The man wore a plain, white tee shirt and dark brown shorts. He had turned and his creepy hand was reaching for the sliding van door. He looked up and saw Sharon barreling toward him. He started to grab the yellow shirt when the banshee scream came out of her mouth.

The sweet, gentle, kind expression on the creep's face switched to ugliness and he shot around to the driver's side as Sharon swept the yellow shirted boy into her arms and kept running down the street. The van disappeared. The boy struggled to get away from her, but she couldn't let go. A patrol car wailed closer and closer. When they pried the boy from her arms, the officers asked questions about the creepy guy and his van. People were watching from their yards.

The boy was crying now. His yellow shirt already had her tears on it.

She felt her knees buckle and Officer Bigelow helped her sit on the curb. He offered the seat of the patrol car, but her feet wouldn't move. It was ridiculous, she thought, that this concrete felt as good as her bed had the night before.

Two women were running down Grafton and one of them scooped up the boy. More tears on the yellow shirt.

Homer, the Happy Dog, had found her and nuzzled up against her.

Officer Bigelow helped her up to the sidewalk as the boy's mother tried to hug her while she was still clutching her son. Sharon kept nodding, but her mouth was dry and no words could be spoken anyway. She was crying. The mother

was crying. And the boy in the tear soaked yellow shirt
squirmed to get down.

Yes, thank you, she and Homer would like a ride home
in the police car.

As she locked the front door behind her and took
Homer's leash off, she considered making her way to her
bed. But it seemed too far away and the sofa looked too soft.
She would call Steve later. She pulled the quilt from the back
of the sofa and grabbed a pillow. She dropped to the carpeted
living room floor and curled up, still wearing her sneakers
that felt melted to her feet; still seeing the creepy hand on the
van door; and still hearing the banshee scream shaking in
every part of her body and mind.

The End

The Dungeon of Despair

A fictional account of a true story.
Judy G. Burford

Kevin quivers, partly from the cold, but more from the blackness. "I don't think it's fair."

"I don't think it's fair." It isn't an echo. It's a completely different voice, Brandon's voice.

"It isn't fair, at all." Connie says.

"Yeah." The final comment comes from Patrick.

Then silence. Kevin shivers. He pulls his legs up as close to his torso as possible and stuffs one hand under each armpit. His belly rumbles. *I sure hope the food comes soon,* he thinks. The dogs shove their bodies against Kevin's trembling body. *They help me feel warm, but those mutts have fleas!* Kevin's arms itch with the bites.

Connie, on the other hand, is hoping the food will never come again. With it comes terror, for her. *Those two men. They do things. Things I don't like. They hurt me. It isn't fair.*

Brandon wonders why Stephanie hasn't come to take him away from these terrible people. Stephanie is Brandon's older sister. *She doesn't come often, because she lives a long drive away, but wouldn't she wonder where I am by now.* Brandon doesn't know how many days he's been in this dark place, but too many. *I hate it here.*

Patrick's head still hurts. *Why did that bad man hit me? I didn't do anything wrong. I just told him I was hungry. What's wrong with that? I hope he doesn't hit me ever again.* "I'm scared."

"No, you're not, Patrick, you're not scared," Kevin doesn't want to think that Patrick is scared. *If Patrick is scared, then maybe I'm scared too.* Goose bumps start to form along Patrick's arms and he feels a shiver up his spine. "I'm scared, too, Patrick."

"Me, too," says Connie. "I wish those bad people would never come here again."

"Yeah, stay away bad people," says Brandon. "Excuse me, I farted."

"That's okay," says Connie. "You're allowed to fart. It's okay as long you say excuse me."

"That's right," says Patrick, "You gotta say excuse me."

"Excuse me," Brandon says again.

"Oh, that's very stinky," says Patrick.

"That's okay," says Connie. "You're allowed to be stinky, as long as you say excuse me."

"Excuse me," says Brandon.

They hear other voices coming from the outer sanctum. "Jesus Christ, Lydia. Give it a rest."

Sometimes, I can't figure that broad out, thinks Thomas. *Nothing pleases her. She's some bossy bitch.*

"I mean it, you two, no more. We're doing this for the money, not for you two to get your rocks off," Lydia says.

"But, for a dummy, she ain't that hard to look at," Thomas protests.

"I don't care, leave the bitch alone."

Clinking metal is the signal the four captives have been anticipating. Their predators are back. They are about to open the steel door. Connie shields her eyes from the onslaught of light she knows is about to spring on her.

Patrick's stomach rumbles, in a kind of Pavlovian response to what he knows is coming.

Whoosh. The door opens and light fills the empty cavity splaying itself on the four frightened individuals within.

"Oh, that stench, it's disgusting," says Aaron.

"Excuse me," says Brandon, one more time.

"Shut-up, idiot." Aaron kicks the limp figure lying next to him on the cold dirt floor.

"At least he has manners, asshole." Lydia punches Aaron's arm.

Patrick flinches. *I hope they don't hit me.*

"Here, you retards, eat your dinner," Thomas takes the lid off one of the four plastic containers he brought and shoves it across the floor toward Connie. He winks at her with a grin. She pushes herself as far back into the darkness as she can, hoping to make herself invisible.

In turn, Thomas shoves containers to each of the remaining three. "Eat you idiots."

"Take that pail of shit out back and dump it into the gully," Lydia tells Aaron.

"Hell, they make the stink, let them live with it." *I'm sick of being pushed around by this bitch. Who does she think she is? She isn't the boss over me. We're partners. What will it take to get that through her thick skull?*

"I said, empty it," Lydia gets right in his face this time.

"Okay, okay," he isn't really backing down. He just doesn't feel like getting into a big fight right now. He'll deal with her later.

Kevin hates having to share his food with the dogs, but they are hungry too. *They help to keep me warm, so I owe them,* he thinks. *Funny, they never make a sound, even when the chains are rattling outside of the door. I had a dog when I was a little kid. It barked like crazy every time anyone came near the front door. These dogs stay quiet. They're too scared to bark, just like me.*

Lydia sees the look in Thomas's eyes. She places herself between Thomas and Connie. His craving for sex makes even a bitch like Lydia cringe. *We started this endeavor for the money. We're after the moron's Social Security checks. Why can't Thomas stay focused? Because Thomas is an idiot, a sex-crazed idiot.*

Thomas gets the message and heads toward the door. "Let's get out of this shit-hole."

Returning with the empty shit pail, Aaron tosses it down, then has to bend over to put it upright. *The dummies will never be able to figure out how to use the thing if I leave it on its side.* Then, he heads toward the hallway outside. Lydia follows.

The four frightened captives watch as the infringing light narrows until it is a sliver, then nothing but darkness. They push the food into their mouths with filthy hands that haven't seen water in days, maybe weeks. The food lacks flavor but fills the yearning spot that's been crying out to be filled for the past several hours. Patrick lets the dogs lick the last specks from his plastic container. He wishes there was more, his gut still growling. The darkened wait begins again.

Soon, silence envelopes all four and soon becomes heavy breathing, then rhythmic snoring.

Connie is startled awake when she hears the chains rattle once again. Her abdominal muscles clench. *Are those bad men coming back to do those awful things to me? They forgot to do them last time.*

The door whooshes open, and the light pierces her eyes. It happens too fast for her to shelter her eyes from the onslaught. Patrick rubs the sand man's residue from his eyes with both fists. When he opens his eyes again, he sees a huge figure silhouetted in the light from the door. The man has a piercing voice, "Police, everything's going to be okay, we're here to help you."

A lady officer follows the large man into the room, "Oh, the stench," she says.

"Excuse me," says Brandon.

"Oh, sweetheart, it's okay." *She's a nice lady*, thinks Connie.

It isn't Stephanie, but that doesn't really matter, thinks Brandon. *At least somebody is here to save me.* His eyes become moist, then he hears a guttural squeak come from his own throat. His shoulders start to tremble. The tears flow. *Safe, at last.*

Patrick has never been so happy in his entire life. "Police officers save people. They're here to save us," he squeals. Even the dogs seem to know what is going on, they jump into Patrick's lap and lick his face in unison.

The police officers use a big cutter thing to break through the chains that tether each of them in place on the cold dirt floor. It feels good to stretch and stand, even though Kevin's right knee nearly buckles when he puts pressure on it. *I'm not going to let that trick knee get in the way of safety,* he thinks, as he bolts upright and heads toward the light.

Patrick tells the lady officer he's hungry. "We'll get you a nice hot meal, right away," she says.

"And my dogs," Patrick adds.

"Sure thing."

It's the first time Patrick smiled in a very long time.

The End

Hermit Crab

Standing outside myself
Searching to get back in
My life force
Animating
This husk of a body
An idea looking for a home

The Real Thing

A fruit fly would rather die
In a glass of wine than dive
Into a diet Coke.

Fish Quick

Fish quick I swim above the stones
Snatch a fly from a spider's web
And watch the shadow above my head

Mosquito

I don't need a name—
Just rain in a cup,
A sun-baked day,
Stinger sharp,
and a belly full
of blood.

River Run

Rolling to the boat launch
Old kayak
Eighteen foot stiletto knife
God's breath held
Plunge into the river's cut current
Old red blade flies through liquid air
Reflections on tannic water
Gliding over treetops, around

Mirrored roots
Each canopied bend, the silence of
Opening an abandon room
Or one where someone died
Intimate impersonal space
Fingers sliding into darkness
Oars moving through virgin light

Listen! The swish of water
Flap of wings down the channel
Blood up a vacuum tube
Ibis eating jumping mud frogs
Twisted earth masquerading as
Exposed tree roots above the sleep line
Travels past gurgling bone where turtles
Bask unalarmed. Distant dreams of
Mother's mud, milk of sun's saved heat

They slept in that ooze.
We stacked them like stones. Lived in
That house all winter. Danced by the
Fire, careful not to let flames
Touch the stones. Sleeping in their shells
While the occupant was somewhere else
Coupling: sweat between breasts
Blood pressure pounding

March Sky

>Green hair hanging
>red eyes shining
>sunset glimpsed through
>a sabal palm

Winter Drought

>Down the hill through palm grass
>Frostbitten firespikes, caught
>with early morning mist
>slip through my fingers
>
>Summer ooze gone
>from the dry riverbed
>A soft green mattress
>tastes of July mixed with saliva
>chews through new grass
>Pillows of snail shells
>filled with mud
>snake-tangled sheets of roots
>cover the riverbanks
>
>High water stained tree trunks
>thousands of cypress knees pattern
>where water once flowed
>The power of absence hibernates
>
>Clouds foreshadow sodden rain
>drops dimple the sugary sand
>tap on my hair run down wet cheeks
>Turtles shift in deep mud
>Herons sense the frogs

Shore Birds

Coco-plum tree,
Sweet sprawling grasses
On the distant shore
Clouds rolling over the sun
Sanderlings peck at a long foamy ribbon
Refreshed by wave on wave

Black-bellied Plover
Its *pee-a-wee* call
A child's squeal of joy
Carried on the beach wind

Flocks of black-capped terns
Fan out
Thoughts of flying
Last longer
Than water over stones

My Love is Hid

My love is hid behind a screen
A silhouette in soft cold flame
The paper screen falls away

In cool fall mornings, trees gone bare
I walk through restless paper leaves
And read the dates upon the stones

Al Svoboda

Esperanza's Sorrow

Jill V. Svoboda

On the April day when two uniformed patrolmen knocked on the front door of her Rogers Park bungalow, Esperanza Marchita Marquez knew that they had come to confirm the fear that had haunted her for the past three months – the fear that her only child was lost to her forever.

The taller of the two introduced himself. "Mrs. Marquez, I'm Sergeant Hector Diaz, a homicide detective for Chicago police department, and this is my partner, Jesse Reyes. I'm so sorry–

Esperanza clasped her hands together and raised them to her mouth, praying that she might awake and find that her nightmare had fled in the light of a new day.

"I'm so very sorry," Sergeant Diaz continued. "On a tip from one of our informants, we located the remains of a young man and a young woman in a Glenview water retention pond. Our crime investigation unit has identified the woman as your daughter, Narcisa. The male was a known drug dealer. We believe both were murdered, though we don't have an autopsy report as yet."

Esperanza did not shriek at the news, nor did she weep, although her heartbeat stuttered, and for a long moment she could not speak. But then her renegade heart resumed its steady rhythm, insisting that her life continue despite the death of her beloved 18-year-old daughter. Willing her emotions to be still, Esperanza quietly thanked the officers for their concern.

When the officers had driven away, Esperanza did what she always did in times of trouble: She went into her little dressmaking studio, where she had spent years sewing fine apparel for some of the city's wealthiest women. Inside, lengths of fabric were stacked neatly upon shelves; garments in progress hung on racks; and sewing machines and sergers waited on tables, ready to be called upon.

Esperanza didn't know what she intended to do in the studio until her hand fell upon her keenest pair of shears. Taking them up, she went next to Narcisa's room, where she pulled her daughter's garments from the closet and spread them out on the bed. All the colors of a summer garden, all the colors of youth, she thought. So beautiful, as her wayward Narcisa had been.

Tears would not come. Esperanza raised her shears and began cutting Narcisa's skirts into random pieces. The newer skirts were so short and the tops so skimpy that there was scarcely enough fabric in them to make her efforts worthwhile. All the girls wore clothes like these, Narcisa had assured her. It was the American way. Esperanza had believed her daughter. What did a mother so far from her birthplace in Michoacán know about what was right for girls in this cold and alien city?

She picked up Narcisa's prom dress. Narcisa had made it herself, a sophisticated gown in shades of turquoise and ecru. Esperanza glanced at her daughter's dresser, where Narcisa beamed from a photo in which she was wearing the dress and standing beside her prom date, Jorge Ramirez.

Jorge was a nice young man, not like the Norteamericano punks Narcisa had been seeing lately. Esperanza's shears slashed into the dress, severing threads of memories. Next came the ivory-white dress from Narcisa's quinceañara, the festive celebration of her fifteenth birthday. Esperanza sighed as her scissors reduced it to scraps. The sharp blades made short work of Narcisa's gray and navy blue school uniforms, of her pastel Sunday dresses and of her flowered nightgowns.

By the time Esperanza finished cutting, the streetlights were casting their harsh orange light into the darkened neighborhood. Esperanza piled the scraps of Narcisa's short life into brown paper bags, lay down upon her daughter's bed and slept.

Daylight awakened Esperanza. She rose from Narcisa's bed and went to the bathroom to splash water on her face and then to the kitchen. There she fried up a plate of eggs and tortillas, forcing herself to eat before taking the bags of newly cut scraps to her dressmaking studio. The task she had set herself would require strength.

Esperanza owned several newer sewing machines, each one more electronically elaborate than the next, but she chose to sit down instead at her old Kenmore. She had bought that machine soon after she and her husband, Carlos, got married, five years before Narcisa's birth. Carlos had made good money working construction jobs until the night he went out with his friends and drank a little too much. After he left the bar, he crashed his pickup truck into a viaduct. Narcisa had just reached her second birthday.

With Carlos gone, Esperanza used her sewing skills to become a custom dressmaker. She worked hard with that Kenmore machine and managed to provide herself and Narcisa with an adequate living. Now she selected a cone of daffodil-yellow thread and led its bright filament through the machine's loops and into the needle. The Kenmore was ready.

Esperanza fingered the scraps of fabric in one of the paper bags, lifting out a random handful. She took a blue polka-dotted cotton patch–a piece of Narcisa's favorite Sunday dress–and stitched it to a multicolored swatch of tropical print cut from a swimsuit cover-up. She added a semicircle of lime-green linen that had recently been part of a skirt. Then she sewed on a bright red scrap, left over from one of Narcisa's first sewing projects.

As she guided the pieces under the needle, grief flowed from Esperanza's heart down her arms and through her fingers into the thread and the fabrics and the bed of the sewing machine. The machine throbbed imperceptibly as each unshed tear reached it, and microscopic flakes of its plastic casing broke loose and fell to the table.

Around ten in the morning, the doorbell rang, interrupting Esperanza's desperate patchwork. It was Father McCarthy, the parish priest, calling to offer his condolences and to discuss a funeral mass for Narcisa. At the priest's urging, Esperanza telephoned the director of the funeral home he suggested. The funeral director made time in his day's schedule to help her select a casket. She came home with a sample of the golden satin that would cushion Narcisa's eternal bed.

By the time Esperanza returned to her house, the daylight was almost gone. She reheated a bowl of leftover picadillo and ate it sitting in front of her television set, watching stolidly as the news channel broadcast videos of the scene where Narcisa's body had been found. Again that night she slept in her daughter's room as though she could absorb her child's essence from the bed in which the girl had slept.

Early the next morning, Esperanza resumed her patient stitching. The satin sample from yesterday's visit to the funeral home was the first piece she added to her slowly growing patchwork. Her sorrow flowed with the fabric into the machine, but unlike the stitched pieces, it never emerged from under the presser foot. It chipped away at the

Kenmore's bobbin mechanisms, its tension controls, its feed dogs, its wiring and its gears.

After Narcisa's burial, Esperanza's days took on a routine. She rose early in the morning and worked for awhile on the patchwork of scraps. Now and then a tear she'd been unable to suppress dropped onto the Kenmore and vanished into its workings. When that happened, the rise and fall of the needle hesitated imperceptibly, then resumed its rhythmic motion.

Around ten most mornings, one client or another would call with a request. Despite her sorrow, Esperanza could not afford to say no. Most difficult were the days when mothers brought their lovely young daughters to be fitted for their coming-out dresses. Now and then Esperanza would select scraps of fabric left over from the construction of these festive gowns and stitch them into her patchwork.

Sometimes the police detective, Sergeant Diaz, called to bring Esperanza up to date on the investigation into Narcisa's murder. The police were working on it but had nothing definite as yet. But they would solve the case, of that he was certain. Sergeant Diaz was a Chicano, and Esperanza trusted him because he spoke to her in Spanish.

Every evening after her supper, Esperanza walked to the cemetery. If the florist on Ridge Avenue was open, she bought flowers. At first it was narcissus, Narcisa's namesake flower. As spring moved into summer, it would be daisies or gladiolus. Sometimes she laid a single yellow rose on Narcisa's grave. Then she knelt on the grass and prayed for justice.

As autumn approached, Esperanza's patchwork fabric took on a vaguely rectangular shape. Piecing it together was slow work because she had cut the scraps so small, but she felt no urgency. Esperanza didn't notice that her reliable Kenmore sewing machine had developed rust spots here and there, nor that its once-glossy case had become discolored and shabby as her fingers continued to release more and more of her grief into her work. She saw only her careful lines of stitching and the bits of Narcisa's garments she used. There were swatches from the ivory quinceañara dress interspersed with strips from a flowered pink blouse, navy oblongs from a school uniform, a scrap of blue bathrobe, and fragments of a very old T-shirt printed all over with images of Snoopy. The sewing machine labored on, putting thousands of stitches into the patchwork history of Narcisa's brief life.

When all the scraps had been sewn together, Esperanza cut a piece of fluffy batting to fit the patchwork rectangle. For backing, she took a piece of Narcisa's yellow bedspread. She basted the layers of patchwork, batting and backing together on the Kenmore. Then she began stitching the lines of quilting. It seemed random at first, but before long the lines resolved into interlaced outlines of narcissus blossoms. Every stitch diminished her grief by a fraction, although Esperanza did not yet recognize that.

Late in the afternoon on a chilly November day, Sergeant Diaz came to Esperanza's bungalow. He told her that Narcisa's killers had been caught–four young men who trafficked in all manner of illegal substances.

"Norteamericano?" Esperanza timidly asked.

"No, Colombian gangbangers," Diaz said. "They shot your daughter and her boyfriend and threw their bodies into that Glenview pond."

"These young people, no good," muttered Esperanza. "Doesn't matter where they come from. Will they go to jail? What will happen to them?"

"They'll be in jail for awhile, and then they'll go to trial," Sergeant Diaz told her. "Maybe they'll be convicted. Maybe not. Sometimes, if they can pay for a good lawyer, they get off. These Colombians, now, they have money–"

"Where is justice?" Esperanza asked.

Diaz shook his head. "It's in God's hands."

On the following day, Esperanza sewed the final stitches into the quilt she had assembled from memories of her daughter's life. When she had finished, she released the

quilt from the old Kenmore machine. It was hard to raise the
presser foot, and the corroded mechanism dropped dull
metallic shards on the fabric when it finally relaxed its grip.
She lifted the cloth from the machine and tied off the last
line of stitching.

The finished piece was an artistic masterpiece, but to
Esperanza, its beauty resided only in what it represented–
what she had been able to salvage of her daughter's severed
life. Standing up, she shook out the fabric and wrapped it
around herself. As its warmth enveloped her, her tears finally
flowed.

But as Esperanza made peace with her sorrow, the old
Kenmore sewing machine broke down. The presser foot fell
off its corroded mounting, dropping to the rusted needle
plate. The tension discs froze in place, immobilizing the
thread path. A massive Gordian knot jammed the workings
of the bobbin case. The hand wheel stalled, and the teeth of
the gears sheared off. A network of fine cracks spread
through the shabby plastic case. The filament in the
machine's light bulb crumbled, and the light went out.

The old Kenmore had struggled to take away
Esperanza's grief. When its work was completed and it could
do no more, it perished of Esperanza's sorrow.

The End

Highland Woman

John Boyle

"Tis the next corner you'll be turning at."

Bruce Camden tapped on the steering wheel. "Left or Right?" Without looking up from the scrap of paper with scrawled directions, his wife pointed left. Bruce smiled and slowed the Mercedes, thinking how Shannon knew that once again she'd let slip her Scottish brogue despite those expensive elocution lessons he'd insisted she take. Still, as trophy wives went, Shannon was several cuts above any of the other junior partner's cohorts at his investment firm. Her perfect figure and long blond hair might meet their match with a few of the upper level executive's companions, but no women he'd ever met could boast of those sparking deep-blue eyes. Wild Scottish eyes that hinted of a deep and barely-restrained sensuality.

This back road was garbage-strewn and narrow. Bruce hated driving his Beamer anywhere in upper Manhattan, and somehow, Shannon had steered him into the worst neighborhood on the island. At least it wasn't Brooklyn or Queens. He'd been quite firm in telling her that they'd never go garage sale scrounging in those neighborhoods. He glanced at his Rolex, four more hours of this foolishness and they could return to their house in Connecticut.

One wasted day humoring his wife's strange compulsion to check out garage sales and tomorrow he'd be flying to Las Vegas for two weeks of non-stop gambling. It wasn't a bad compromise. He had never understood her need to poke around in other people's junk. However, she called his gambling foolish and would spend her time in Vegas going to shows like *Chippendales* and *Thunder from Down Under*.

"Stop!" Shannon shouted. "Look there."

Bruce turned to where she pointed and saw a dirty graffiti-covered wall. "What, look at a stupid wall?" he said. "This area is a dump, we should get out of here."

"No look carefully. It's a shop. Antiques and used goods. Let's go in, just for a minute."

Bruce looked again, this time picking out an old, weather-beaten and almost graffiti-disguised shop. How could he have missed it? He would have sworn he'd seen a wall when he'd first glanced over. Reluctantly, he pulled the Beamer to the curb. Shannon was out of the car almost before he'd stopped.

His eyes took a minute to adjust to the shop's dark interior, although his nose was well entertained by a variety of strong and unusual smells. Lilac, wood, leather, and turpentine all flashed through his nostrils in turn as if they'd been standing in a queue. By the time his eyes could make out anything in the dim light, Shannon stood in the far corner of the store opening small drawers and peering at the contents. Bruce looked around, noting that the only light came from three flickering oil lanterns hanging from the ceiling. Clever Goth ambiance, but the New York Fire Marshal would shit bricks if he ever inspected this joint. There were other things hanging from the ceiling, the most obvious being a stuffed fifteen-foot crocodile. He stopped looking at it when the flickering light made it appear as if one of the animal's glass eyes winked at him.

Every nook and shelf held some unidentifiable knickknack; the wall behind the counter appeared entirely devoted to glass carboys filled with various herbs. He walked over to the counter with its ancient mechanical cash register and a stuffed bird in a wicker cage alongside it. The stuffed bird had large multicolored butterfly-type wings which made him bend down to examine the artist's creation more clearly. Viewed closely, the body appeared to be a naked female, and he jumped back when some hidden sensor caused the figure to hiss and open its mouth to display a multitude of shark-like teeth.

Surrounded by so much unexplainable junk, his hand reached out to grab the one thing he recognized: one of those magic eight-balls. He shook it and watched as the little device inside rose to visibility. It said: *Beware the pool boy*. He shook his head. It figured a place like this would carry some sort of gimmicky knock-off.

"Tis a question you'll be asking it first," his wife shouted from the other side of the store.

"All right," he decided to humor her. "What number will come up first when I start playing roulette in Las Vegas?"

The answer slowly rose from the depths and Bruce readied himself to shout out the incongruous result.

Twenty-two.

"Oh," he muttered and quickly put the ball back on the counter.

"And what might I interest you fine people in buying?" Bruce looked down; a small man dressed in a sequined robe and pointed stocking hat seemed to have appeared alongside him. The store's proprietor looked, for all the world, like a garden-gnome statue. Bruce pushed his non-PC thoughts back, and had begun his "just looking" line when the little guy grabbed Bruce's hand, slid back his jacket sleeve and inspected the watch.

"Ah, a gentleman of means," the gnome said while nodding excessively. "I have just the thing for your household. It will solve your servant problems and impress your friends. It's right over here."

He pulled Bruce to the opposite side of the store and yanked the canvas cover off what might have been a brass and leather model of a movie robot, if the designer hadn't gone crazy with tubes, valves and exposed clockwork bits that served no function. The thing's mechanical eyes were seriously overdone, two brass protrusions behind a toothed wheel inset with six different glass lenses. A clockwork screw device sticking out where the eyebrows should be was obviously placed there to rotate the lens-wheel. The thing sat, if that was the right word, on a crate that said: Professor Darwin's automanitrons.

"Just let me insert an aneither ball into the boiler and you can see some of its functions." The gnome continued talking as he opened a small metal box to remove a glowing blue ball which he inserted into a slot on the robot's back. "One aneither ball will run the pistons for over a month. Ah, there we go. Once the steam's up to pressure, I'll demonstrate some of its abilities."

Things began to happen. Valves clicked, screws turned, a clockwork mechanism rose out from a hatch in the top of the head and began moving in complicated ways. One of the arms slowly rose to its chest and pressed a lever. Steam shot out of the mouth opening. It sounded similar to the last squeal of a mouse as the trap sprung closed. Bruce took a step backward.

Just as the automanitron reached a standing position, it gave out a long hissing sigh that ended up sounding like a child blowing a raspberry. Then it stopped dead and tumbled over. Several brass cogwheels rolled across the floor.

"What?" shouted the gnome? "This can't be. That was a new aneither ball." He bent over, opened the hatch and pulled out the ball which had turned a reddish brown. "Exhausted. Totally spent," he muttered.

"Excuse me," said Shannon. "How much do you want for this?" She held up a sparkling blue crystal pendant whose color perfectly matched her eyes.

"That's a witch's talisman," said the Gnome. "Only a powerful witch can even pick...." He stopped, stared at Shannon and then turned to Bruce. "Your town," he said hesitantly. "It's Londinium, right?"

"New York, Manhattan to be precise. Lived here long, dude?"

"Oh shit," muttered the gnome. "I've got to leave, now!"

"The pretty crystal," interrupted Shannon. "How much?"

"It won't leave you now that it's found an owner," muttered the gnome. "Your damn power must have pulled me here instead of the steam world. So I guess it's free...wait! Stores like mine rarely stop on science planets because they drain aneither power so quickly. Things from places like this are really rare, how about trading that clever watch for the ladies' crystal?" He pointed to Bruce's Rolex.

"No way," said Bruce. "This watch cost me more than thirty grand."

"You'll be giving the nice man your watch now," said Shannon, her hands tightly clasped around the crystal.

Bruce, without losing contact with Shannon's flashing blue eyes, removed the watch and handed it to the gnome. The little guy kissed the watch while jumping up and down. Then, like any good tradesman who did his business across the multiverse, ushered the two of them out of the store before they regretted the deal.

Bruce, sans watch, sat in his Mercedes, stared at the graffiti covered wall and wondered what had just happened. He turned to look at Shannon who smiled and gently rubbed the pendant that now hung around her neck.

"Bruce dear," she said quietly. "Go have your silly fun in Las Vegas. Bet all you have on twenty-two like the magic ball said and make lots of money. I'll not be going with you this year. I have a number of things I need to arrange." Her blue eyes flashed, cold, brilliant and most of all determined.

The End

The Hunt for Sam Bass's Gold

Jerry Cowling

Hogg Nubbins had been a cowpoke for most near all his life. He wasn't much good for anything else. He couldn't read or write, not that he was interested in reading anything that would give him ideas. If he could write he wouldn't know what to put on the paper. Hogg had just one goal in life: to find Sam Bass's gold.

Riding up and down the Chisholm Trail in Texas all he ever heard was the Ballad of Sam Bass. Other cowpokes said the song was written to lull the cows into walking the same direction and to keep the cowboys from falling asleep. It was quite a yarn, that Ballad of Sam Bass.

Sam had one hell of a life, yessiree. Born in Indiana, he came to Texas as a young man, filled with piss and vinegar, and set out to make himself some money. This was all in the song. The guys on the trail filled in facts left out because the songwriter ran out of notes. Sam and his buddies started robbing trains and banks all the way from Central Texas to the Dakotas and points in between. One time they robbed a train, beat a man to a pulp before the guy gave up and opened the safe.

"Sixty thousand dollars," old Pete, the chuck wagon boss, said. Pete was a youngin' when they finally shot Sam to death at Round Rock, Texas, so he should know. "All in mint twenty dollar gold coins. The biggest train robbery ever."

The ballad said Sam was like some kind of Robin Hood, stealing from the rich and giving to the poor, being loyal to his friends and all.

"The only poor people Sam ever gave money to was bartenders and whores," Pete said.

"The whole sixty thousand dollars to bartenders and whores?" Hogg asked, his mouth falling open.

"Oh hell, there ain't enough whores in Texas to spend sixty thousand dollars on," Pete said. He doused the campfire, and that was the end of the story.

The next morning on the trail the cowpokes around Hogg started singing the Ballad of Sam Bass again. He went back to thinking about that sixty thousand dollars. Damn, he thought, if I had that much money I might buy me some of those fancy false teeth I hear talked about. Hogg didn't have a tooth in his head. They had all rotted out by the time he was thirty.

That night as he gummed his chili and corn pone Hogg asked Pete, "Well, if Sam Bass didn't spend all sixty thousand dollars on whores what do you think he done with it?"

"He hid it," Burly piped up. Burly was almost as old as Pete, but he was still spry enough to ride a horse and herd cattle. "That's what I always heard."

"Where?" Hogg was getting excited now. If somebody can hide a bunch of gold coins then somebody else can find them.

"Sam's last words were, 'I bet those folks in Cooke County will be huntin' a long time for that gold.' So it must be in Cooke County," Burly said.

"Where's Cooke County?" Hogg asked.

"Aww, that's bullshit," Pete said as he spooned out the last of the chili. "Sam's last words was 'The world is bobbing around me.' And I had fellers who was right there when he died tell me that."

"It ain't no bullshit at all," Burly shot back. Pete and Burly hated each other for years. Some said they once fought over a woman. Others said they were just a couple of sonovabitches that couldn't get along. "It didn't have to be the absolute last thing Sam said. Hell, it took him a full day to die after they shot him. He probably said a lot of things before he actually died."

"I still say bullshit." Pete looked at the cowpokes around the fire. "Anybody want the last cornpone?"

"Now where is this Cooke County?" Hogg asked again. He figured he could spend the gold coins on whores just like Sam did.

"Everybody that got a lick of sense knows that Sam Bass hung out in Cooke County as much as he hung out anyplace else in Texas," Burly continued in a loud defiant voice. "I know for a fact Sam and his gang hid out in Cove Holler. That's in the southwest corner of Cooke County, and hardly nobody lives there."

"Only a idiot would hide out in Cove Holler. It's so thick with oak and walnut trees and vines and brush the sun can't shine through at noon day," Pete countered.

"Well, nobody said Sam was the brightest man around," Burly said sullenly. "And the holler is all riddled with limestone caves, just the place to hide a bundle of gold coins."

"Where is this Cooke County?" Hogg said for the third time. If anybody could find Sam Bass's gold, Hogg knew he was the man to do it.

"Hogg, you must be the dumbest sonovabitch I ever done seen. Cooke County is three counties due west of here." Pete doused the campfire, and the conversation ended right there.

When Hogg mounted up the next morning he kept
looking due west toward Cooke County and then at the
cattle. He had been herding cattle all these years, and what
had it ever got him? A calloused ass and a wallet full of
nothing. All he has to do is ride west and keep asking folks
along the way where this Cooke County was.

"Hogg! Get movin'! We gotta get across the Red River
by night fall!" Burly shouted.

Hogg looked west and then at the cattle one last time,
and then he lit out full gallop heading west. The gallop
eventually became a trot, and he started laying out his plan to
find Sam Bass's gold. He didn't want to be none too eager to
talk about it, Hogg told himself. When he stopped for the
night he ought to be real casual about his conversations with
folks. Didn't want nobody to know what he was up to. That
Cove Holler seemed to be the place to look, all right. After a
couple of days he found himself in Gainesville, the Cooke
County seat. He settled into a chair at the local boarding
house dining room. Hogg tried to start up a conversation.

"Nice little town you got here."

"Wouldn't know. I'm just passin' through." The man
had on a nice suit of clothes and had his hair slicked down
with something that smelled mighty sweet.

"Then you wouldn't know about Cove Holler."

"Everyone in North Texas knows about Cove Hollow,"
the man replied with a sniff. "The worst land in the whole
territory. Not worth a dime."

"That's what I heard too," Hogg said. "Lots of
underbrush and limestone caves. Sounds like a place you
wanna to keep away from. Just where is it so I can go in the
opposite direction?" Hogg thought he was being very clever.

The fancy dude with the perfumed hair gave him perfect
directions -- southwest of Gainesville along a long ravine.
The nearest ranch was miles away.

When he woke up the next day Hogg checked out of the
boarding house and went southwest until he found the
beginning of the ravine. When he couldn't ride any further

into the thick underbrush Hogg tied up his horse. The prickly bushes and vines surrounded by oak and walnut trees made walking slow going. He didn't know exactly where he was or how he would find his way out. All he knew was that he was on the hunt for Sam Bass's gold.

Soon the foliage thickened so the sun was completely blocked. Only mottled areas of dim light appeared here and there. Hogg squinted from side to side and saw hints of limestone caves in the distance. Suddenly his foot slipped and he fell straight down. At the bottom of the hole Hogg took a moment to regain his senses. He must have fallen into one of them limestone caves. There was so little light he had to wait until his eyes adjust a bit. Then he began to reach his hands out to touch something. Mostly limestone. Smooth, moist limestone. Then he felt something else. Leather. Hogg eagerly grabbed at it. A leather bag. No, two leather bags. No, more than that.

Hogg clumsily clawed at the belt tying one of the leather bags shut. Opening it he frantically stuck his fingers inside. He felt coins, lots of coins. Hogg pulled them out of the bag and peered at them. They were gold coins. Twenty dollar gold coins. And they still looked as new and sparkly as the day Sam Bass took them off the train.

Laughing loudly he quickly opened the other leather bags. They were all filled with gold coins. Enough gold coins to get him some good false teeth and all the whores he'd ever want.

"Glory hallelujah!" Hogg shouted. He looked up. "I found ..." Hogg stopped as he stared at the steep slippery limestone shaft above him. He finished in a whimper, "...Sam Bass's gold."

The End

IRS

Mary H. Sheldon

Jed looked out over the yard. The last refrigerated truck pulled into its bay and the door creaked when Ron English got out. Ron limped to the steps at the end of the dock and pulled himself up each step. Jed had been invited to Ron's 60th birthday party last summer.

"Man, he looks like he's hurtin," Jed thought. "I wonder if he'll make it to retirement age?"

That wasn't the only reason he wondered if Ron would make it to retirement age. Jed wondered if his South Hadley Ice Company would still be in business next year.

He heard his receptionist, Sheila, talking with Ron as he brought in his slips for the day. He ought to go out and wish Ron a good weekend. But he couldn't make himself go out there.

"Have a good weekend, Ron," he heard Sheila say.

"You too. No bar hoppin now, Sheila." They both laughed.

Sheila's chair slid back. A file cabinet opened and closed. The copier chortled and shut down.

Sheila poked her head through the doorway. "I'm ready to go now."

"That's fine, Sheila. Have a good weekend."

"Do you have everything you need for Monday?"

"As far as I know. If I don't, I'll find out on Monday, won't I?"

Sheila started to turn and then said, "I shut the copier off, but if you still need it, I'll turn it back on."

He shook his head. "No, I'm going home, too, in just a little bit. There's not much more I can do to prepare. Thanks for all your help this week, Sheila. It's been a nightmare."

"Try to get your mind off it, if you can. See you Monday morning. He's coming at nine am, so I'll be here by eight to make sure everything is neat & tidy & coffee is made."

"Sheila, what's the guy's name that's coming?"

"Lemme look." Papers shuffled in the file folder Sheila flipped through." The Notice is signed by an Agent Carter. Good night."

Jed nodded as Sheila grabbed her sweater and quickly closed the door behind her.

Jed went back to the window. He had always liked the second floor office where he could keep an eye on the place. Sheila's dusty car backed out and tore out of the driveway. She sure was glad to get out of here, wasn't she, he thought.

Apparently, he had stood there for longer than he realized when his cell phone startled him.

Holy crap. I'm in for it.

"Hi, Midge," he tried to say cheerfully. "No, no I didn't forget. I just wasn't ready to leave here, yet."

Midge wasn't happy. The Greens had invited them to dinner at the Club and they were all tired of waiting for him so they were going into the dining room without him.

"That's OK, Dear. What do want me to do? Come out there now or just go… OK."

Midge didn't really care where he went or when. He tapped the phone and slid it in his pocket.

Jed looked sadly at the boxes of receipts and reports and tax returns brought up from the storage room. Stuff from three years ago.

Shit, I'm not going to remember anything from three years ago. Agent Carter is going to start digging into these boxes and ask me something, and I'm going to say the wrong thing. How am I going to do this?

His phone rang again. He looked at it and debated whether to listen to Midge's tirade again.

"Yah ... Okay ...That's alright ... Okay, I'm leaving for home now ... That sounds good ... Mushrooms and onions? Sure ... Bye"

Midge was sorry for being snippy and was bringing a steak and potato home for him.

He shut off the lights as he went out, locking the doors behind him. The freezers chilled the entire building outside of the office and break room. The compressors hummed and vibrated on their platforms. But it was the smell of the packing room that he had loved since he was a kid. When he got to the loading dock and reached for the railing, he thought he might look like Ron dragging himself around. All his muscles were tight as tortoise shells.

❀

It was a busy weekend. Jed talked with the kids about summer camps. He smiled at the neighbor's jokes at the neighborhood cookout. He hung on to Midge as she slept and snored. He fixed the patio door. He went down to the plant twice each day and stood and looked at the boxes and piles of papers stacked in his office. He didn't know why, but he just needed to look at them. He had decided not to call his accountant again, since he was so mad after the last call.

"Why do I pay that guy as much as I do and end up having to figure it out myself?" he yelled as he slammed the phone down.

Sheila had come in and quietly shut the door between the offices.

Harry Zabrinsky, his lawyer, got him wondering if he should just shut the doors and close the business.

"This isn't going to be pleasant, Jed," Harry said. "But keep in mind, you are the taxpayer and you pay his salary. Don't let him intimidate you. Don't give him *anything* you aren't *absolutely* sure of. Keep him waiting as long as you can. Make him think you'll give him whatever he wants, but stall him, if you have any doubts, we'll go through what he's asking for. Call me whenever you want, day or night. Oh, yeah, I'm going to Reno that weekend, so leave me a message and I'll get back to you."

"Thanks, Harry."

Jed stared, eyes wide open, at the ceiling over the bed on Monday morning. He'd been awake since 3:30 and was rehearsing answers for Agent Carter. Why would he be audited? He hadn't made any big changes and that was a question he was going to ask, "Why?"

At 5am, he swung his legs to the floor and quickly got dressed. Midge thought he should wear a sport jacket for the big day, but Jed put on his regular chinos and polo with the company logo on it. "I'm an iceman not a pencil pusher."

He quietly shut the doors behind him as he left the house. He'd pull through McDonalds for coffee. Waiting for a pot to brew seemed like an eternity this morning.

Remembering Ron English, he forced himself to bound up the steps and stroll briskly to his office.

The men started coming about quarter to seven. After he heard a few come in, he went to the top of the stairs and called down to them, "Have a good day today, guys. After the warm weekend, you should have a lot of restocking to do." They all nodded and waved. They were whispering, probably wondering how long they would have a job.

Well intentioned as she was, Sheila didn't get there until 8:30 and spent the time rushing around making coffee and turning things on and listening to the voice messages.

Midge was on the phone when Sheila came to the door and made all sorts of hands signals. He told Midge he'd call her when it was all over. "Love you, too."

He took a deep breath and walked out to greet the IRS agent. He smiled as he put his hand out. Whatever he had planned to say went out the window. He could barely speak. He sounded like a cold was coming on.

Agent Carter smiled broadly back at him.

"Very nice to meet you, too, Mr. Hawkins." Agent Carter was hauling in plastic tote boxes with holes in them.

Oh, gees. He's going to take away my files. Damn. I only made a few copies. I should have copied the whole pile. Damn. Damn. Damn, Jed thought.

"Thanks for making time to see me today, Mr. Hawkins. I'm sure you're going to find this to be a fascinating day. Where can I set up my displays?" Carter said.

"Displays?" Jed puzzled.

"Why, yes. I have brought three different specimens and I'd like to see which one you are most compatible with before we can assign it to you and your family." Agent Carter addressed each of his file boxes: "Calm down, Molly. You'll be fine. Boris, wait just a minute. Wake up, Annie. No time for a nap" he said as he lined up the totes.

Sheila was staring from the doorway and making that circular move with her finger to her temple. "He's nuts!" she mouthed.

Jed moved to the man. "I'm sorry for the misunderstanding, sir, but I've got a very important meeting here in a few minutes. You must have gotten the wrong address."

The man looked at his notebook. "Jed Hawkins, South Hadley Ice Company, 9am Monday, April 1st. That's you, isn't it?

Jed thought he had entirely lost his mind.

The man continued, "My mother had a sense of humor and she thought by giving me the first name of Agent that a lot of doors would open for me. And then when I got a job with the IRS , it was perfect."

"What?" Jed whispered.

"Why, yes. The International Rodent Society is the perfect group to raise the esteem and dignity of the world's sorely misunderstood rodent family."

"What?" Jed croaked again.

"Now here's Molly, a cute little Delicate Deermouse. She's from Mexico originally. She's a little excited right now, but..." Agent clamored on.

"If you open any of those cases, I'm going to call the police," Jed bellowed.

Sheila was sitting at her desk now with her head on her folded arms as she rocked with laughter.

"But you requested information about our No Kill Rodent Shelter, and I think you owe me the respect of hearing the rest of my description of our work. You may warm to taking Annie the Guinea Pig into your home." Agent Carter pleaded.

"No, I'm not going to warm to it and my wife is not going to warm to it. Sheila!" he bellowed.

Sheila peeked, unable to even try to cover her downright amusement.

Jed looked at Agent Carter and then at Sheila and heard a roar of laughter from downstairs. "Sheila, grab a hold of this case and be careful with it because cute little Molly Deermouse might bite you with her cute little sharp teeth! Help Agent Carter down the stairs."

"But Boss, I can't touch a, a, a.....rodent," Sheila stammered.

"You'd better figure it out fast, Sheila, because you are going to repack and re-file ALL of these files and storage boxes. I'll be taking Midge to the Club for lunch, and then

I'm going take a long ride. I expect you'll have it all cleaned up by tomorrow morning when I get back here.

Jed flew down the stairs and vaulted off the loading dock. He put the windows down in his Ford 150 as he headed out. It might have been 20 years ago since he felt this good. The IRS was off his back and he was *free!*

The End

Jumbo

Based on a true event
Judy G. Burford

"It was a somber day. Children on two continents wept. Grown men pulled their hankies from their pockets to wipe away elephant sized tears. Even Queen Victoria and the Prince of Wales were in mourning."

Albert Copeman's great-grandchildren leaned in close to hear the story their great-granddad was about to share for the umpteenth time.

"Tell us about the 'Jumbomania,'" Alex said.

He was the youngest of the three children. His sister Emma sat to his right, wriggling with excitement. The oldest boy, Lucas, sat to his left nodding in agreement with his younger brother's request.

"There were venders on every street corner selling trading cards, prints, hats, bracelets, earrings, canes, cigars, fans and numerous other trinkets to remember the day that Barnum & Bailey's circus came to town."

Albert grinned from ear to ear. He enjoyed telling the tale as much as the children enjoyed hearing it.

"What did your mother get?" Emma asked in spite of the fact she'd heard the story before.

"Her mother, my grandmother, took her to one of the stands and allowed her to pick out whichever trinket she wanted."

Emma let out a squeal in anticipation.

"She picked a print that had a picture of Jumbo and Tiny Tim," Albert said.

"Show us granddad, show us," Emma said.

Albert held up the well-worn print, dating back to that unforgettable day, September 15th, 1885.

"Ohhh," all three children responded at once.

"And what did your mother think of the circus?" asked Lucas.

"She thought it was the most magnificent thing she'd ever seen in her entire life," Albert said. "She especially liked the giant elephant who danced about the center ring."

"It was her best day and her worst day, wasn't it Granddad?" asked Alex.

"Indeed it was, Alex," replied Albert.

All three children leaned in closer in anticipation of the part of the story that always made them jump nearly out of their skin.

"When the circus was over, my grandmother took my mother down to the rail yard. It was way past my mother's bedtime, but it was a special occasion. There were hundreds of other people lined up close to the track hoping for one last glimpse of the animals before they boarded their rail cars for the journey to their next show town. Before very long, the crowd started to cheer. They could see Jumbo's trainer, Matthew Scott, leading the elephants through the opening that had been made in the fence along the track. The excitement was building and my mother could barely contain herself. She was only seven years old, so she had to push her way toward the front of the crowd in order to see. Then, suddenly, the flagman started running and waving his red lantern. Everyone in the crowd turned their heads to see what he was running toward. That's when they heard the warning horn followed by a trumpeting screech."

The three children jumped in unison as Granddad's voice reached a feverish pitch.

"And instantly a swiftly approaching train ran into Tiny Tim throwing him into the nearby ditch. That's when Jumbo seemed to get disoriented. He started running along beside the track and darted right in front of the oncoming train. By the time he realized his mistake, he turned just in time to see the train hit him. Several cars jumped the track and the crowd ran in fear of being part of the accident. When everything settled, Jumbo was lying on the track, his trainer sobbing by his side. The giant animal reached up with his trunk and pulled the trainer close to him. The two embraced just before the giant beast took its last breath."

Emma wiped a tear from her face with the back of her hand.

"Scotty loved Jumbo didn't he Granddad?" Emma asked.

"Yes, he did, Emma," Albert replied. "He did indeed. And so did most of the people across two continents.

"North America and England. Right, Granddad?" said Lucas.

"You're right, Lucas."

"And nobody will ever forget Jumbo the greatest elephant in the whole wide world," said Alex.

"Can we go up to see Jumbo's statue," the three chimed at once.

"We can indeed," said Albert. "Grab your jackets and get in Granddad's car."

"I call the front seat," said Lucas, even though he knew the other two were too young to ride in the front.

"Emma took Granddad's hand in hers and walked with him to the car," being the little lady that she was.

The bubbly foursome buckled themselves in and Albert started the engine. They were off to see the famous pachyderm atop the hill at the west end of St. Thomas, Ontario, Canada.

Albert wondered who would be the first to ask for ice cream. His story always ended with the same ritual.

The End

Karma

Karen Ann Wilson

Kathy's husband, Steve, was in a 4x6x8-inch box on the top shelf in the hall closet. The box, itself, was in a thin blue nylon bag bearing the name of the funeral home. Randall and Davis. The bag was blue, rather than red, or even green, presumably to denote serenity, although sadness is what the color meant to Kathy. She could almost hear 13 year-old Leanne Rhimes singing that old Patsy Cline song that made her so famous.

Kathy glanced up at the bag every time she got out the vacuum cleaner. She felt guilty that she hadn't done anything with Steve's ashes. His parents were dead, and his brother was farming somewhere in Central America. And, as Steve liked to put it, he wasn't growing broccoli. Her parents lived on the west coast and after Steve's murder, didn't seem inclined to talk about him at all. Certainly not about what to do with his remains. Or, more specifically, cremains.

Although he did have a will, fortunately, Steve hadn't
made any funeral plans. He was, after all, only 50, and such
matters are hard enough to discuss when you're 75. His
health was good, he ate right, ran three miles every day after
work and did not smoke or drink (well, except for an
occasional glass of red wine with dinner.) He just hadn't
counted on being shot in the back by Gregory Fuller.

Steve worked for Bingham Environmental Consulting,
Inc. He was their reptile man, which meant a lot of plastic
lizards and snakes adorned their refrigerator and Steve's
office, many of them Mother Nature never envisioned, even
in her wildest dreams.

Indigo snakes, gopher tortoises, scrub lizards, anything
endemic to a sand hill, were his specialty. Which meant a lot
of people in Florida had it out for Steve. Developers mostly,
because sand hills were where you wanted to build stuff.
Good drainage, fewer mosquitoes, no alligators. Cheaper
permits. No wetland vegetation to worry about. Of course,
that meant the natural inhabitants of the sand hills were
rapidly becoming threatened, even endangered. And the last
thing a developer wanted was for Steve Young to find any of
the aforementioned species on his or her property. Because it
cost money, on the order of three grand per tortoise, to move
the critters to some other suitable habitat, mostly because
suitable habitat meant sand hills, which were, themselves,
endangered. You had to hire a professional biologist (not
your unemployed brother-in-law) to do the moving and you
had to pay a fee for the use of the land where the tortoises
would end up. Also, for a time, it became difficult to move
gopher tortoises anywhere because of the diseases they
potentially might transmit to gopher tortoises already
residing in the new location.

So when Bingham Environmental was hired by Fuller
Enterprises to assess the environmental impact of their
proposed Sandy Hills Mall (required for issuance of a
construction permit), Steve was sent out to the site on Old
Wayne Cross Road, where he discovered not one or two

active gopher tortoise burrows but fifty-six. Whereupon
Gregory Fuller et al. saw the grand opening of their little
mall quickly fading into the sunset, along with the contents
of their bank account.

Gregory Fuller decided to go out to the site one Sunday
after church and cover the burrows with enough fill material
to suffocate the little bastards, or at least impede their ability
to dig themselves out. That way, when the state people came
to verify Steve's findings, a second environmental
assessment would be necessary--a second opinion, if you
will--because by then it would be a "he said, she said"
situation, and the new expert could honestly say there
weren't any burrows or, at most, just a couple.

Unfortunately, Steve liked to work on Sundays,
mapping out the locations of the burrows and taking
pictures, without having the property owners tagging along.
About the only dangers he ever expected to encounter that
fateful day were the occasional rattlesnake or nest of yellow
jackets. So he was armed with only a machete and a can of
insect repellant. He had his cell phone on him, but it's hard
to make a call when you're laying face-down in the sand,
bleeding out.

Gregory Fuller eventually was arrested for Steve's
murder, but not before he and his brother and their little band
of illegal immigrants managed to fill in a majority of the
burrows. His brother, Samuel, went ahead with the project,
and the grand opening was on the horizon, tarnished a bit,
perhaps, by the murder, but still a big deal for the locals who
didn't even have a Wal-Mart to call their own.

Kathy continued to fret over a final resting place for her
husband. They lived (well, Kathy at least) in an old
farmhouse on ten acres of land, and had a nice garden where
Kathy grew vegetables. She thought about scattering Steve's
ashes over the garden, where they might nourish the
tomatoes, but decided that when she died, the Fuller family
would probably buy the property, then pave over it, since the
farm was located on a sand hill. *Some final resting place that*

would be, she thought. And then, it struck her. The idea was so wickedly wonderful, that she took the blue bag down from the shelf and danced around in the living room, holding the bag close and singing *I'll Be Watching You*, by Sting. "Every move you make, every step you take..."

The very next day, Kathy, with Steve sitting beside her, sans blue bag, drove out to the site of the Sandy Hills Mall. She hadn't been there since before Steve's death and hadn't planned to ever go there again, no matter how badly she needed a new pair of designer jeans.

The transformation was awe inspiring. Where once a sand pine forest stood, there now was a desert in the middle of which sat the Sandy Hills Mall, a series of interconnected concrete buildings surrounded by tiny little live oak trees set in planters, which, Kathy presumed, were intended to make up for the lost pine forest. The 'Mall' was surrounded by an asphalt parking lot the size of New Hampshire. Kathy was pretty sure there weren't enough people in the whole county to fill it up, even at Christmas.

She parked her car at the far left side of the lot. Fortunately, there were half a dozen other cars parked nearby, so she wouldn't be drawing attention to herself. She scanned the area, looking for a suitable place to scatter Steve's ashes.

It was twelve-thirty, and most of the workers were taking a lunch break. She could see them sitting on a picnic table in front of a store with "Coming Soon!" printed on a giant piece of white paper taped to the inside of the window. From where she sat, Kathy couldn't make out exactly what was coming soon.

A large concrete truck was positioned at the edge of the asphalt, its huge oblong barrel slowly turning around and around. A long sluiceway extended from the barrel down to what was obviously a sidewalk under construction.

Kathy stared at the concrete truck, as if the slowly rotating ovoid had some special hypnotic powers. The she smiled, picked Steve up, and got out of her car. And froze.

Maybe she hadn't drawn attention to herself while in her car but now she was out of her car, and she would have a hard time looking the part of a large, grizzled man in coveralls. At least Steve wasn't in a flowery $600 urn.

The men at the picnic table didn't see her as she approached the concrete truck. She was acting as nonchalant as possible, but her heart was pounding in her chest and she felt faint. Nauseous even. But she continued on until she was behind the truck. She looked up at the opening to the rotating drum.

"Well, Steve," she said. "This is it. For eternity, or at least until the mall is leveled to make way for something grander, you can haunt the place. Cast spells, scare customers away. Drive the Fullers into bankruptcy."

She opened the box and looked inside. The contents were a mixture of ashes and small bits of bone, much like the small rocks and pebbles that were mixed with cement to produce concrete. She said a little prayer, more for herself than for Steve, because now she was shaking like the proverbial leaf, then stepped on the bumper of the truck and hoisted herself up just far enough to pour the cremains through the opening in the drum. Then she hopped down and quickly headed back to her car, fully expecting someone to shout, "Hey, you!" at her. But no one did.

❁

Two weeks later, Kathy drove out to the new mall. A grand opening celebration, complete with fireworks and free hotdogs was scheduled for that evening.

Kathy walked along the sidewalk, studying the nice new concrete. A couple of sections had tiny footprints in them, foxes probably, and one had the usual sidewalk grafitti in the form of a child's hand print. She didn't know what she was looking for. After recovering from her brief little foray into misdemeanor vandalism, it had occurred to her that maybe Steve hadn't been deposited in the mall sidewalk after all.

That maybe the concrete truck had gone to another job after pouring the sidewalk. Maybe Steve was now resting in the floor of someone's garage. *At least make it someone with a classic car collection,* she thought.

Then Kathy stopped. Something embedded in the concrete caught her eye. It wasn't something you'd notice unless you were looking down at that very moment and the sun was just right and you were hoping for a sign. Any sign. She knelt down and ran her finger over the tiny object. It was smooth and metallic and very shiny. Like the white gold backing on one of Steve's incisor crowns.

Kathy giggled. The section of concrete with the gold nugget was right in front of the leasing office for the Sandy Hills Mall. 'Fuller Enterprises' was written on the door. It was so fitting, so perfect, it brought tears to Kathy's eyes. She drew in a deep breath, then smiled. "Every step you take...."

She put her index finger to her lips, then put it back on the little gold nugget. "Rest in peace, my love," she said. "Rest in peace."

The End

King Willy

Dennis Pupello

If a sex-crazed king or his power-hungry wife asks if you want to be the royal Wizard-Adviser, I would have to say, tell them you'd rather be spat upon by a pack of newts.

Being a naïve dunderhead, I took the job. Back when King Willy and Queen Billary gained control of the throne of Amiracle from King George, I wasn't experienced enough to have the benefit of this sensible warning.

A vocal minority of his subjects who were disenchanted had deposed King George because of his handling of domestic issues. When questioned about domestic affairs, he'd look confused and say, "Who cares about who's cheating with whom?"

At the end, noblemen were openly referring to him as 'the King who would be man.' And one bright November day, he was ousted.

Into this void slid Duke Willy Lint, hips-a-swingin', eyes-a-winkin', with Billary at this side. He would make the peasant women weak in the stomach, with their knees all aflutter. Or maybe it was the other way around.

Duke Willy slipped into the throne of Amiracle like Don Juan stealing into a mistress's window. You see, he was much practiced at the latter.

But now, one year into his reign of love, King Willy was besieged by complaints. He couldn't tell the truth. He couldn't make up his mind. He couldn't pay for all the state-run medieval barbers.

King Willy, at the urging of Queen Billary, called for a "town meeting" in the grandiosely named Monte Hall. There he would listen to the people's complaints, make good eye contact, get in touch with the common folk. Especially the young, attractive blonde girls.

It was with much trepidation and nausea that I listened to Willy rant about how I would have to work 'security' at the town meeting, casting this spell or that if the crowd got out of hand.

I'm the Wizard/Adviser damn it, I don't do security! That's the Secret Squires' job! But he would have none of it. Then I shut up, remembering how a member of his court had recently been found dead, victim of 83 self-inflicted saber wounds.

The medieval barber's report had proclaimed it a suicide.

So now the day of reckoning had come. I watched as Monte Hall filled up with the rich and the poor, the screwed and not-yet-screwed, the Willy-supporters and Willy-opponents, and the attractive young blonde girls.

As I stood beside the dual marble thrones, trumpets bellowed and a purple velvet curtain was swept back revealing His Highness and the queen. He wore his usual white cape, pants, and pointy-boots. Billary was dressed in a peach robe and iron vest. Simple, yet business-like. Smiling, she walked majestically across the platform, and took her royal seat. He shimmied for a few seconds and sat down with a flourish.

I had to admit there were some cheers amid the catcalls

and hissing.

"I feel your pain..." the king started, making a gentle fist.

Because of his long, diamond-studded cape, no one could see the queen's firm grasp around His Highness's royal jewels. No one, that is, except me. Having such a view is not what I would call a perk.

"...and I care about each and every one of you, my lowly, er, *loyal* subjects." He looked out on the gathering compassionately, if not because he felt their pain, because he felt his own. The queen had just flexed her grip.

"We realize that old King Ronnie, at least when he was awake, was much beloved. He made us feel all warm and gushy about ourselves as we crushed the very life from our opponents." Scattered applause. "But Ronnie's gone now..."

In more ways than one, I thought.

"...banished to the Hills of Confusion. Let him live out the rest of his life in peace, searching for Bozo..."

"Bonzo," I whispered.

"Bonzo, Bordeau, whatever. Let the old man live out his dreams, is what I say. And I..."

The queen gave him a squeeze. "...*we* won't even go into his successor, King, King..."

"George, sire," I said.

"King George. His lack of accomplishments makes one forget he even existed. Tell me, can anyone in this hall name one good thing King George did for our great land?"

One of the merchants yelled out: "The Persian Rug War!"

A mercenary: "Captured the bandit Manuel Norieggo."

A philosopher: "Gave the final tug that brought down the Steel Curtain."

A priest: "Kicked the living shit out of..."

"We get the idea," said King Willy. "I am listening to you. I care. You know, you're right, George wasn't so bad." Loud cheering.

Watching my liege bask in the sounds of approval, I

marveled at how quickly he could change his mind. He flip-flopped more than the little morsels in old' MacDonald's tadpole stew.

"Now we must address the reason we are here," he said, looking at the queen, who, it must be said, gazed at him adoringly. Not that she released her grip on his manhood.

It was at this point that I caught King Willy winking at one of the underage damsels. Afraid that the queen would castrate him on the spot, I cast upon the King one of my favorite spells, Limp De La Salt Peter. More powerful than Homely Maiden, simpler than Cold Shower. Does the trick every time. Willy looked down furtively, and then continued.

"Er, uh, I've come up with a plan to solve our problems," he said.

"Whose problems, yours or ours?" cried a bloated stand-up prophet. To his followers he was known as Flush, the most dangerous man in Amiracle.

Before he could cause any more trouble, I conjured furiously, at last creating Dispel Hot Air. His mouth continued to move, but no sounds escaped it.

Only now I grew tired, weary even, having cast two strong spells in succession.

"My beautiful wife Billary and I, and members of our residue…"

"Retinue, sire" I corrected.

"…*retinue* are working hard to improve the quality of life," he said, "for everyone! Peasants included!"

Cheers and applause.

"And we will do it with no further taxes levied on our fine citizens to pay for it!"

I had to roll my eyes at that one.

It was then that several conservative Dukes made obnoxious noises from their balcony seats. I could see Prickly Dole pounding his one good arm against the rail. Next to him, Mad Dog Buchannon foamed at the mouth and barked unintelligibly. Court speaker Newturd Gingrich yanked on multiple patches of white hair, including some not intended for family viewing. Leaning forward in his seat, the wide-eyed William F. Buckler, resident intellectual, removed a quill from its usual place in his mouth and flung it at my liege.

Undaunted, King Willy finished, "Today we are proud to announce our new tax plan. Whitewash!"

Oh, to be spat upon by newts.

The End

What's Ahead

To stop dying I move my fingers
then my arms. Climb out of bed
Vertical is best. Open door

Walk the road, trail memorized
Moon lights the way
past black heaps of tires
tipped barrels, frost-drooped husks.

Last May a thin bitch suckled her
pups here. Our eyes met
Surprise spotlight, a slap in the face.
I'm a short bad dream
dissolved in the scent of the day.

Rooster shouts the call
Honeysuckle trumpets its scent
Yellow the sun, fresh warm
eggs
yolk, butter delicious
fills me up.

The Best of Both Worlds

I ate a quart of ice cream
and didn't have room for cake
I was so fat
Fat walks away bearing the weight
of starvation. Don't feed it

It feeds on itself. Being stupid is harder
than being nothing

Figuring out where I live is as difficult
as a boiled potato. Finish the story
when you get here. Watch the head butt
the cut above the right eye
Bleeding makes the crowd go wild
Eating makes them sleepy

For Goodness' Sake

For goodness' sakes, it's Judy Jakes, as thin as a
dime
And light as a feather.
Lipstick, bubble gum
And rouge hold her together.
She travels around with an entourage of ten,
Judy, eight men, a cat and a hen.
Bim, bam Bacardi, let's crash a party.

The eight muscled guys wear black and white ties,
Rooty tooty Judy shows off her curvy beauty.
Cat and hen, Judy and eight men,
Out for adventure again.

Judy pulls up in her Coupe de Ville
They all get in, they know the drill.
To the Higginbottom party at the top of the hill.

The joint is jumpin' and the band is hot.
Judy wiggles to the beat, she hits the jackpot
When the eight guys do a rowdy fox trot.
But where's the hen?

The hen's from Aruba, by way of Paris, France,
She lays an egg in the tuba, looking for romance.
When the tuba player starts playing,
The egg goes a-sailing clear across the hall,
Lands with a splat on the mirrored disco ball.

The cat hides behind the glittering punch bowl,
Eats all the brie and filet-de-sole.
When the crowd sees what happened
With the egg, the fish and the cheese,
They fume and fuss and are not pleased.

Judy shoots a glance at the cat, the men and the hen.
They all take to the floor and dancing begins
All the way out a secret back door.

The Coupe de Ville stands waiting, black and slick,
The crowd is looking for a bone to pick.
Car doors fly open, they all jump in,
Hooting and shouting at the crowd's chagrin.
Laughing and singing at their clever caper,
They disappear into the night's mysterious vapor.

Picture Perfect

Look at the photo, old man,
six brothers and me.
The newspapers printed it.
We were celebrities.
Stare at it.
Your memories,
air escaping from a balloon.
The family thinks you've lost your memory.
No such thing.

We're here,
around your tired old bed.

Look at Howie, standing on a chair.
You'll always be the shorty, Howie.
Ma, please don't hit me. Don't hit me!
Danny did it. Yeah, you did, Danny.
No, he didn't. Thanks, Danny.
And you, Darrell, dead at sixteen
and it wasn't you driving.

Sally, he's smiling.
Do you think he remembers?
Harry, he's looking
at paper—not the photo.
Dad, it's me, Sally.
Dad?
Come on, remember.

We remember you, Sally,
all of us do.
Uncle Darrell, Pig Face Pauly,
Little Leo, fat Danny.
We love you, sweetheart, and your mother too.

You're a beautiful woman, Dora,
more than any man deserves.
You're not in my dreams anymore.
I can feel you right here,
sitting by the lake, talking and drinking wine.
Dora, it's just a bug.
Come here, sweetheart. Okay, I'll kill it.
I won't leave you, Dora.
Push, Dora, push!
Yes, doctor,
To the hospital now.

Sally, please stop crying. He looks happy.
Something's going on in his head.
He's looking at you.
Sally?
Turn out the light.
No.

Christmas Down South

In the morning, slippers glide
over grassy path
Popcorn, cranberry garlands
strewn around the chicken run
Thumps of hens land
fly out the coop door
Peck holiday leftovers

After school, young feet dance
climb bus stairs
clutch plastic bags of food
to eat over winter break
Not enough food at home

Buzzards tear rotted fruit in my neighbor's yard
Not enough dead animals on the road
They roost—dark ornaments on a dried up tree
Moving as the world moves
Creatures of balance
Motion within motion

New Day

We'll have to take this plate of bacon
Off your tray
It's not meant for just one person
Besides this is a church
Listen to the sermon and pray before you eat
Why the weird hat and the dirty raincoat?
The lining is hanging out
Your legs are bare
Sneakers and no socks!
Did you expose yourself in the parking lot?
I'm hungry
I want to eat

Al Svoboda

The Lily of the Mohawks
Michael Goldman

This is the true story of Kateri Tekakwitha (1656 –
1680). She was born in the eastern woodlands of North
America, a member of the powerful Mohawk tribe of the
league of the Iroquois. As Kateri grew it became apparent
that she was on a unique path, but one that is not always
understood by the average person. She was a mystic, and a
mystic's path has been called either the dark way -- the way
of the shadows -- or the way of divine love. It is not open to
everyone, only to those chosen by God. Orphaned, half
blind, scarred by small pox, and considered of little worth in
her world, she was yet destined for greatness.

Kateri's mother, an Algonquin woman named Kahenta,
was captured during a Mohawk raid. She was judged worthy
of being a slave and thus was allowed to live. Eventually
Kenhoronkwa, the Mohawk chief, took notice of her and
married her, conferring full rights of being a Mohawk upon
her. Kahenta was a Christian, having been baptized at the

Catholic mission in Quebec. She showed kindness and tolerance, and even with her captors, always behaved with good will.

In 1660, when Kateri was four years-old, disaster in the form of a small pox epidemic struck the village. Many people died including her mother, father, and small brother. Kateri also caught the disease, but survived. Although it left her half blind --able to see only shadows -- and badly pock marked.

A warrior named Iowuano was chosen to be chief in place of her dead father. The new chief and his family adopted her. Kateri loved her new step father and mother very much.

At this time the whole tribe decided that the old village was a place of too much unhappiness. They decided to build a new village someplace where the water was pure and clean. They also needed a place that was easy to defend. The Mohawks got along well with the English and Dutch, but were constantly warring with the French.

Moving was a major undertaking and everyone had a part to play. Longhouses were stripped of their bark, poles were pulled up to be used at the next site, and food stuff was packed. Families even gathered up the remains of their dead ancestors so they could be reburied at the new village.

Although Kateri was small and too weak to help the move, she did have useful skills. As well as being wise for her years, she showed great skill in decorating items of clothing. She could use beads and quills to fashion beautiful designs.

As Kateri grew older, the matriarchs decided that she should be married. They invited a young warrior to the longhouse and Kateri was ordered to serve him some food. She refused and fled to the forest. Because of this disobedience, she Instead she walked out of the longhouse into the forest. After that, the women began treating her very badly. They gave her the worst chores to perform, and even struck at her and treated her cruelly.

Kateri suffered all this bad treatment in silence and kept a smile on her face. She was given the task of cleaning the hides, working extra long in the fields, and any other dirty chore that came along. Because she bore all this without complaining, however, after a time the women began to respect her again and stopped treating her so badly.

When the Mohawks made peace with the French, the Jesuit priests were able to return. The first was Father Boniface, although he wasn't received warmly. In fact, the Mohawks resented all things European. They did not understand the need for elaborate churches, shrines, and formal rituals. Instead they felt the presence of the Great Spirit in the beautiful mountains, icy streams, and still deep forests.

On Christmas Father Boniface made a manger and placed the Christ child in it. The figure was made with its arms reaching out to the people. For some reason, the Mohawks liked this. Kateri especially took this as something profound. In this figure, she glimpsed the vastness of Divine Love and felt that love surging through the wilderness and into her life.

Father Boniface converted at least thirty adult Mohawks at this time. He was helped by the great chief Kryn who lived at Mission Sault.

Father Boniface died suddenly in 1674. His replacement was Father Jacques De Lamberville. When Kateri had a chance to talk with him she asked to become a Christian. He did not discourage her, but told her to study and learn the Catholic ways first. She was baptized on Easter Sunday, 1676, and, because she was a prominent member of the clan, all the Mohawk population attended. Father De Lamberville named her Katherine or Kateri in honor of St. Catherine of Sienna. She was twenty years old at the time.

After her baptism her soul opened and she sought solitude more and more. She spent long periods in the woods praying. She had never liked the celebration of the Mohawk's traditional yearly festivals, finding them pagan, unchristian. The young men and women of the tribe made fun of her for this, and that made her turn more and more to the Church.

Father De Lamberville was concerned when he saw that Kateri's faith was making her an outcast. He prayed for her and an answer to his prayers arrived in the person of an Oneida chief called Hot Powder. The chief suggested that two Christian men he trusted should take Kateri by canoe up the Hudson River to the Sault mission where she could practice her religion in peace.

Setting out on her journey, Kateri carried a letter from Father De Lamberville introducing her to the father at Sault Mission. The letter read "I send you a treasure, guard it well."

Kateri was excited and felt elated the closer they came to the Sault Mission. She also admired the two men who accompanied her for their daily prayer rituals. They were moving through rugged wilderness, dangerous because of hostile tribes, but all three kept the spirit of Christ alive in their hearts.

At Sault Mission Indians and French sat side by side worshipping in the chapel. Kateri set about earning her place in this community by working in the fields and the house. She was coming to life at last, blossoming in the beauty of the mission site and supportive atmosphere of the city. A large cross had been erected in the woods by the river, and she prayed before it every day as well as attending all the mass services in the chapel.

Many of the Mohawk converts had once been guilty of torturing and killing prisoners, and other pagan activities. At the Mission they repented for their actions in the past. Kateri had never done these things, but she had remorse for the years she spent without the sacraments. Imitating the others she began a series of physical punishments to atone for her sins, using switches to beat her back and shoulders, walking barefoot in the snow, and eating only one meal of porridge each day.

On the morning of Christmas day 1677 Kateri made her first holy communion. Even though she was shy and humble, her face wore such an expression of rapture that all the people there were transfixed. She was one with Christ.

By the time the winter snows began falling in 1680 Kateri's health was failing. She was wracked by pain and very weak, and seldom left her cabin. Father Cholonec visited her bringing holy pictures and writings from the old and New Testament inscribed on birch bark. Others in the city including the Indians there, began visiting her as well for they knew she was about to leave them.

Finally the priest decided to bring her the Viaticum, the communion offered to the sick and dying. This was seldom taken out of the chapel for fear some harm might come to it, but since Kateri was so weak they brought it to her. She was delighted that such a blessing was going to be given to her. She knew the hour of her death and died soon after the ritual reciting the names Jesus and Mary. She was only twenty four years old.

The body of Kateri was laid on a pallet, but to everyone's amazement, it was no longer frail, dark, and scarred. In death, her skin lightened and became radiant, while her disfiguring scars vanished. People were astounded for before them lay an exquisite creature. The priest's made a special coffin for her, and she was buried by the big cross by the river.

People visited her grave, kneeling to pray or weep. Soon they noticed that lame and sick people who came there were cured. People started taking dirt from the gravesite, and soon these packets of dirt were being used to cure people throughout the territory.

That was the first of the miracles. The next was her visitations. Father Chauchetiere was the first one to see her after her death. Six days after she was buried he was working in the church and looked up to see her standing beside him radiant and smiling. She had two images with her, a church turned upside down and a Native American tied to a flaming stake.

Three years later a tornado ripped thru the area picking the chapel up and it landed upside down with three priests inside. The priests were unhurt but the church was destroyed. Also about the same time an Onondaga war party raided the Mission taking one captive with them. They later related that while burning him alive at the stake he preached to them through all his dying torments begging them to accept Jesus, and forgiving them for his death.

Anastasia, Kateri's adopted mother at the mission, was the next one to see her. She opened her eyes to see a beautiful and radiant Kateri standing next to her bed holding a shining cross. The wife of Hot Powder, the chief who had helped years before, was terribly ill and in danger of dying. After she was wrapped in Kateri's coverlet, she was instantly cured.

In time, a monument to Kateri was erected at Auriesville N.Y. where the former Sault Mission stood. It reads: Catherine Tekakwitha April 17, 1680, the most beautiful flower that ever bloomed for the Indians. This is how she came to be called the Lily of the Mohawks.

Since all the many cases of her healing were documented, Kateri was declared blessed by the church in Rome in June 1980. Then, on October 21, 2012 Pope Benedict XVI conferred sainthood on her making Kateri the very first Native American saint.

The End

Love Slightly Skewed

Mary Cooper

Billy Keene went about his morning routine
systematically. There was nothing odd in that, nothing dull
or tedious. He liked having a set way of doing things. It
made him feel safe, comfortable, gave him a sense of
control. Control was something else that Billy liked.

One, two, three, four... Billy counted as he stirred the
sugar and milk into his coffee. Eight swirls clockwise
followed by eight counter-clockwise. That was the right
method to ensure a perfect blend every time. He tapped the
spoon against the mug's rim and set it down. Billy smiled
and raised the cup to his lips. He had life down to a science.
It took exactly six pulls on the handle of the paper towel
dispenser at work to get the right amount of paper to dry his
hands. Five was too little and left his hands damp afterward.
Seven was too much and some of the paper would be wasted.
Once he established a count for something, he could forget
about it and save his brainpower for important tasks. Billy
once read that Einstein had taken a similar approach to life,

filling his closet with many copies of the same clothes so he wouldn't have to think about what to wear each day

Great minds think alike, Billy reasoned.

Other people didn't understand his meticulous nature. As a child, Billy's mother had dragged him to doctor after doctor, searching for a "cure" for his behavior. She'd complain and commiserate with her friends, coworkers, and every relative she could get to listen. Over the phone or over tea, she would tearfully, tragically relate her son's 'crazy' exploits, how he went ballistic if the towels weren't folded just right (*Heaven forbid if a tag shows!*), how he washed his hands more than he should (*Until they bleed! They actually bleed!*), and she never, never forgot to mention the dog incident.

That hadn't been Billy's fault, not really. A clean and orderly house was simply no place for a dirty animal. The shedding hair, the chewed shoes and toys, the licking and drooling and fleas...it had been more than he could stand. Billy's mother was fiercely intent on him loving that dog and caring for it 'like a normal boy'. He knew she wouldn't reconsider the idea so Billy did what he had to do. It was quick and relatively painless; little Fido never even saw it coming.

After that, there were weekly visits to the psychiatrist, medications, and therapy sessions. Billy learned to change his behavior around other people. Billy learned to hide.

But at least, thank God, there were no more dogs.

None of that mattered now. Billy had grown past it, become a productive member of the community. He finished his coffee and retired to the bathroom to get ready for work. When he was freshly scrubbed and shaven, Billy donned his perfectly pressed garments and checked his reflection in the mirror. He smirked at the ordinary man that met his eyes. Average height, average weight, nondescript features set in a forgettable face. He may as well have been named John Doe. And that suited him just fine.

A familiar tug arrested his thoughts and focused them onto the vision that rose in his mind. A lovely woman with fair skin, blonde hair, and blue eyes. Ashley Crenshaw, the new teller at the bank. Billy never knew when someone would catch his interest, never looked for it intentionally, but he didn't fret over women. He had a system for that too.

He stepped to his closet and slid open the doors. Stretching up, he slipped his hand past the stacks of folded sweaters and jogging pants to the very back corner of the shelf. Desire passed through him as his fingers touched the metal box hidden there. He didn't have time right now to pull it out and examine the contents but this was enough. Billy closed his eyes and imagined what it held: Jenny Blazack's mother of pearl watch, Danielle Campbell's silver butterfly necklace, Courtney Breckenridge's gold wedding ring. He didn't want to keep the wedding ring, a reminder that she'd loved someone else, but she had worn no other jewelry. There were other mementos inside the box, other women represented, but it was getting late and he needed to leave.

"Bye, ladies," he whispered to the box, "See you after work." He pictured Ashley's face. Soon there would be a new trinket added to his collection. Whistling, Billy grabbed his car keys and headed out the door.

※

"Hey, Billy, I really like that shirt," said a stocky brunette, leaning over the cubicle partition. "It looks sooo good on you."

Billy tried not to wince. He answered without looking up. "Thank you, Vanessa. Sorry, can't talk. I'm right in the middle of something."

He heard the pout in her voice. "Aw, Billy, I wouldn't want to get in your way or anything."

Vanessa Cicero was the bane of Billy's existence. She had recently been hired and placed in the cubicle adjacent to his. She began by asking him questions about work related issues—the proper procedures, where to find supplies—but had quickly progressed to personal questions and dropping not-so-subtle hints about asking her out. That had been irritating enough but things had become insufferable after the office luncheon. The only available seat had been next to Vanessa. She'd treated the mandatory meeting like a date, flirting outrageously with him the entire time. His fellow employees had noticed, how could they not? He'd been teased and prodded about it ever since. Now everyone expected him to take her to dinner. Vanessa was not his type. She was the opposite of his type, the exact opposite. Worse still, she seemed to think they were in a relationship of some sort. The woman was delusional.

"Silly Billy. I could never stay mad at you. Where do you want to go for lunch?"

Billy kept his eyes glued to the computer screen. "Lunch? I brought my lunch. Maybe Andy will go with you." *Go away, go away, go away.*

"Oh, that will work out perfectly!" Vanessa exclaimed brightly. "I'll just grab a sandwich from the vending machine and we can sit together in the cafeteria."

"I'm working through lunch today, eating at my desk, so…"

"I'll be glad to help…"

"Not enough room…"

"But I…"

"No thank…"

"Fine! I can see that there's just no talking to you this morning. Well, I have things to do too!" She flung her nose in the air and disappeared behind the partition.

The hairs on Billy's arms and neck were standing on end. His hands curled as he imagined gripping Vanessa's thick dusky throat and squeezing. The thought thoroughly repulsed him. Not the violent act—it's not like he'd never done it before—but that Vanessa was all wrong. She didn't fit his profile, went against his own personal aesthetic. His

system was fixed and he couldn't deviate from it. Vanessa
was olive-skinned with dark eyes and hair and her compact
frame was solid, what his mother referred to as 'big boned'.
His girls were all pale blondes with blue eyes, slender and
delicate. Like Ashley. The familiar tug pulled a bit harder.
Yes, just like Ashley.

Billy knew he'd better get his work done while he
could. Despite Vanessa's disgruntled departure, it was only a
matter of time until she started up again. He turned to his
computer screen in earnest, tapping the keys with effectual
strokes.

❀

"Hey, Billy, Vanessa's really cute. So when's the
wedding?"

Billy looked up to see the leering grin on his coworker's
face. "Funny, Brian. Why don't you ask her out if she's so
cute? She's definitely available."

"Well, she *is* cute... What, you got some other
girlfriend nobody knows about? I figured you two were
already a couple."

You're not the only one. "Not interested. Please, feel
free."

Brian backed away, palms raised in mock surrender.
"Oh, no, *Silly Billy*, She's all yours."

Billy's jaw clenched. Silly Billy. He'd managed to stay
inconspicuous during the five years he'd worked here, stayed
under the radar in every way. Now he was singled out for
attention, being eavesdropped upon so that "the guys" could
laugh at his expense around the water cooler. Thanks to
Vanessa, his carefully crafted persona was compromised.
Something had to be done.

❀

A heavy shroud of humidity oppressed the otherwise beautiful day. Billy felt perspiration bead his forehead as the sun burned its brilliance into the back and shoulders of his dark suit coat. He crossed the parking lot to the bank's entrance. A rush of chill air hit him as he swung open one of the glass double doors. Billy stood at the counter reserved for customers who lacked the foresight to make out their deposit slips ahead of time. He took a blank slip and a pen and slowly transcribed his information, using the occasion to cool down and to catch surreptitious glimpses of Ashley Crenshaw.

Once he was certain he was perspiration-free, Billy got in line. He was in luck. When his turn came, Ashley was the open teller.

"Good afternoon, Mr. Keene. How are you today?" Ashley gave a quick professional smile.

"Fine, thank you. And you?" Billy replied, taking in her creamy complexion and pretty blue eyes.

"Very well, thanks. Just a deposit today?"

"Yes." Billy's gaze fell on her bent head, her wispy blonde hair, her freckled décolleté. He smiled. "That's a beautiful necklace. Is it an antique?"

Ashley glanced up at him, unconsciously fingering the diamond heart pendant. "Oh, thank you. It was my grandmother's but I don't know if it's an antique or not."

"Well, it's lovely," Billy said. "I've always been a bit of a jewelry buff."

Ashley straightened and handed Billy his receipt. "Here you go, Mr. Keene. You have a nice day."

"Thanks. You too." Billy pocketed the receipt on his way out the door. The familiar tug had become an ache.

❈

Billy was almost to his car when he heard his name called in an uncomfortably familiar voice.

No. Not here. You've got to be kidding me.

"Billy, I think we need to talk," Vanessa said rushing toward him.

"Vanessa, what are you doing here? What could we possibly have to talk about?" Billy glanced around. No one was paying them any attention. He continued to his car.

"I saw the way you were flirting with that blonde. Don't even try to deny it." Her voice was getting louder.

Billy couldn't allow a scene here. Nothing could jeopardize his access to Ashley, especially not *this woman*. He stopped and turned to her. "Alright, just calm down. What blonde? What are you talking about?"

"What blonde? The bank teller, as if you didn't know!"

"Please lower your voice. This is my bank. It's Friday. I was depositing my paycheck," Billy spoke in short sentences that he figured even a mentally unbalanced female could follow. "I'm sorry if that upsets you. I didn't know this was your bank too."

"This isn't my bank," Vanessa pouted. Her eyes glistened and her voice cracked. "I followed you."

"You what?" Billy seethed, "You're *following* me?"

Vanessa crossed her arms over her ample chest. "Well, you didn't give me much choice! You've been so distant lately. I had to find out if you were seeing someone else! Now I find you flirting with that skinny blonde bank teller!"

Billy remembered where he was and what was at stake. He took a deep breath and quieted the violent urges that vied for dominance. Several people were now openly watching them. This was turning into a nightmare. He forced his lips to smile. "Look, Vanessa, how about we have lunch tomorrow and talk about it? This is hardly the place to have a private conversation."

Vanessa sniffled loudly and dabbed her eyes. "Well, okay, I guess so." She smiled coyly. "I can't stay mad at you, Silly Billy, but this doesn't mean you're completely off the hook."

Billy got into his car and gripped the steering wheel until his knuckles turned white. The woman was stalking him. He might be able to get a restraining order but the very idea of going to the sheriff's office made his skin crawl. Police were his enemy and he knew enough to steer clear of any involvement with them. He took the bank receipt from his pocket, precisely matched the corners, and folded it in half. He repeated this process again and again until the paper was too small to fold. He put it back in his pocket and wondered what to do.

❄

Billy sat in the restaurant, ostensibly enjoying his lunch. Vanessa gushed at him from across the table, making the food stick in his throat.

"This is such a beautiful place and everything is delicious. You're so good to me, such a sweetheart to bring me here. It's sooo romantic!"

"Yes, well, I'm glad you like it." Billy took a drink of water and leaned in. "Vanessa, about yesterday—"

"Oh, that's as good as forgotten. We don't ever have to mention it again." She giggled and took another bite of Steak Diane.

"But I think we should talk about it. We need to talk about it. You admitted you were following me. I want you to promise me you won't do that anymore."

"How about this? I won't follow you if you don't give me a reason to," Vanessa replied and took another bite.

Stay calm, Billy thought. "You can't just follow me around everywhere. It's called stalking and there are laws against it."

"Stalking?" she laughed, incredulous. "I'm not stalking you, Silly Billy. I care about you, that's all. Why are you making such a big deal about it?"

Billy dropped the subject. It was pointless to continue and he wanted to avoid another scene. During the remainder of the meal, Vanessa spun fantasies about them as a couple, suggesting vacation spots for romantic getaways and plans for introducing him to her family. He let her talk, hoping she would eventually run out of steam, which, of course, she didn't.

He paid the bill and they stepped out into the bright day. The downtown sidewalk was bustling with people hurrying to and fro in the summer heat. As they stood at the corner waiting for the walk sign to blink on, Billy caught sight of a city bus coming up the street. The driver was going too fast, trying to make the light. In a subtle move, Billy positioned himself behind Vanessa. On and on she rambled, saying things he couldn't care less about. It didn't matter; he wasn't listening anyway. He shifted his body forward, causing her to take a step, then she was standing on the curb. When the bus was almost upon them, Billy feigned a stumble and bumped Vanessa out into the street.

Things happened very quickly.

"Bill-eee!" Vanessa shrieked, her arms pin-wheeling through the air.

Billy felt himself yanked forward. Some of Vanessa's long, dark hair had gotten tangled around his wristwatch. He pulled back hard to keep from falling into the street. Vanessa's head followed suit, jerking sharply toward him. One of her flailing hands caught his sleeve and clamped down tight. She pitched wildly, fighting for balance and careened into Billy, knocking him backward onto the sidewalk. He hit the concrete surface with a thud and Vanessa landed on top of him. The bus swerved into the far lane and passed by, the driver sounding the horn.

Vanessa raised her head and looked at Billy with an expression of wonder. "You saved my life. I love you, Billy."

❀

The television cast a bluish glow over the room. Billy sat on the couch and tried to concentrate on the program but his mind was in confusion and he was miserable. The control he valued so highly was slipping away and everything he did to regain it only seemed to push it further out of reach. He didn't know how to correct the problems that plagued him, didn't know what to do next. Visions of Ashley popped into his head at regular intervals and without conscious effort he formulated systems that would bring his fantasies to life. The ache within him was now a persistent throb, like an itch he couldn't scratch. Intermingled was a hatred for Vanessa and his frustrating inability to deal with her. She was a weed that overtook everything in its path; one that defied any conventional methods of extermination. She stood in the way of what he wanted most, directly opposed him and his plans, but what could he do about it? Nothing. Nothing at all.

Billy rocked back and forth holding his midsection. He stood and paced the room. He stalked into the kitchen and flipped on the light, grimacing at the trashcan and the objects it held—unopened cards from Vanessa. He took a glass from the cupboard and filled it with ice and water. He sipped then pressed the chilled glass to his forehead.

Get a grip, he chided himself. *You'll figure it out*. After all, he'd managed things perfectly up until this point, hadn't he? But how? What could he do? His efforts to direct Vanessa's enthusiastic attentions to other men at the office had met with utter failure. For some reason, she was fixated on him. She had no concept of personal boundaries or that her affections were not reciprocated. She lived in a fantasy world that no hint of reality could penetrate. He'd tried several times to devise a way to end his suffering, and her life, but was infernally bound by his systematic codes. The one time he'd been presented an opportunity, it had backfired badly. Vanessa spread the story far and wide that she'd tripped into the street and he'd saved her life. She actually believed it happened that way. *Silly Billy, my hero*.

My God, thought Billy. *I'm going to lose my mind*.

He set the glass in the sink and ran his hands down his face. His desperate sigh was cut short, however, when he

spied a pair of brown eyes staring at him through the
windowpane.

"Vanessa!" he yelled.

She beamed at him. "I'll come around front." She
quickly disappeared from view.

No, no, no! The woman was like a disease, a
metastasizing cancer running rampant and destroying his
life. The weed metaphor came back to him. Billy imagined a
monstrous sea of green flowing over his yard, growing up
the sides of his house, covering everything in a leafy jungle.
He pictured thick tendrils vining up the brick chimney and
spilling down into the house, over the hearth, the rug, the
furniture. He felt weed shoots twine around his legs, slither
up his torso, and squeeze his throat. He couldn't breathe; he
was being smothered.

Impatient knocking snapped him out of the
hallucination. The suffocating sensation lingered and he
grabbed the counter for support. He had to get away from
this woman, had to get her out of his life somehow. Then
he'd be okay again. He could make things right, concentrate
on Ashley, satisfy his need, and be in control.

The doorknob turned but was halted by the lock. "Billy,
sweetheart, I'm waiting," came Vanessa's muffled voice.

Billy wanted to cry.

Vanessa pounded on the door.

Billy made his way to the front of the house, slid back
the lock, and cracked the door open.

"What took you so long?" Vanessa complained. "Hey,
aren't you going to invite me in?"

Billy turned on the porch light. "It's late, Vanessa. Go
home."

"Oh, Billy! You look awful! What's wrong? Are you
sick?"

"If I am, you could catch it. Go home."

"Aw, you're sooo thoughtful! But no, you need
someone to take care of you. Lucky for you I stopped by."
Vanessa tried to push her way past him but Billy stood firm.

"I just need some sleep. I'm fine."

"But—"

Billy tried a different approach. "If you care about me as much as you say you do, you'll let me rest. Please leave." He saw the argument on her face. "I'll see you tomorrow at work. Maybe you can help me organize my desk drawer."

"Well, I dunno…I guess so. But you have to promise to call me if you need anything, okay?"

"Yeah, sure," Billy replied. He watched her walk to her car and drive away before shutting his door and locking the deadbolt.

❋

Billy stared, disgusted, at the haggard man in the bathroom mirror. He briefly considered calling in sick but knew that Vanessa would camp out on his front porch if he did. She practically did that anyway. Every time he turned around, she was in his face. He felt constantly shadowed. She had invaded his life completely, a cloying presence that made the air thick and hard to breathe.

The vision of weeds encroaching and burying him alive became a regular occurrence, filling him with fear, competing with thoughts of Ashley. Ashley. He'd gotten no closer to his plans for her, though his hunger was a burning ceaseless pain. He was living a nightmare, being pulled in all directions at once, jumping at the smallest noises. He couldn't go on like this.

He went to his closet and removed the cherished metal box. He sat on the edge of the bed and sifted the contents through his fingers. One at a time, Billy examined the pieces of jewelry, closing his eyes and reliving each moment of its procurement. He thought about Ashley's diamond heart pendant and how badly he wanted it in his box.

Billy went to work and bled out his day in a state of perpetual fog. He felt removed from the world around him, unable to concentrate on even the simplest tasks or conversations. His coworkers went from teasing to giving him odd looks and asking if he was okay. That he was coming down with the flu was the general consensus and fellow employees stopped by his cubical throughout the day, offering him advice and homespun remedies. At least it was Friday and he could rest over the weekend. No one got too close but everyone wished him a speedy recovery to which Vanessa would invariably poke her head around the partition and explain her part in things. "I'll take good care of my Silly Billy, don't worry about that. He saved my life, you know."

After work, Vanessa said that she was going to do some shopping, pick up the usual foods of the infirm—orange juice, chicken soup, saltines, ginger ale—then meet him at his house. Billy gave no reply, just picked up his paycheck and headed to the bank. When he arrived, he went through the same procedure as always, going to the table and filling out the deposit slip; however, this time when he glanced at Ashley she was looking right at him. She averted her eyes and anxiously pulled her sweater over her shoulders. Billy got in line and when it was his turn Ashley was the open teller. Without waiting for her to ask, he stepped up to the window. She quickly pushed a "closed" sign in front of him, whispered something to the adjacent teller, and scurried to the ladies room. Billy got a sinking feeling in the pit of his stomach.

"Next," announced a slouching middle-aged teller. Billy walked to the window and handed her his papers.

He had to know what was going on. "Is she okay?" He indicated Ashley's vacant window with a jerk of his thumb. "She doesn't seem like herself today."

The teller gazed balefully over her bifocals. "Well, what do you expect after your girlfriend came in here carrying on like she did."

"My g-girlfriend?" Billy stammered. The sinking feeling was becoming a black hole, sucking him down, down, down. "I don't have a girlfriend."

The teller harrumphed and leaned in closer. "That little hot-head of yours came in here screaming like a banshee. Practically accused Ashley of seducing you, said she caught you two doing something or other and that Ashley had better steer clear 'if she knows what's good for her'—scared the poor girl half to death. The manager didn't like it one bit, I can tell you that. He put us all on the lookout for you and your nutty girlfriend." She leaned back and handed him the receipt. "You might want to use the drive-thru from now on."

Billy took the receipt and left.

❃

Ashley was out of his reach. He was most certainly on the radar now. Like an addict denied a fix, pain stabbed him, coursed through his blood, radiated from his fingertips. He wanted to howl and rave and beat his chest. He wanted to set fire to entire neighborhoods and laugh at the conflagration. He wanted to cry and wail and moan. He believed he was imploding, that every fiber of his being was ripping apart as he was drawn into the black hole inside him. He drove like a madman, finally screeching to a stop in his driveway.

Billy ran into the house, slammed the door, and forced the deadbolt. He rushed from room to room locking windows and doors, yanking every curtain closed. He pushed chairs in front of the main entrances and ran up the stairs to his bedroom. After securing the door he dragged a dresser in front of it and collapsed onto the bed. He lay motionless, taking quick, shallow breaths, eyes darting erratically. His ears were alert, attuned to the sound he dreaded; the one he knew would come.

It didn't take long.

Knock, knock, knock. "Bill-ee," Vanessa said in a singsong voice, "I'm he-ere."

Cold sweat prickled Billy's skin. Goosebumps rose on his arms.

The knocking got louder. "Open the door, sweetheart. I'm going to make you dinner."

Billy closed his eyes and saw the black hole. Only it wasn't black. It was green.

"I've got groceries out here. Frozen stuff, too. C'mon, Billy, open up."

The monstrous sea of green was outside. It was trying to get in.

Vanessa pounded the door. "Hey, Billy! Can you hear me? What's going on in there?"

Billy saw vines climbing the outer walls, looking for a way inside. He heard glass breaking, shards clattering on the tile kitchen floor. He started to tremble.

Vanessa dropped the rock and used her purse to knock the rest of the jagged slivers out of the square door panel. "You'd think he would have at least left me a key," she muttered.

She felt around for the inside handle and sprung the lock. As the door swung toward her, she saw the stack of dining chairs that barred the way in. She pushed them aside, stepping around the sprinkling of glass on the floor, and passed slowly through the kitchen.

"Billy, where are you?" She surveyed the interior rooms and noticed the wingchair wedged against the front door. "Why is everything so…?"

It was in the house. It was coming for him.

Billy's eyes flung open. He had to do something. He sat up and looked frantically around the room. He could see it as plain as day—the creeping mass of green, carpeting the floors downstairs, flowing over tables and chairs and sofas, slithering up walls. It would choke out everything; erase his very existence if he let it. He grabbed the phone from the nightstand.

Vanessa moved the chair away from the front door and brought in the grocery bags, setting them in the kitchen. She ticked off her responsibilities on her fingers. "One, I'll check on Billy and make sure he's alright. Two, I'll sweep up the broken glass. And three, I'll make chicken soup."

"Billy?" The house was quiet. She headed up the stairs. "Billy, are you sleeping, sweetheart?"

Billy cowered against the headboard and cradled the phone in his lap. Thick green shoots, like leafy pythons, twisted and coiled up the stairs, closer and closer. There was nowhere left to hide. He'd imagined this a thousand times, felt the monster wrapping around him to squeeze and smother, and now it was happening for real.

Vanessa stood before the bedroom door and knocked. "Billy, are you up?"

Panic washed over Billy in a great wave, stealing his ability to move or think.

Vanessa tried the knob. Her bottom lip pouted. "Aw, why do you make things so hard for me?"

She located the bathroom and rummaged through drawers until she found a bobby pin. Smiling triumphantly, she straightening it, pushed it into the lock, and jiggled it until it clicked. "Easy peasy lemon squeezy," she giggled.

I'm going to die. The words popped into Billy's mind of their own volition, startling him. No, it was worse than that. He wasn't just going to die. He was going to be buried for eternity under a colossal green terror, one that would swallow him whole and slowly suck the life out of him. A memory flashed of a dead beetle he'd swept off his porch. The inside was gone leaving the exoskeleton a pathetic empty husk. He gripped the phone and stared at the door.

Vanessa frowned when the door refused to budge. "There's something in the way, Billy. Maybe you can move it from the inside."

"Go away!" Billy screeched. "Leave me alone!"

"Oh, sweetheart," Vanessa cooed. "You don't have anything to worry about. I'm here. I'll take care of you." She hunkered down and thrust her shoulder against the door.

It was battering down his door. With each blow the dresser shifted, allowing the crack to widen. Billy watched in horror as tiny green fingers poked through and wound around the jamb.

"No! Please!" Billy began to cry.

Vanessa was using her full weight and her efforts were beginning to pay off. She stood on tiptoes to see over the barricade and popped her head into the room. "Almost there, Silly Billy."

Silly Billy, Silly Billy, Silly Billy.

Billy screamed. The door banged against the dresser. It was almost in. He punched numbers into the phone but his hands were shaking badly and he misdialed. He shot a glance at the door and saw wispy vines snaking up the wall. He held the phone tightly and pushed the numbers again, this time with success. The call rang through.

"Pick up!" Billy pleaded.

"9-1-1. What's your emergency?" asked the nasal voice on the other end.

"I killed them all -- Amanda Walczak, Courtney Breckenridge, Danielle Campbell, there's a whole list! I can prove it! I have their jewelry! Please come and get me!"

"Someone will be right there, sir."

The distant wail of sirens could be heard as Vanessa burst through the door.

The End

Love Story

C. J. Goldman

That afternoon Liam and I lay naked in front of the fire on a thick bear skin rug, while it snowed outside. We'd had a severe storm, and there was deep snow everywhere.

It was warm and cozy by the fire and the crackle of the logs as they burned was soothing and restful. The smell of the wood burning infused the room. I could almost forget, as I lay in his arms, that he would soon be gone. When we made love I clung to him as if by holding him tight I might be able to keep him with me forever.

Afterwards, while he drowsed, I traced the long lines of his beautiful lean body with my fingertips, admiring each curve and hollow, each strong muscle, and the curling dark hair on his broad chest, the smooth belly and taunt loins, the entirety of him. He opened his eyes, took my hand and kissed my fingertips.

"Liam," I said slowly, "There is something I need to confess to you."

"What is that, my little angel?"

"There is someone I loved before I met you."

He smiled and stroked my hair. "Yes, and who was this lucky man? Don't worry. I may envy him but I won't challenge him to a duel."

"My stable boy, Eric," My voice was very low. "We never really made love, but…"

"Yes, I understand, it was a beautiful, innocent young love. I'm glad you told me. And I must confess, dearest angel, that I too have had loves of my own."

"Have there been many women in your life Liam?"

"Many. But only a few that I have truly loved. I have a friend, a very dear friend, Clara Monroe, she lives in Cape Town and I treasure her company. I have known her for a long time. Then there is my friend, Carlotta Lewis, who is far less lovely, but she has a warm heart and a generous spirit. She is fearless, and always true to herself. I admire her very much. She has taught me a good deal about life."

He saw that I was crest fallen, and said, "Ah, my little angel, I would never want you to think of them as rivals."

Taking my face in his cupped hands, he looked at me, and kissed me with a long lingering caress that took my breath away.

"I have never treasured any woman the way I treasure you now, this moment. You are all I think of, all I want. If only we didn't have to part."

We stopped talking then and made love again and slept and ate and talked some more.

I wished I could make him stay here in this warm room. His long lean suntanned body was gleaming in the firelight. Afterwards as usual, he seemed to be in a hurry.

"My darling little angel, keep me in your heart until I return, we'll keep this a ritual every weekend."

"But, Liam, when will we marry? It's been two years now, you promised." Ignoring my question as usual, he slipped from under the soft down comforter and stood naked in front of the fire yawning.

I felt the anger explode inside me and I thought you lying rat you've used me for the last time. I flew from under the comforter with my teeth bared and charged at him screaming and raking my nails down his back. I maneuvered him towards the cabin door. I loosed the latch and gave his naked ass a swift kick out into the deep snow and slammed the entry and locked him out.

Caring not of his plight I shivered under the comforter and cried. Hours later I heard a familiar voice; it was Eric my stable boy who had pledged his love to me forever. I threw on my chemise and opened the door. He tumbled in and said with concern "I've been worried about you since the snow storm."

Turning my face up to him he gathered me into his arms and kissed me with a soft slow hungering kiss. He held me thus for a long time, his mouth against mine, his breath rustling across my cheeks, his free hand tracing the line of my body from my breast to my hips.

He held me until the blood began to move warmly through my veins again. I melted and leaned into him. Our bodies formed together like the fit of a fine leather glove. Then he lifted me against him and carried me to the bear skin rug. He laid me down, gently cradling my head in the hollow of the pillow while he ripped off his clothes and slipped under the comforter running his fingers through my tumbled cascade of dark curls. He kissed my neck and trailed kisses over my entire body as I lay in ecstasy and drank in his essence with every pore of my flesh.

I'm in love with you he said softly, I've wanted and dreamed about you forever.

I smiled into his shoulder as a calming peace filled me. He really means it I thought as I gave into our ravenous passion. Afterwards, bending his arm behind his head, he whispered we shall plan our wedding as soon as possible. I agreed and snuggled my head into the crook of his arm and put my arm around his waist. He cradled me close and we made love again.

Three months has passed since our marriage and we are expecting our first child. If a boy we'll call him Eric, and if a girl we shall call her Erica.

The End

Mac

Sam Kafrissen

I have always enjoyed watching baseball. There is
something about the easy flow of a baseball game that fits
nicely with the soft rhythms of a summer's day. It moves
slowly as we all should whenever the temperature exceeds
eighty degrees. There is no sense of urgency in a baseball
game nor does it have to adhere to a time clock like most
other sports. Baseball sets its own pace based solely on the
actions in the game itself. And like life, a baseball game ends
only when the final out is made. For me baseball will always
be a game played outdoors in the bright sunshine of a
summer's day. This, of course, is seldom the case nowadays
with professional games being played mostly at night.

I played baseball briefly as a boy but was never very
good at it. The hand-eye coordination needed for hitting and
fielding just wasn't part of my skill set. I would later
gravitate to sports like football and wrestling that valued
more macro-type skills. I did play on a Little League team
for a couple of years though I suspect that I was only chosen

to be part of the Garden Hardware nine because my older brother Don was the team's star. In our town there were two Little Leagues, an American League and a National League. Each consisted of four teams that oddly never played against one another during their regular seasons. The teams were sponsored by local businesses and usually bore the name of those enterprises in one manner or another. We were supported by a local hardware store, but had no nickname – we were just Garden Hardware. Other teams were the Hornets, the Eagles, the Pioneers, etc. None of the teams in either league bore the moniker of one of the major league teams of the day. There were no Yankees, Red Sox or Dodgers in our town.

Don was two years older than I and had very quickly acquired some valuable baseball skills after he turned eleven – the most prominent of which was that he could hit for power. That year he knocked out a league leading seven home runs in the short Little League season to help the Garden squad win the American League championship. He also hit over .600 while playing a very slick fielding first base. He had one of those giant claw-like first baseman's mitts that would gobble up throws from his fellow infielders. I admired the way he would position himself in anticipation of their pegs with his right foot on the bag and his left stretched out across the baseline. At the last minute he would flick his glove up to stab the tosses from across the diamond. If a throw were low he would casually dig it out of the dirt with great finesse.

His last year in the league would be my first. I played third base, or at least tried to. I must say I always found it alarming when I took my position to be standing so close to the hitters. Hot caroms smashed my way would often be caught, or rather "knocked down," off my chest, my knees or that more vulnerable area of the body in between. Unlike Don, I was at best a Punch and Judy hitter who would occasionally rope a single between third and short. More often, however, I would pop up weakly or strike out. I could tell that our manager, Mr. Nash, was disappointed that Don's baseball genes had not been passed on to his younger brother. But since my mother was driver in the team's car pool I became an accepted, if not vital member of the Garden nine.

When it came to baseball Mom was another story altogether. To say she was a rabid fan would be an understatement. There were four different Little League fields in our town, including one directly across the street from our house, where ironically, we seldom played. My mother never missed a game and once she had transported a third of our team to the game in her gigantic Mercury station wagon she would set up her folding aluminum chair and join the other parents on the sideline. Then she would proceed to berate everyone on the field in her loud, husky voice. She had no truck with players trying to get on base via a walk so she would loudly tell a hitter to "take the bat off his shoulder and swing like a man" - a heady message for an eleven or twelve year old boy. If a player tried to steal a base and was thrown out standing up she'd loudly criticize him for not sliding. Mom was an equal opportunity heckler so she had no compunction about criticizing players from either team. Batters or pitchers who took too much time getting down to business particularly incensed her.

My mother reserved her most outrageous taunts for the poor umpires, those stout members from the community who had to call every play, including balls and strikes, while parked behind the pitcher's mound. It was not uncommon for her to repeatedly question the quality of their eyesight. One evening she so riled the man in blue that he marched across the field to where she was sitting and insisted that she leave the field lest our team be forced to forfeit the game. At that point Mr. Nash intervened and mom angrily folded her chair and watched the remainder of the game from the front seat of her station wagon.

During these Little League years news began to circulate around town about a phenomenal player who competed for the DeLuca Hornets in the rival National League. While my brother Don may have been the star of our team, and perhaps even our league, the kid from the Hornets was talked about as if he were the star of all of baseball. His name was Mario Pagano, or Mac as everyone referred to him. He pitched for the Hornets and when he wasn't pitching played shortstop. In those days Little League teams played twice a week, three times at the most if there was a make-up of a rained out game. However, a pitcher could only pitch once a week. This was a rule instituted to save their young arms from serious injury. I think there may still be such a restriction.

It just so happened that on a day when our team was not scheduled to play the Hornets, who were sponsored by the DeLuca Nash Rambler dealership, had a game at the field adjacent to our house. It was on that day that I got my first glimpse of the great Pagano. What I saw that evening has stuck with me all these years. Mac Pagano took the mound in his white uniform with purple trim, his purple hat brim perfectly curled. There was nothing physically imposing about him He was just a touch taller than most of the other players but no bigger in terms of bulk. In his windup he would bring his two hands up to the tip of his cap, lift his front leg a bit higher than your typical Little League hurler and then bring a stinging fastball in over the top with such velocity that you could hear the ball loudly pop into the catcher's glove. The batters would either be frozen in their tracks or would weakly swing long after the ball had entered the catcher's mitt.

Although there was a good-sized crowd on hand I moved around the outskirts of the field throughout the game so I could watch this pitcher hurl from every angle. The Hornets scored two runs in the first and there was never any doubt as to the game's outcome after that. Inning after inning Mac Pagano poured his sizzling fastball by each opposing hitter, and each quickly went down on strikes. By the fourth inning it dawned on me that no one had even hit a foul ball.

When Mac struck out the final batter word went round the field that he had not only pitched a perfect game but had struck out all eighteen batters he had faced in the six inning game. It was by far the most dominant pitching performance I'd ever seen, even if it was by just a little leaguer.

The next time I saw the Hornets play Mac was not pitching but holding down the shortstop slot. There are two things I remember vividly about that game: Mac hit two titanic home runs and in the last inning when an opposing hitter smacked a long fly between the left and centerfielders Mac backpedaled from his shortstop position to snag the fly before it passed over the fence.

I was now hooked on the Mac Pagano story. Meanwhile, my brother continued to crush the ball as our Garden Hardware squad marched inexorably toward its second straight American League title. In addition to Don, our scrappy catcher, David Nash (the manager's son), provided some additional firepower with his bat, while Jay Houston (was there ever a better baseball name) our pint sized pitcher continued to hurl victory after victory. Each week we would wait in anticipation for the delivery of the local newspaper to read Don's press clippings and to check the standings and the stats. He was well on his way to leading our league in batting and home runs and was sure to break his home run record of the previous season. Then I would sneak a glance at the National League stories where Mario Pagano continued to throw no hitter after no hitter. He likewise led his league in batting and home runs but with numbers that were slightly less than Don's totals, much to my brother's satisfaction.

At the end of each season an all-star team made up of the best players from each league would meet to see which squad would go on to regional, statewide and perhaps even national competition. All of these elimination games would culminate at the Little League World Series in Williamsport, Pennsylvania. First our American League all-stars would have to face the Nationals where no doubt the great Mac

Pagano would be hurling. In addition to Don, Dave Nash, Jay Houston and our shortstop, and later my best friend, Bruce Filler, would represent Garden Hardware in the all-star contest. As always Don brought his trusty bat, Old Betsy, with him for the game. He had named this piece of lumber after Davy Crockett's rifle from the Disney TV series. He'd even used a wood burning set he'd gotten for his birthday to etch the name Betsy into the thick part of the bat. With black tape wound around the handle it was a formidable looking instrument. Few players used their own bats in those days, as we often just chose a comfortable stick from the bag our manager brought to each practice and game. But Don wanted his own weapon and thought it was Betsy's special powers that brought him such great success.

As expected Mac Pagano did hurl for the Nationals that day, though he did not set our boys down as easily as he had the other National League teams during the regular season. In his first at-bat my brother Don struck out after pulling a couple of hard fouls down the left field line. The Nationals scored three runs early off Jay Houston and Mr. Nash was forced to yank his prized hurler in the third inning. A few hits and a costly error later and Pagano had a 5-0 lead and was cruising. In the sixth inning Don came up for what would be his last at-bat in the red pinstripes of Garden Hardware. This time he was not to be denied as he caught hold of one of Pagano's blistering fastballs and drove it deep over the fence in left center field. Don trotted slowly around the bases clearly savoring the moment. He had knocked out the only home run hit off Mac Pagano in that pitcher's Little League career. It was Don's twelfth home run of the season and as he rounded third Pagano tipped his hat to my brother. It must have been one of the greatest moments of Don's life.

The National League all-stars advanced to the Rhode Island regional finals, where they won the deciding game on a Mac Pagano one-hitter in which he struck out thirteen of his opponents. They then moved onto the New Englands where they reached the semi-finals. Unfortunately, they were eliminated by a team from Swansea, Massachusetts. In that final game Pagano was prevented from pitching but he did hit three home runs in his team's 7-5 loss. Things might have been different for the Nationals if Mac could have pitched every game.

The next year my brother and Mac Pagano teamed up on the Bain Junior High School baseball team. Mac immediately became the school's ace hurler but it took Don an extra year before he could crack the starting line-up. By then other boys had grown bigger and stronger and Don began to morph from the Babe Ruth of Little League fame into a line drive hitter. The fields were bigger and there were no fences so outfielders could play as deep as they wanted. Home runs were at a premium in this league and Don wisely made the necessary adjustments to become an effective singles and doubles hitter. Pagano still played shortstop when he wasn't pitching though Coach Frank Tanzi would often put him in right field to save his arm for future pitching assignments. One day the coach summoned Pagano in from right to relieve in the third inning. He had already pitched a one-hitter earlier in the week. On this day he proceeded to give up no hits in his four innings of relief.

I didn't see too many of these junior high contests as I had begun to develop my own athletic and social life. However, I was there one day when the team was facing its archrival from the other side of town, Park View Junior High. It was a hard fought game that went into extra innings tied 4-4. Pagano was not pitching that day. He did lead off the bottom of the eighth with a double but was stranded on second as the next two batters struck out. But then Don, batting seventh in the order, cracked a single through the middle of the infield to score Mac and win the game. He was mobbed after the winning run crossed the plate. I ran all the way home to tell my parents about Don's heroics. That night my father took us all out for steak sandwiches at the Jolly Chef to celebrate.

The next year I entered junior high and Don and Mac Pagano went on to Cranston High School. Mac became a star quarterback on the football team, a high scoring guard on the basketball team and the ace hurler on the baseball squad. Don continued to play baseball but his interest in the sport and school in general was waning. He soon discovered girls and hot cars and then got in with what my parents referred to as "the wrong crowd." In terms of baseball he fully expected to be the starting first baseman his junior year after laboring the previous season on the JV squad. But the team had a big lummox of a kid who could hit the ball a country mile but couldn't field worth a damn. There was no designated hitter in those days so slow, weak fielding players were often put on first base by default. Much to his disappointment Don was relegated to right field where mostly what he caught were mosquito bites. Halfway through the season Don packed up his glove and spikes and quit baseball for good. It was symptomatic of a lot of unhealthy changes he was going through at the time - but by then my parents had more serious concerns about the direction of my brother's life than about his baseball career.

I had grown up as a baseball fan, thanks to my mother's interest and to my baseball card collection. Each year we would make one or two trips to Fenway to see a then hapless Red Sox team, which featured an aging Ted Williams and little else. I saw Williams hit a couple of prodigious home runs during those years. We even made a few one-day pilgrimages to New York to see the famous Yankee Stadium and the juggernaut that was the Yankees in the 1950s. I saw the great Mickey Mantle, Yogi Berra, Moose Skowron and Whitey Ford. We once drove to Brooklyn to see the Dodgers and the equally famous Ebbets Field. There I watched Jackie Robinson, Duke Snider, Gil Hodges and the portly Roy Campanella cavort. Occasionally when our family went to Philadelphia to visit relatives my great uncle Sid would take my mother and me to Connie Mack Stadium to see the perennially second division Phillies play some National

League rival. One time I saw the Cardinals' Stan Musial hit a grand slam home run. I also saw a triple play there but can't recall the details. Suffice it to say as a youth I got to see some of baseball's greats up close and personal, but on a day in, day out basis the greatest baseball player I ever saw was Mac Pagano. Maybe it was because I knew him, as for a while he was a friend of my brother's who occasionally came to our house to play HORSE with my brother and some other guys on a hoop in our driveway.

I continued to follow Mac's career at the high school. By his junior year he was one of the most talked about pitchers in the state. That year he racked up seven one hit games and pitched the team into the state finals where he was outdueled in a 2-1 contest by a kid who had already been drafted by the Milwaukee Braves. The sky appeared to be the limit as Mac entered his senior year. Major League scouts were already flocking to the town stadium where the team played its home games. On Friday night the games were played under the lights and when Pagano was on the mound the crowds were enormous. You could actually feel the buzz in the air. But then the worst that could happen did happen. Mac had injured his right shoulder during the football season and had not let it heal that winter while he played basketball. By spring he had what they now call a "dead arm." Not only was his senior season in jeopardy but also any prospects of playing professional ball.

The high school team muddled through the first half of the season at about .500 with Mac playing mostly shortstop or right field. He could still hit better than most of the other players but it was his right arm that had brought him glory over the past seven years. By mid-season, however, he began to recover. He pitched a five hitter here, relieved three innings there and little by little regained his old form. Likewise the team started to win as well.

One Friday night in the middle of the season Cranston Stadium hosted a high school all-star game to raise money for something called the Athletic Injury Fund. All the best high school players from the Suburban League would face off against those from the Metropolitan League. At the time our high school was part of the Metro League. It was scheduled to be a nine-inning game and no pitcher could toss more than two innings. The game was a wonderful exhibition of baseball filled with sharp hitting, slick fielding and excellent pitching. The stadium was packed that night and what most of the locals were anticipating was when Mac Pagano would enter the game. As the night marched on there was no sign of our local hero, not even at shortstop. In the bottom of the eighth the Metros jumped ahead 4-3 and word quickly passed through the crowd that Mac had gotten up in the bullpen. In those days the stadium had the kind of bullpens you seldom see outside of the major leagues where the pitchers warm up outside of the crowd's view.

When the Suburbans came up in the ninth for their last whacks Mac Pagano slowly made his way in from the pen. A green warm-up jacket was draped over the right shoulder of his green and gray uniform. The Cranstonites in the crowd stood and cheered wildly. As he warmed up you could see the snap of the fastball and hear that familiar pop when it hit the catcher's mitt. I can still see him that night as if it were yesterday. The hands going up to the brim of the green cap, the left leg rising into a high kick and then the right arm coming over the top and extending toward the plate. And the ball, well the ball was just a blur as it hurtled toward the catcher. The question on everyone's mind was "Does he still have it?" After all, this night he would be facing some of the most formidable hitters in the state. What happened next should go down into Rhode Island sports lore forever. Mac Pagano threw only nine pitches to three batters. All of them were strikes; none of them were even tipped or fouled off. He just blew it by his opponents as if to announce that he was back. When he and his teammates exited the field the entire crowd stood and gave them a three-minute standing ovation.

Mac was indeed back as he took his turn for the high school nine every other game tossing shutout after shutout. When he wasn't pitching he was at short and smacking the ball all over the yard. The team made it into the playoffs, easily winning games that Mac pitched and scratching and clawing to victories in ones when he didn't. Eventually the Cranston squad reached the state championship game as they had the year before.

The final that year was held at Deering High School Field in West Warwick. It was the town Don and I had grown up in before moving to Cranston and where my brother had first played Little League ball. The game was played on a cold, windy day, not what you'd expect in early June. My brother and a group of his friends were going and at the last minute, much to my surprise, he asked me if I wanted to come along. The contest was going to be broadcast on the radio and one of his buddies brought along his transistor so we could listen to the commentary as we watched. Mac, of course, would be pitching for the Cranston nine and another highly regarded prospect, Johnny Zielski, would hurl for West Warwick.

Each team put up a single run early on but then the game ground into an epic pitcher's duel. With his devastating fastball Pagano struck out hitter after hitter, while Zielski was mixing speeds enough to keep the Cranston batters off balance all afternoon. The game passed through the high school seventh inning barrier still knotted at one apiece. It remained that way through the major league nine-inning limit. Still both pitchers labored on, seeming to get stronger as the game progressed. When afternoon moved into evening it turned bitterly cold. Players on either bench hunched together and wrapped their hands in towels to keep them warm. The two pitchers wore hooded sweatshirts under their warm-up jackets while they waited to take the mound again. The game went into the fifteenth inning and was now over four hours long. In Deering's bottom half of the fifteenth their first batter drew a walk. I wondered if Mac was tiring. I was reassured when he struck out the next hitter. The radio commentator announced that this was Pagano's *thirtieth* strikeout of the game, which must be, he said, some kind of record. The next batter hit a hard shot at the third baseman – a made to order double play ball under most circumstances. But it was late and the boy's hands were cold. The ball caromed off his glove into left field and the runner went all the way from first to third. Now more than ever Mac needed strikeout number thirty-one. I crossed my fingers and lowered my head praying for an out. He got an out all right, on a lazy fly ball to short center. It was just deep enough to entice the runner from third to bolt toward the plate. The Cranston centerfielder made a good throw and it was a close play at the plate but the runner was safe and the game was over. Deering High had won the state title and their supporters went crazy with excitement. Mac Pagano slowly trudged off the field, head bowed in defeat. He had given up three hits all day, had struck out thirty batters over fifteen innings and had lost the most important game of his life on an unearned run.

I never saw Mac Pagano again. That summer he was signed by the Red Sox and sent to their minor league club in Pittsfield, Massachusetts. I tried to follow his minor league career in the Providence Journal and Sporting News. For a while he pitched well as a reliever but then came up with a sore arm. He kicked around the minors for few more seasons but eventually his arm just gave out. My mother always said he should have tried to make it as a shortstop instead of a pitcher, and maybe she was right. But I knew once you had commanded the mound as Mac had, it would've been hard to relinquish that domain.

As for my brother, shortly after high school he enlisted in the navy, where he served four years, including a short tour through Vietnam in the early days of that war. As far as I know Don has never played another inning of baseball in his life. At best, he may have played some catch with his son or daughters when they were young.

I still enjoy watching baseball as much as I ever did though I readily admit that I don't know all the players as I once had nor can I remember any of their batting averages. Occasionally these days I'll be taking an evening stroll and come across a Little League game in progress. I'll stop and watch for while wondering if there's a budding young Mac Pagano among the boys on the field. And if I listen closely enough sometimes I hear the faint echo of my mother's voice suggesting that the umpire needs to get fitted with glasses.

The End

A Mayor for Catfish
Linda Welker

Doctor Manfred Gunther walked into the bar in a huff;
his cheeks flushed cherry red and his ears white, as if his
face stole all the blood out of them. He slammed his hand on
the bar-top to command the attention of the bartender.

"Tom, who is Barney Zinger? I grew up in this town,
I've been mayor for the past four years and I thought I knew
the names of all three hundred and fifty-two residents. I
never heard of a Barney Zinger. Zinger is your last name. Is
he a relative of yours?"

"I guess you could say that." Tom was a good six
inches taller than Doc and outweighed him by about seventy
pounds. He leaned over, his head a few inches from Doc and
wiped the bar with a rag. "You, want a drink, Doc?"

Tom owned the Catfish Bar as his father had before
him. It looked the same as it did fifty years ago when it
opened - bare wood floor, small round tables, and cowboy
pictures on the walls. Tom always had a toothpick hanging

out of the corner of his mouth and he was an expert at talking using only one side of his lip.

"This Barney guy has to be a resident to run for mayor. Where does he live?" Doc asked backing up a step from the bar and Tom.

"Right here at the bar."

Doc looked around the room; the only occupants were a young couple sitting at a table in the corner.

"Where is he? I want to meet him," Doc demanded. He was no longer a doctor; he'd lost his license to practice medicine ten years ago, for showing up at the hospital drunk. He retired to his hometown of Catfish, California, still referring to himself as Doctor Gunther. Immediately he became involved in local politics, trying to bring progress to Catfish.

The town stagnated in the early 1920s after all the catfish were fished out of the pond. Then the state built the highway to bypass Catfish by six miles. The bar was the only business the town had. On Sunday afternoons Tom offered half price beer, dollar hot dogs, dollar chili, and free pool, which tempted the bikers off the interstate.

"Where is Barney Zinger?" Doc repeated the question, his impatience beginning to show. A ten-year veteran of Alcoholics Anonymous, he was embarrassed by the bar being the only entertainment in his town. He tried to get it shut down after being elected mayor, but the bar was a landmark in Catfish. He wasn't able to get the support he needed from the locals, who thought of it as their community center. The feud between Tom and Doc split the town into two unequal parts; the drinkers supported Tom and non-drinkers supported Doc. Doc's group was the minority.

"Come-by, Sunday afternoon. Barney will be here. Think he's going to make a campaign speech." The toothpick wiggled in Tom's mouth as he spoke.

"I'll be here and I demand the right to make a speech as well."

"That's only fair." Tom said as he washed glasses. "Sure you don't want a drink, Doc? You look like you could use one."

"I'll see you Sunday." Doc stomped out, pausing long enough to step over a fat basset hound sleeping in the doorway. The hound was sort of the town mascot, a stray everyone on Main Street fed. On cold nights he would bark at a door until the resident let him in to spend the night, but in the morning he'd leave to wander the streets looking for handouts. Doc allowed the dog to spend an occasional night in his house. He knew the bar was one of the hound's favorite places, especially on Sunday's with hot dogs and chili around.

Doc scratched the dog's huge elephant-like ears, his most impressive feature. "Hey, boy, come with me and I'll give you something to eat." He glanced back at Tom in the bar. "Why don't you give this dog a bath? He stinks."

"He's not my dog. He just thinks he lives here."

The hound followed Doc down the street, the tip of his ears an inch off the pavement.

The next day Tom made a banner eight feet long and hung it in front of the bar.

Sunday Noon, Catfish Bar - Candidates for Mayor Dr Manfred Gunther & Barney Zinger will debate the issues.

Doc spent the week preparing. He thought about the things he planned to do for the town in his second term as mayor. Four years ago he was the first person who actually wanted to be mayor. There was no pay. Doc spent his own money for office supplies and gas to attend the county commissioner's meetings. He fought for road repair and a stop light for his little town. He was trying to negotiate a contract with a major, upscale restaurant chain to build in Catfish. The last thing he expected was to have an opponent in the election this time. *Who in the hell was Barney Zinger?*

Sunday the bar parking lot filled with motorcycles and cars. All the locals showed up to see the candidates, the bikers for the food and half price beer. The place was jammed. Tom had to hire a waitress for the afternoon. Doc entered with two of his closest friends from AA to give him support. They pushed through the crowd to the bar.

"Tom!" Doc yelled.

An assembly line of glasses waited by the tap, Tom poured draft beer as fast as he could, foam spilling over his fingers.

"Yeah, Doc?" he said without looking up.

"Where is he?"

"Over by the food."

Doc and his friends headed toward the food shelf along the wall in the back, behind the pool table. The pool players parted to let them pass. All Doc saw was the hound sitting under the shelf, wolfing down a hot dog.

"Doc, meet Barney Zinger," Tom yelled from the bar. Suddenly the crowd shut up. All eyes watched Doc, as he glanced from face to face in confusion. Someone giggled, another laughed with gusto, and soon the whole place roared like canned laughter on a television sitcom.

A woman standing next to Doc put a hand on his shoulder. "It's the dog. We named the hound Barney Zinger."

Doc's face glowed red as a streetlight, his ears as pale as paper. Even the two friends who came with him started laughing. Doc turned, marched out and down the street. He could hear the hilarity coming from the bar all the way to his house.

The election was held two days later. Doc went to the elementary school multi-purpose room to vote. It was a short ballot, a couple of county commissioners' positions were open, a judge, and of course the Mayor of Catfish. He grimaced while reading the name Barney Zinger: Occupation Unemployed. A hand full of people came in to vote, watching them; Doc wondered if they knew his opponent was a dog.

In the evening Doc received a call from the county elections supervisor. "I'm sorry Doctor Gunther, but Barney Zinger was elected Mayor," she said. "I don't have a phone number for him. Do you know how I can reach him?"

"Barney Zinger is a dog," he growled.

"A what?"

"A damn dog. A basset hound stray dog."

"Oh."

Doc hung-up, put on his jacket, and walked down to the Catfish Bar. It was ten o'clock on a quiet Tuesday night. Tom and a local were playing checkers at the end of the bar.

"Hi Doc," they said in unison. Tom came over to where Doc sat.

He put a fresh toothpick in his mouth and asked, "Can I get you something?"

"I'll have a coke."

Tom filled a glass with ice and coke and set in front of Doc. "Are you okay? It was all in fun and I sure made some money on Sunday."

"He won. The damn dog won."

"He did? Oh, my god. I never dreamed he'd win," Tom chuckled.

"Catfish now has a dog for a mayor." Doc said with disgust, his face glowing.

"This town doesn't need a mayor anyway. You know, Doc, you never ordered anything in here before. Every time you come in here you're upset over something. The noise, the bikes on Sunday, things nobody cares about but you."

"You made a joke out of the election." Doc glared at the big man. Suddenly he reached out, grabbed the toothpick and threw it on the floor.

Tom's eyes widened in surprise.

"Look, Doc, you tried to shut down my bar. This is the only business in town. It's my taxes that pays for the road and the new stoplight. People around here don't like change. We like things the way they are. We don't need a fancy restaurant."

"I wanted to help the town," Doc said, his voice quiet and a little sad.

"The town doesn't need any help. We're ten minutes from the interstate. It can take us anywhere we want to go for dinner. Let Catfish be Catfish."

"You won, a dog for mayor will stop progress," Doc said, shaking his head.

"Don't take it so hard. Barney will make a good mayor. He's everyone's friend and all he does is eat, sleep and scratch. Just like all politicians."

Doc felt a chill in the air as he walked home. Barney was waiting for him on his front porch. "Hello, Mayor," Doc said, "Guess you want to spend the night with me, you traitor. Well, in the morning I am going to give you a bath. We can't have the mayor of Catfish stinking like a barroom."

The End

Monty Python Had No Idea!

Marlene Becker

Gary raised an eyebrow in concern as he looked at his friend's pet. "Wilson, What the hell did you do to that rabbit?"

Wilson shrugged. "I fed it?"

"Where'd you get the rabbit food? Cheronobyl?"

"Hey, don't blame me for the rabbit! I didn't do anything!! If you want to place blame, then blame the rabbit!"

The bunny in question, who was a gun metal gray that glowed a burnished blue, slowly raised his head from the pound of carrots he was munching contently and looked from one human to the other as if to question if he were to receive more food. After all, the carrots were almost gone.

"When you asked me to take care of your pet rabbit for a few weeks when you went on vacation, I sure didn't expect . . . this!"

"It's only a *rabbit*, Gary!"

"It's bigger than my dog!!!"

"Yeah, well, just don't let him play with your pooch. I wouldn't want him to get hurt accidently."

"Ladybug, wouldn't hurt the rabbit."

"I wasn't talking about Ladybug. I wouldn't want Baxter to hurt your dog. Ladybug only weighs about what, fifteen, twenty pounds?"

"Yeah, around eighteen. How much does Baxter weigh?"

"Thirty-nine," Wilson said softly.

"Rabbits are not supposed to weigh thirty-nine pounds. They're supposed to be cute, cuddly little fuffy bunnies that can be picked up with one hand."

"It's not that bad. Honestly. Baxter is leash trained. And litter box trained. Of course, his litter box is pretty big."

"Of course."

"But I'm providing the litter," Wilson added hopefully, going to the hall closet and opening the door. "A 50-lb bag."

"Uh, yeah."

Wilson paused with the unopened sack halfway into the hall.

Hands on hips, Gary looked from the giant rabbit to the giant bag of litter. "Looks like I'm going to get in shape whether I want to or not."

"He likes to go for an evening stroll."

"Of course."

"And he's very sweet."

Gary eyed the rabbit suspiciously.

Baxter finished the carrots, sat back on his haunches, looked up at the human, then began to wash his face with his front feet. Gary stared at the fluffy paws in amazement, each was as big as a mitten.

"I figure he's either a Flemish Giant, a German Giant, or a Continental Giant," Wilson stooped down to stroke the soft fur on its back. "The Continental can get as big as 50 pounds."

"That's not normal," Gary shook his head in wonderment.

"Well, they're not found in the wild, that's for sure. It seems to be a European thing." Wilson reached behind him to a nearby end table to snag a large harness which he snapped securely around the rabbit.

"Of course," Gary held the leash his friend had passed up to him lightly draped over one hand, not quite certain what to do with it. "Your brother was stationed in Europe last year, wasn't he?"

"Yeah, he sent Baxter to sis' kids last year for Easter. When Bax almost sat on the Chihuahua, Vi had a fit and I ended up with him."

Gary sighed, resigned that the giant bunny did seem to be quite docile and he'd about run out of arguments. "My landlord agreed to my keeping a bunny, not a buffalo. I'm not sure how I'll explain a forty pound, four-foot rabbit."

"Hum-m-m-m." Wilson straightened and let his eyes wander around the room. When they found a hinged basket, he let out a quick, "Ha!" and pounced. "I thought Vi left this the last time she was here." He dug through the contents until he found some bright red ribbon. Quickly returning to the rabbit, Wilson gathered Baxter's long, fluffy ears together and tied them carefully. Then, he fluffed the fur around it and stood back smiling at his handiwork.

Gary watched in amazement. "What the hell is that for?"

Wilson took the leash, clipped it to the harness and handed the end to his friend. "I want to thank you for taking care of my poodle while I'm on vacation. With his deformed back end, I just couldn't leave him at a boarding kennel." He grinned.

Gary couldn't help it. This was going to be one of those great stories to tell in the break room at work. He smiled back and accepted the leash. "Com'on Bax. Do you like riding in the front seat or the back?"

Dragging the sack of litter out the door after them, Wilson said, "Just don't let him hang his head out the window, he gets bugs in his teeth."

The End

Morning Ride

Grass flows from an old hayfield,
swelling beyond its banks
onto a two-rut road where green
laps my buckskin's hooves. Sun releases
moist air that grows into waves of heat
above heavy ground. Vultures appear,
not in their usual floating coil, but hovering
in a circular formation, as if looking down
into a well. Rounding a curve past the cattle
gap, we stop, see them again, a gathering
of old men, wearing black tie and tails,
standing slightly stooped in a hushed
squabbling over the bloated
carcass of a yearling calf. Hot breath
mists from my mare's nostrils as only
a few bald heads turn. They speak in low
murmurs as they tear strips of darkly-blooded
backstrap from a long, supple spine.
Though I cannot hear, furred ears flick
toward their conversation. It may be of
sun-baked flesh or memorable thermal
rides, but my guess is pity. For no matter
how far we lean toward wind or how
much sweat froths down her flanks,
my mare and I can never gallop
upward onto great roiling currents of air.

Christine Cock

My Dear Friend

Jerry Cowling

You may remember the news reports surrounding the death of best-selling novelist Irving Stone in 1989. He was found slumped over his desk, dead from an apparent heart attack, with his hand still holding a pen as though he were in the middle of a letter. On the paper he had scrawled, "My Dear Friend."

Literary authorities debated for months who this dear friend was and why had Stone had only one other word written on the page before he died and what was the meaning behind it. Irving has been gone several years now and I myself am an old man, so I think it is safe to reveal that I was his dear friend.

It was late 1978, and I was flying to Virginia to join my wife and son at my in-laws' house for Christmas. I looked forward neither to the flight nor the visit. I didn't know to be afraid I might die in a plane crash, or to fear surviving the flight and have to endure my wife's parents for two long, cold weeks. The last thing I needed was a grumpy old man plopping in the seat next to me and start mumbling to himself. His comments became louder and unfortunately more distinct. When he got to the part about how it was intolerable that first class was filled to capacity, I could no longer contain myself.

"Well, I'll try not to breathe on you."

One of my worst character flaws was opening my mouth and letting fly words that I wish I could immediately grab and cram back in. Not only was I subjected to a disgruntled aristocrat generally angry at the airline for not accommodating him but also was going to be the personal object of his disdain for the next three hours. Glancing over at him, I watched his face change from shock, anger and incredulity to surprise, humor and relaxation. He laughed out loud for about half a minute, which in a crowded tourist class airplane section was exceptionally long. Several fellow travelers turned to see what was going on.

"This is the first time I've laughed in at least three days," he said. "Thank you."

"You're welcome."

Smiling, he stared at me, which made me uncomfortable. I decided I would have preferred to have him angry and ignoring me in excess than have all this attention.

"You don't know who I am, do you?"

My first impulse was to ask, "And why should I care?" Instead I restrained myself. "I take it you are a person who prefers to fly first class."

He chuckled again. "And why should you care in the first place?" Settling into his cramped seat, the man looked straight ahead. "I apologize for being an insufferable bore. I assume everyone knows who I am and will try to convince me he has written the next best-selling novel in the world if only he could get a foot in the door."

I had written a novel and sent the first three chapters to Doubleday. An editor replied he liked them and wanted to see the rest of it. By the time I mailed it, he retired and the next editor didn't like it at all. Since I didn't want to add

another rejection to my list of achievements, I refrained from
telling the author my story.

"You don't have a novel, do you?"

"Oh, no," I lied. "Used to work for newspapers though.
But that's not real writing, is it?"

"All writing is real writing. I admire how you people
can write a full story, zip like that and have it published the
next day. I could never do that."

"It's called a deadline. And the necessity of being paid."

He laughed again. "None of the reporters I've talked to
have ever made me laugh. Why is that?"

"The deadline." I paused. "I interviewed a famous
author once. One of the Haileys. Not the one who wrote
Roots but the other one. You know. Hotel. Airport."

"Yes, I do know him."

"He acted like he was a character in one of his own
novels."

The man giggled.

"And he looks like he has a personal tanning bed in his
house and uses it daily."

"He does, he does."

Three hours passed quickly as I tossed out random
comments about writing and writers while the man laughed
all through it. I never felt so clever in my life. By the time
we were circling the airport, he pulled out a note pad and
pen.

"Please put your initials and address on this," he said. "I
would like to hear from you. But I think it would be better if
we kept our identities to initials. It would ruin it, don't you
think, if you knew exactly who I was."

It was just as well. I didn't think I wanted to be on first
name basis when anyone that eccentric anyway. By the first
week of the new year I received a handsome letter on
personalized stationary. At the top of the paper were the
initials "IRS." He apologized again for his rudeness on the
plane and reiterated how much he had enjoyed our
conversation.

"By the way, I was at Hailey's house for New Year's Eve and giggled at him the entire evening. He was quite put out by it and asked what the matter was. I couldn't tell him that he was acting like a character in one of his novels, so I just said I had had too much wine. Please keep me informed about what you are reading. I don't get honest opinions often."

This put me in a rather odd situation because I was going through a period when I wasn't reading much of anything. The last novel I had picked up I hadn't even finished.

"I tried to read Irving Stone's book about Sigmund Freund, Passions of the Mind, but couldn't finish it. I supposed it was over my head. I can't read William Faulkner either."

In the return mail I received this note from IRS:

"I agree about William Faulkner. He tried to be the American William Shakespeare. Stone was just lucky. He needs to remember to be appreciative of what he has been given."

At the time I thought he was bit rough on Stone, but since he knew all these people personally I didn't want to dispute his opinion. Through the years we corresponded, and I resisted the temptation to talk about my own writing. I wrote a few more novels, some plays and screenplays, none of them getting past the standard rejection slip. Every now and then I did pump him for gossip. For example, I asked if he thought Ernest Hemingway actually committed suicide or was it murder.

"Hemingway was crazy," IRS wrote. "He could have been a great writer if he wasn't always trying to prove he was a real man, whatever a real man is."

By the middle of 1989 I had a huge stack of handwritten letters from the anonymous novelist. In September not one single letter came in the mail. Perhaps he had grown tired of connecting with a common man. On October first, however, I received this:

"My dear friend, I am sorry I have not written lately. My health is beginning to fail. Not to bore you with details but I've been hospitalized for the last month. I fear I have written my last novel, which is a shame since it's all I've done for the last fifty years. Once again I feel remorse over our relationship. I regret having taken advantage of your good nature and humor. In the ten years we have corresponded I should have dropped my self-defense mechanism to reach out to help you with whatever dreams you have. To make up for it, I want you to feel free to ask me for one favor. No matter what it is, I will do everything within my power to grant it."

This put me in a particular bind. While my heart raced a bit with the prospect of finally being published by a real publisher, I didn't want to ruin the good feelings of our ten-year relationship by having him try to sell my books and fail. However, I've always felt it was bad manners to reject someone's offer to do me a favor, so I wrote back this:

"My dear friend. Corresponding with you for ten years has been an honor and a pleasure, I think, made even more special by the anonymity. Therefore, my only request is that you share with me what your middle name is. That way you can keep your privacy and I can have the joy of knowing a private fact about a public person."

Another month passed without a letter. Again I assumed I had presumed too much and lost this special relationship. The next morning I read the local newspaper. Irving Stone, author of bestsellers Lust for Life, Agony and the Ecstasy and Passions of the Mind, died at his home, leaving an enigma—an unfinished letter to "my dear friend." I smiled when I read the only word on the letter.

"Rebecca."

The End

New Neighbors

Johanna M. Bolton

Almost all of the families in our wonderful old
neighborhood had been there for generations. Over the years,
the houses have developed distinct personalities as they were
built onto and embellished to suit the individuality of their
owners. People cared about their houses. Paint was renewed
regularly and the roofs maintained. Manicured lawns were
bordered by trim hedges and generous gardens spilling color
over picket fences. Ancient trees lined the street, spreading
their branches over the pavement and turning it into a shady
tunnel.

It was very unusual for one of these houses to be for
sale, but last year, that's just what occurred. One spring day
the house next door changed hands and almost before
anyone knew what was happening, we had new neighbors.

The moving van came, disgorging cartons and shrouded
furniture that briefly littered the lawn before being carried
inside. Soon curtains appeared in the windows and potted
plants on the front porch. On Monday morning a stack of
flattened cartons tied with twine stood beside the trashcans

to be hauled away by the garbage truck. And that was that! The new neighbors were installed.

Beyond their names, however, I didn't know much about them. I assumed we'd have more time for chatting now that they were settled in. I was delighted they were an older couple, no teenagers with loud music -- nothing to disturb the peace of our suburban enclave.

Or so I thought.

Alas, I couldn't have been more wrong.

Mildred Cunningham introduced herself one day as she worked in the side yard. She proved to be an avid gardener, ruthlessly pruning the neglected beds of prized roses that once flourished around the house. The woman who planted the shrubs had been my mother's best friend, but she died years ago. After that, her husband lived alone, and he let the gardens go. Now Mildred seemed determined to bring them back to their previous glory. She worked long and hard, hoeing, weeding, and digging. Lately she was making a hole by the back fence, moving dirt out of the compost heap there to spread on the annual beds. Beyond the compost heap, rambling over the back fence, were several varieties of climbing roses. I remember my mother telling me that the red ones were called Scarlet Bess. The blooms were sparse this year, but they just needed some fresh mulch, water, and plant food to come back to the dense mass they had once been.

Mildred was all right. It was her husband who turned out to be a problem.

I didn't see very much of him, except every morning when he made his way across the backyard to his workshop in the detached garage. But I could certainly hear him. In fact the whole neighborhood could hear him. He was back there hammering something metal -- oil drums, maybe. I couldn't begin to guess what he was making, but the noise was horrible!

Then Mildred got into it. The more noise he made, the more she yelled at him to be quiet.

"He says he's building a rocket ship," his wife confided to me one sunny afternoon as I leaned over the fence. "He's driving me crazy with the noise," she added, "but at least it keeps him out from underfoot."

"Rocket ship?" I repeated. "You mean one of those toy rockets people shoot off behind the high school?"

"No, a real rocket," she corrected me. "He says he's going into space." She shook her head and pursed her lips. "Good riddance, I say."

Her words were interrupted by what sounded like an explosion from the garage. I jumped, but Mildred just turned around.

"For crying out loud, Vernon! What did you blow up now!" she called.

"Nothing," came a reply, muffled by garage doors. "Everything's all right. Don't you fuss!"

"I'll 'don't fuss' you, you old..." she muttered under her breath. She gave me a strained smile. "Well, better get back to weeding. Be dark soon. Sorry about the noise."

A couple hours later I heard another explosion, this one twice a loud as the last. Mildred came running from the back fence where she had a sizable hole going, and raced into the garage.

"What in hell did you do now?" she yelled.

"None of your damned business,' came the reply, cut off short as she slammed the door after her. I could still hear voices, though, raging up and down, punctuated by her shrill arguments. I closed the window and went into the kitchen to make a cup of tea. These neighbors were going to be interesting, all right. But something had to be done about the noise!

The next day, however, a hush fell over the neighborhood. There was no banging and crashing, and no explosions from the garage. When I stepped outside, I saw Mildred placidly working among the roses dressed in her usual baggy overalls and a huge straw hat. She was singing softly to herself.

I called hello as I went to put the garbage out.

She raised a smiling face. "Isn't this just the most beautiful summer day?" she commented.

"Beautiful." I agreed. "How's Vernon's rocket?"

"Oh, he finished it," she told me.

"Really? Can I come over and see it?" I wanted to know.

"Oh, no, she replied. It's gone. He left last night."

"What do you mean 'left'?"

"On his trip. To Mars." She beamed at me. But you can come over anytime and see my roses," she invited.

From that day on it was quiet and peaceful in the neighborhood again. Mildred's flowers won prizes every year at the state fair. Some of her biggest and best blooms were the Scarlet Bess roses that grew around her compost heap.

The End

The Pig Did It

Joan Donohue

The swirl of cold, sharp air told Melania that it was near to freezing as a light drizzle began to fall. She was finishing her walk home from the bus stop after work.

Getting indoors would not come soon enough, except for one thing. Russell was there.

Several years ago, maybe five, Melania changed her name from Mary. Mary Clark, perfectly forgettable. So she told herself, "Make a statement!"

She made up something melodic or exotic, whatever and it was done. Mary became Melania and that was that. No argument was worth hearing and she would have none though her mom whimpered and whined - her name was Mary, too. Her brother John endlessly told her she was a fool for all the hassle it would bring with changing forms and documents. "Yes," he said, "It would even confuse the darn postman."

That was the same time Russell came to live with them.

John brought the pig to his mom from a farm store in eastern Pennsylvania where John worked as a rep for a big pharmaceutical company. The owner was really happy to part company with Russell and gave John the little pig for free only saying he'd make an interesting pet. Now, Mary, the mom, automatically hated all animals no matter what but Russell was strangely different.

"Oh, Ma, look what I've got! Ain't he great?"

Mary took one look at Russell and just fell in love. Nobody could explain it so it was more than strange when Russell got the spare bedroom.

These days, Russell stood about two and three-quarter feet at the shoulder, had an enormous snout, and a rather long tail that only curled up when he was mad or thinking of mischief. He was a pig but a pig smart as the devil. More than once did Melania see sausage and bacon instead of Russell, looking or rather trying to look innocent after some disaster, like the fire in the basement last Christmas Eve.

Or there was the time Russell tried making spaghetti but instead managed to flood the kitchen trying to put water into the pot. Melania got stuck cleaning up that mess because her mother's leg was broken after Russell tripped her running after the neighbor's cat. Melania said that the cat knew Russell was some sort of freak and the cat did disappear shortly after.

Melania pushed open the front door of the old brownstone. Russell was right there at her feet. He fluttered his eyelashes, and grunted as Melania stood aside to let him out.

"Don't do anything stupid, Russell," she said as he squeezed passed and threw another grunt over his shoulder, which sounded a tad derisive.

She shook it off. "Ma, I'm home!" she called. No answer. "John?" Silence. Tom the canary fluttered wildly in his cage when Melania came near. "Hey, hey... What's up with you?"

She stopped in the front hall to look at the mail, expecting some literature on a place to live in Virginia. She had a new job lined up and was planning on getting out of her current situation and making a fresh start. Melania was only twenty-four but felt years older. She picked up a fat envelope. It was from her mother's lawyers, Ghetsam and Goode. Her mother had changed her will, again. Melania wondered. Was she in it, out of it? This event happened twice a year and really, she ceased to care. Every change was precipitated by a big fight her mother picked and predictably, this last was about Russell.

Suddenly, two gun shots exploded from the rear of the house. Melania froze for what seemed like minutes though it was only a moment or two. Finally, she tiptoed toward the kitchen and just at the door on a chair sat a revolver on top of some books. "What the hell..." She reached for it and held it up by the handle. Just then, Russell appeared, his tail tightly curled up as he chortled . She stumbled into the kitchen and screamed.

Another loud bang blew in from behind but it was the police coming through the front door.

She saw her dying mother pointing at her and then collapse on the kitchen table; John already shot dead on the floor. "Oh, my God ! I'm going to kill you, Russell !" The pig just backed away as the police tackled Melania.

"You have the right to remain silent..."

"Russell ! Tell them !" Melania thrashed. "Show them, damn it!"

"Hoo, boy," said one of the cops.

Melania's head was pinned down to the floor as they cuffed her.

Russell nuzzled her face and then looked at the cop holding her down with a very worried look, making little squeaky noises.

"You little piece of garbage," she managed to say though almost muzzled. "It... was... the... pig !"

"Man, this is a new one on me."

"Yeah, nothing surprises me anymore. Hey there, little pig. I'm going to take you home. I got a little farm out in Jersey, my mother's place.

You'll like it there."

Russell shrugged his shoulders, sat down, thought for a moment and then grinned. He'd certainly be very well off. Why not?

The End

Reincarnation of an Acorn

Incarnation begins
as deer nibble and browse. Acorns pass
through long, tawny bodies, landing among
steaming, pebbled piles. Sun, soil, water

stir a spiraling alchemy of growth, rings overlap
rings, rooted energy erupts into leafy crowns
housing countless wanderers.
Wind, woodpeckers, and lightning fire

wear into creased bark. Branches wither,
beetles leave behind crumbling skirts
of sawdust; downed, desiccated limbs split
under trembling force of muscle and bladed

steel. Even though we can only know this
moment, even though ash seems weightless,
as it leaves fire, rising before it falls, it rises
again, and then again, as root, trunk, branch and crown.

                                          Christine Cock

Richard's Revenge

Judy G. Burford

As the sound of Jane's footfalls approached the kitchen, Richard gripped the largest of the knives from the counter, and slipped behind the door. His palms were sweaty and his heart was racing. The very thought of Jane being this close brought back memories he'd been trying to forget.

The contusions on Richard's face and forearms were yellow now, as they made their way through the color spectrum of healing. The eleven stitches above his eye pulled at his flesh as though it were an elastic band.

The divorce, the restraining order, nothing seemed to keep her at bay.

It wasn't bad enough that she referred to him as her "Dickless wonder", among other defamatory remarks. Over the years, her tirades had increased in intensity. Early on, he believed it was his fault. He'd perturbed her so.

He recalled that first time. The redness rose up Jane's face like lava rising from a crater. The veins in her forehead bulged and her fingers clenched into fists. Her strides seemed to levitate above the carpet as she lunged toward him. The pain cut through his nose the instant her knuckles made contact, spewing blood everywhere.

"You son-of-a-bitch," Jane said. "You took my car."

"Jane, I had a flat. I didn't have time to wait for assistance."

"I have a job to get to too."

He had to admit, she had a point.

"I'm sorry, Jane, it won't happen again."

"Promise me, Richard. I need to know I can trust you."

Relief washed over him. Was she calming down?

Since then, there were numerous other incidents, numerous trips to the ER to get something stitched, bandaged, or casted. Richard got good at making up excuses to protect the monster he called his wife, until one day when his mother dropped by unexpectedly. He didn't have time to disguise the damage. He felt so humiliated, emasculated, forlorn. It wasn't long after that that he decided to go into therapy. His therapist taught him people need to be responsible for their own actions. He didn't make Jane act that way, she did.

The hairs on Richard's forearms stood at attention, as the swinging door between the kitchen and the dining room inched open. He hated the power she still possessed over him.

The sound of the doorbell and the reverse swing of the door happened in unison. He exited through the other kitchen door, to see who it was.

"Hey, Larry, what can I do for you?"

Larry had been Richard's next door neighbor for nearly nine years. Recently, Richard shared the horrors of his relationship with Jane.

Larry pulled Richard out onto the stoop and reached behind him to pull the door closed. He didn't want what he was about to say to reach Jane's ears.

"Richard, I saw Jane come down the street an hour or so ago and go around back. I assumed she got inside the house.

I didn't want to interfere, but I got worried so I decided it was best to call the police. They're on their way. He'd barely finished speaking when a squad car pulled up in front of the house.

"Is one of you Richard Cummings?" said the officer on his way up the front walk.

"That's me." Richard said.

"Your neighbor called to let us know that your wife was lurking around. You have a restraining order, right?"

"That's right."

"Are you in any danger now?"

"No, everything's fine."

Larry looked at Richard with a stunned expression on his face. Ignoring his look, Richard turned back to the officer.

I'm just getting dinner ready." Richard nodded toward the knife still clenched in his right hand. Without intending to, he tightened his grasp on the handle of the knife. "My neighbor was just telling me about his call to you. He thought my ex-wife had broken into my house. But it's all a misunderstanding. I gave her permission to stop by to pick up some of her personal items. I just asked that she be gone before I got home from work. I told her I'd leave them on the back patio."

He turned toward Larry, "I'm surprised you didn't see her leave again. Her things are gone."

Larry let out a slow sigh. His shoulders relaxed as he realized Richard was not in any eminent danger.

The three men said their goodbyes, and Richard headed back inside determined to put an end to his on-going nightmare.

The End

Run, Smitty, Run!

Linda Welker

"Run, Smitty, run! Come-on boy, run!"

Smitty smelled the strangers. They were too close. He heard another bang. Old Dad fell. He lay on the trail while blood spread across his shirt and seeped into the dirt. Smitty licked the blood.

Old Dad pushed him away. "Run, Smitty," he gasped. His limp hand flopped to the ground.

Smitty heard the crunch of the two strangers' footsteps on the trail. He dashed into the trees a few yards before whirling around to see if the predators were following.

The two men hovered over Old Dad. Smitty jerked when he heard another bang. He flattened his body under the bushes and watched the enemy.

"It's over, we got him," the tall one said.

"What about the Lab? We should kill him too." The fat one stamped his foot.

"I'm out of bullets. Anyway, he's just a damn dog. Come on, let's get the hell out of here."

After the enemy vanished from sight Smitty crept to Old Dad. He placed his head down on his leader's chest and listened for the beating of the heart or the breathing noises. Hours and hours he waited and waited for the sounds that never started. With a whine in his throat, he rubbed his muzzle under the man's chin and pawed at the unresponsive arm. He wanted Old Dad to pet him, talk to him, get up and most of all, to go home and make dinner.

The second morning Smitty woke with a dry mouth. He wandered into the forest looking for water. Tangles of vines hung on the pine trees, sticker bushes caught in his fur. He squeezed through a pile of rocks and nestled in the shade he found a puddle. Something sharp cut his foot as he stepped into the water to drink. He limped back to Old Dad to show him the injured foot. The man always took care of problems; he'd make it feel better. The smell of decaying flesh reached Smitty's nostrils yards away. His ears and tail drooped in response to the odor of death.

Smitty's hollow stomach sunk into his sides. His left front paw stung every time it touched the ground. He licked the raw pad on his foot, hobbled to a smooth spot beside the trail, and plopped down facing Old Dad. Smitty didn't want to miss any movement, any sign of life, a wave of a hand or a shifting of a foot.

The ache of hunger in Smitty's belly grew stronger and harder to ignore. Which way should he go to find food? In the past, he followed Old Dad. He went where his leader wanted to go. The house sat at the bottom of the hill. The same direction the strangers went. He didn't know what waited ahead; he had never come this far before.

Smitty closed his eyes and thought about how it happened. The smell of terror had zapped out of Old Dad as he ran. The loud boom hurt Smitty's ears. He sensed the fear in the air. They zigzagged through the trees like the rabbits Smitty chased. This time the two of them were the prey.

They rested by a granite rock at the bottom of a steep incline. Old Dad hugged Smitty close to his chest and Smitty heard the heart pounding and the air rushing in and out of the lungs as the man gasped for breath.

"We have to keep going." Old Dad crawled up the slope like a dog, using both his hands and feet. Loose stones dislodged by his shoes tumbled down the hillside. Smitty didn't like the noise. He knew as prey they needed to be silent.

Once on the trail at the top of the hill, Smitty galloped ahead. Old Dad's pace slowed. He staggered in exhaustion until the bang knocked him down.

Smitty licked his hurt paw. A snap of a dead tree branch breaking loose startled him. He jumped up and glanced left and right. Up ahead the trail twisted around a corner and disappeared, with one last look at the man he loved, Smitty headed out. He traveled about two hours before stopping to rest. The heat of the day diminished. The hoot of an owl echoed among the trees. His throbbing paw made sleeping difficult.

When the first rays of sunlight filtered through the treetops, Smitty started his march again. By the time the sun reached directly overheard, the forest began to thin out. Down a grassy embankment sunlight glistening on water drew him forward like a magnet. He collapsed at the edge of the lake soaking his sore foot and drinking his fill. He lay on his stomach, rested his chin in an inch of water and closed his eyes. The cool dampness soothed the heat out of his body.

He dreamed he saw Old Dad in the back yard. "Don't tease; bring the ball back to Old Dad. Smitty, how can Old Dad throw it again, if you don't bring me the ball," he laughed. Smitty liked to hear Old Dad laugh.

"It's a dog."

Smitty opened his eyes to see a canoe on the lake with a man and a boy in it. The boy pointed at him as the canoe glided closer.

"Run, Smitty, run," Old Dad whispered. Smitty charged into the trees.

The man and the boy pulled the canoe on shore and took things out of it. They sat on the grass, with their hands moving from their laps to their mouths. Smitty sniffed the air, the odor of bread and one of his favorite things, peanut butter, floated to his nose.

A three-legged hop positioned him out of the protection of the trees. He paused. A second hop brought him six feet from the man and boy.

"The dog's back and he has a hurt paw," the boy said.

"I know, don't move, Bobby. We can't be sure he's friendly." The man tossed a bite of bread to Smitty.

Smitty swallowed it whole and wagged his tail, hoping for more. The man tossed half a sandwich to the ground. Smitty limped closer as he studied the man's face. The man wore a baseball cap like Old Dad often wore. Hair above this man's lip wiggled when he talked and his eyes displayed a soft friendly look.

"It's okay, boy, you can have it. We aren't going to hurt you." The man spoke in a low gentle voice.

Smitty grabbed the sandwich and hobbled a few feet away to eat it.

"He has a collar on. He belongs to somebody," the man said.

"He's hurt and starving. He must be lost," the boy held a handful of potato chips out. Smitty bit the chips taking care not to touch the boy's fingers. The boy resembled the man, except he didn't have hair on his face. He had the same warm glow in his eyes.

The man slipped his fingers around Smitty's collar. "Get the rope out of the canoe. We'll tie him, so he doesn't run off again."

"Are we going to keep him?" the boy asked.

"No, he has tags on his collar. We can find his owner."

Relief flooded Smitty when they tied the rope to his collar. The man became a leader, someone to tell him which way to go. He licked the man's hand.

Later they lifted him in the canoe and told him to sit. The smell of the water and the breeze ruffling his fur as the boat glided across the lake made him forget the trauma of the last few days. The food in his belly and the companionship of the man and boy relieved the tension residing along his spine. He watched the boy dip a stick in the water and noticed they were getting closer to the shore on the other side of the lake.

"Why do they call it Paradise Lake?" the boy asked.

"When the first white settlers came to this part of northern California and saw the lake they thought it looked like paradise," the man answered.

The boy gazed along the shoreline. "No one lives here now."

"The settlers soon learned the land was too rocky to plant and too hilly for cattle. They moved on."

"How long has it been a park?"

"For a twelve-year-old kid who got a "D" in history you sure are asking a lot of questions about the past."

"In school, it's boring. All they talk about is stuff that happened a zillion years ago."

"Well, I think the county took over the area about twenty years ago."

At the boat ramp, they tied Smitty to a picnic table while they loaded the canoe in a truck. Smitty rested in the shade under the table.

Two men came out of the snack bar carrying drinks.

"Run! Smitty, run!" Smitty heard Old Dad shout. He charged out from under the table toward the water. The rope stopped his forward motion. He couldn't run. He only had one choice, fight. He turned to face the enemy barking and snarling. His upper lip pulled back, exposing his fangs he crouched ready to attack. Hate glaring from his eyes.

"What's the matter, boy?" The man rushed to Smitty's side.

The fat enemy dropped his drink. "It's the dog!" he yelled, "We should've killed him."

"Shut up," the tall one ordered.

"Bo, what do you mean, you should've killed him?" The man took off his hat and glared at the fat one.

"He didn't mean nothing, Sheriff," the other one answered.

The sheriff pulled on the rope and walked toward the truck. Smitty followed, keeping the enemy in his vision. The man picked him up, plunked him in the truck bed, and tied the rope to a truck cleat.

Smitty continued barking and growling at the strangers. He hoped they couldn't tell he was bluffing. He didn't know how to fight. Old Dad never allowed aggression.

"Jack, this dog sure hates you and your brother," the sheriff yelled. "I wonder why."

The tall enemy shrugged his shoulders and both of them went back into the snack bar.

"Who are they?" the boy whispered.

"No one you want to know, Bobby. They've been in my jail a couple of times. They hang out at the snack bar, cause their mother works there and she gives them free food."

❈

The truck moved and Smitty lost his balance at first and fell back on his hunches. He pressed against the metal side for support as the truck swayed. After a quick ride through city streets the truck stopped. The man went into a building.

The boy leaned over the side of the truck. "We're going to find your owner," he said as he petted Smitty.

The man came back and the truck moved again. This time Smitty steadied his body and stood firm. The truck parked in the driveway of a house the color of the sun. A short woman came out, reached her arms up around the man's neck, pulled his head down, and kissed him on the mouth.

"Sheriff Curtis, did you turn your cell phone off?"

"Yes, I did. Mrs. Curtis. It is a wonderful, spring day and I wanted to have an uninterrupted Saturday afternoon with my son."

"You'd better call in. Hikers found a body on Flat Rock Hill." She turned around and smiled at Smitty, sitting in the back of the truck. "What a gorgeous dog. Where did he come from?"

"We found him up by the lake," Bobby said. "His name is Smitty."

"He's beautiful. I've always wanted a golden lab."

"I knew we shouldn't have brought him home." The sheriff shook his head. "We are not going to keep him, he has an owner. We stopped by the pound and they looked up his tag number. He belongs to a George Dickenblocker, of all names."

"Damn, Jules that's the man they found shot to death." Mrs. Curtis scratched Smitty behind the ears. He licked her face as she leaned over the side of the truck.

"Shot! We haven't had a murder in the county in years." The sheriff held his cell phone to his ear. "Ginger, where are you? What's the address. . . .? Okay I know where that is. I'm on my way." He clipped the phone to his belt.

"I know who did it. All we have to do is prove it."

"You are good, but really, how can you know already?" Mrs. Curtis asked.

"He told me." The sheriff nodded toward Smitty. "Bobby, take him in the house and give him some food and water. Janice, he has a hurt paw. Can you see if you can do something with it? Looks like we are going to keep him for awhile."

Smitty knew they were talking about him. He wagged his tail as hard as he could.

Bobby led Smitty into the kitchen. Two dogs rushed at them. A small brown one barked and barked as if her throat was stuck in gear. A black and white one, the same size as Smitty, sniffed noses with Smitty then smelled between his legs. Smitty wiggled his nose under her tail. He stood stiff legged, trying to watch the two dogs and the boy at the same time. The muscles in his back tensed.

"Maggie, Lucy," the woman called from the door. "Come." She held the screen door open. The two dogs went outside and sat with their noses pressed against the screen watching Smitty.

With a barrier between him and the other dogs, Smitty relaxed and allowed the woman to wipe his hurt paw with a wet rag and rub a salve on it. She gave him a bowl of food. Smitty gobbled it down.

For two days, Smitty rested on a blanket in the kitchen only going outside to relieve himself. His paw healed and no longer hurt when he walked on it.

One morning the sheriff sat at the kitchen table drinking coffee. "The only relative the dead man had is a son and he doesn't want the dog."

From the blanket in the corner Smitty listened to the voices and wagged his tail each time one of the humans glanced in his direction.

"Can't we keep him, Dad?" Bobby asked.

"No, we already have two dogs, that's enough."

"He's a beautiful dog," Mrs. Curtis said. She finished her cereal and set the bowl on the floor for Smitty to lap up the leftover milk. "How is the investigation going?"

"No finger prints, no shoe prints, no nothing. The only evidence we have is two twenty-five-caliber bullets. I know Jack and Bo Mercer did it."

"Why? Why shoot an old man walking with his dog?"

"Don't know that, either. They didn't even rob him. He still had money in his wallet."

Smitty finished polishing the inside of the cereal bowl with his tongue and looked up at the man.

"I bet he knows why." The sheriff patted Smithy on the top of the head.

"Let's take him back to the lake, maybe he can show us." Bobby wiped milk off his mouth with the back of his hand.

"That's not a bad idea. But you have to go to school."

"Not today, it's a teacher's work day. I'll get the canoe." The boy jumped up and headed for the door. Smitty followed.

"No, wait. We have to start where Mr. Dickenblocker started with Smitty. He lived near the entrance to the hiking trail that goes up Flat Rock Hill. His neighbors said he hiked there several times a week."

Bobby stood with his hand on the doorknob and Smitty stared at the door waiting for it to be opened.

"Take Smitty out to the truck. I'll call and get a deputy to meet us out there."

The second Smitty saw Old Dad's house he yipped and danced in the truck. When they let him in, he raced from room to room looking for the man he loved. Old Dad's scent radiated from the furniture, but Smitty knew the odor was days old.

Deputy Ginger backed her lanky frame up against the wall when Smitty came near. She stood as tall as the sheriff and weighed about half as much. "Go away, doggie," she said and waved her hand at him.

"Ginger, you are the best deputy I have, always cool in any situation. Don't tell me you're afraid of dogs?" the sheriff asked.

"I'm not afraid. I just have to get to know them."

"Well, this one is as friendly as they come."

In the kitchen Smitty found his water bowl and lapped up the tiny bit of water left in it, before he explored the house for the third time.

The humans went out the back door and Smitty followed them. Old Dad wasn't in the yard either. Smitty's ball lay next to the chain link fence. He picked it up and tossed it into the air.

"The trail runs right by the yard." The sheriff opened the gate. "Come on Smitty, let's go for a walk."

Smitty galloped out the gate and started up the hill. He owned this trail. He knew exactly which way to go and he was sure Old Dad would be up on the hill.

"He's going to be miles ahead of us. Smitty! Smitty!" the sheriff called.

Smitty wanted the man to be happy; he obeyed and stopped to wait for the people to catch up. He wished they would hurry. Old Day waited.

The sheriff patted his head. "Good dog." Snap, he clicked the leash on. "Now, we'll all go together."

The familiar aroma of pinesap and dirt made Smitty's nerves tingle. Excitement consumed him as it did every time he and Old Dad started out on a hike.

They passed the 'Y' where the trail separated. Smitty led them up the left side. A half mile beyond he stopped. A barely noticeable path to the right connected the two main trails. Smitty and Old Dad used the shortcut to circle around back to the intersection. Smitty pulled on the leash as he headed along the path toward the core of a rancid stench. He needed to find out, was the girl still there, did the smell come from her?

The humans followed with the sheriff in the lead. Soon they were able to detect the odor, too.

"What stinks?" Bobby asked.

"I think we are going to find out," his dad said. A few steps more and they saw a pair of blue jeans on the ground. The sheriff stopped and spread his arms out blocking the way. He handed the end of the leash to the deputy.

"Ginger, take Bobby and Smitty back to the house. This is a crime scene, get everybody up here, and call the coroner."

"I want to see, Dad."

"No, Bobby. Do what I tell you. Go back to the house and stay there."

"Yes, Sir." Ginger grabbed Bobby's hand and pulled Smitty and the boy back to the main trail.

Smitty thought about his last walk with Old Dad. They heard noises on the path. Old Dad pushed through the bushes to see the two strangers kneeing over a naked girl lying in the dirt. She kicked at the men. Smitty heard a thump and she stopped moving.

"What's going on here?" Old Dad shouted.

The first bang cracked in the air. The sharp noise made Old Dad run. A second pop, then something whizzed by and slammed into a tree next to them. Old Dad snaked left and right between the trees. Smitty stayed close by his side, keeping in step with every turn.

A tug on the leash brought Smitty's mind back to the present.

"Come on, dog," Ginger said.

Smitty planted his feet, stiffened his legs resisting the pull. He felt a twinge of pain on his ears as the collar slipped off. Freedom!

He leaped away through the trees, retracing the flight burned into his memory.

"Smitty! Smitty! Come back." Bobby yelled.

Smitty ignored the calls. He reached the boulder at the bottom of the hill where he and Old Dad had rested. He sniffed around the rock and lifted his leg, marking it as his own. Right here Old Dad held him for the last time. A faint odor left by their bodies' lingered in the air.

Nose to the ground and panting he scaled the exact same climb up the hill. On the trail, he smelled blood in a patch of dirt. A blend of odors blanketed the area. Many people had occupied the trail, tramping down the weeds, digging in the earth. Smitty lay down, placed his head on his front paws, and closed his eyes.

Daylight was disappearing when he heard someone coming up the trail. He growled proclaiming ownership of this spot and a willingness to defend it.

The sheriff came around the bend and sat down on a log a few feet away.

"Hi Smitty, I thought I'd find you here. I know this is where it happened. I promise you, boy; I'm going to get them. They are not going to get away with two murders in the same day."

The man talked for a few minutes more while drawing lines in the dirt with a twig. Sometimes he rubbed his finger over the hair above his lip. Smitty pretended not to watch him. He wanted Old Dad to be here, not this man. The man's mellow voice droned on. The sound eased the sad ache of his body. .

The man stood and started walking down the trail, "Come on, Smitty, its dinnertime."

Smitty understood the word 'dinnertime' and he followed the man.

Deputy Ginger drove Bobby and Smitty home in a police car. Smitty lay down on the back seat his heart heavy inside his chest.

The first light of morning slid through the window to greet the Sheriff when he came home. He stood over the sink pouring water into the coffeepot, when the woman walked into the kitchen. Smitty stretched the sleep out of his muscles and watched the humans.

"Did you just get home?" The woman yawned, "You must be exhausted. Don't drink coffee. Go to bed."

"No, I can't. I'm going to get cleaned up, eat and leave again."

"Okay, I'll fry you some eggs. What's going on?"

"The stupid assholes raped a girl and beat her to death. She wasn't more than fifteen or sixteen. Dickenblocker probably saw them and they shot him."

"Was it the Mercer brothers, like you thought?"

"Get this, they tied her arms behind her back with a belt and left it there. It's a long, hand, tooled leather belt with the bastard's name cut into it."

"What name?"

"Bo, Boris Mercer's nickname."

"Wow! Sounds like great proof to me."

"That's not all; we got fingerprints on a couple of beer bottles and a shoe print in the dirt. I'm sure the coroner will find their DNA on the girl's body."

The man leaned over and gave the woman a peck on he cheek.
"When this is over I'll take you out to dinner."

"I'll remind you of that promise." The woman broke eggs into a skillet. "What happens now?"

"The DA is waking the judge this minute to get a search warrant. We got enough for an arrest on the girl's murder, but the district attorney says we need the gun to get them for the other murder."

The smell of the eggs cooking caught Smitty's attention. He sat up and sniffed the air. "Who's the girl? " The woman flipped an egg with a spatula.

"We haven't identified her yet. I don't think she's local, there hasn't been anyone matching her description reported missing. Davis, the owner of the lake snack bar, saw her hanging around, asking people for money. He gave her a hamburger and told her to move on."

The sheriff lifted his arm and sniffed his armpit. "I need a shower."

The woman let Smitty out into the yard. Lucy barked as she did every time she saw Smitty. Ignoring Lucy, Smitty and Maggie raced in the yard, mouthing each other's ears. They were best friends now.

The woman had already fed the dog's dinner by the time the man came home in the evening. The sheriff flopped down on the back porch step and kicked off his shoes. The woman handed him a bottle of beer. He grabbed his shirt by the back of the neck, pulled it off over his head and tossed it on the porch.

The shirt reeked of blood attracting the dogs to investigate. They rubbed their noses on it.

"Get away from there," the sheriff yelled. Smitty and Maggie, with tails between their legs, slinked over to lie beside the Sheriff. Smitty placed his nose under the man's hand begging forgiveness for the mistake that made the leader angry. Lucy barked.

"Lucy, shut-up." The sheriff twisted off the bottle cap.

"Rough day, Honey?" the woman sat on the step and rested her arm on his shoulder.

"We arrested the Mercer brothers. Jack pulled a gun. Ginger shot him."

"Damn! Ginger?"

"She's the best shot in the department. They dug the bullet out. He's in intensive care. Ginger is on paid leave for a couple of weeks. Remind me later to call her to see how she's doing." He scratched behind Smitty's ears. "I told you we'd get them, boy."

"What about the other brother?"

"He's at the station, talking like a politician. He blames Jack for everything." After a long swallow of beer, the sheriff stretched his elbows back and up like chicken wings. His wife knelt behind him and massaged his shoulders.

"When I told Bo he left his monogrammed belt wrapped around the girl's arms, he banged his head on the table. Jack waved a Raven, twenty-five caliber automatic pistol at us. The same caliber bullet we found in Dickenblocker. They're both going down for two murders, if Jack survives."

"Where did the girl come from?"

"She's most likely a run-a-way. She told them her name was Renee. We may never know who she is." He glanced over toward the kitchen door. "Where's Bobby?"

"He's having dinner at his friend's house."

"Ginger said her cousin will take Smitty."

Smitty wagged his tail at the mention of his name.

"Go to bed, Jules. I'll call Ginger for you, later," the woman said.

"Thanks babe." The sheriff stumbled into the house.

The woman grabbed both sides of Smitty's face and kissed him on the forehead. "Don't you worry, I got it covered," she whispered.

Smitty watched the woman move around the kitchen. Once in a while, a woman visited Old Dad; they didn't stay long. He liked the way this woman caressed him, soft and gentle. He enjoyed her smell, sweet like the flowers in front of Old Dad's house. He harbored a desire to be near her. Sometimes she and Lucy cuddled together on the couch. Smitty wished he could rest on the woman's lap.

He heard her speaking in the phone. "Hello Ginger. Jules told me what happened today. How do you feel?"

A couple of days later, the sheriff stretched out on the couch, all three dogs reclined on the floor. The woman came down the hall in a bathrobe rubbing her hair with a towel.

"You look comfortable."

"Just waiting for you to get ready to go to dinner. Jack Mercer is going to be okay. He'll be able to stand trial."

"Good."

"I called Ginger to tell her and she said her cousin can't take Smitty."

"Oh, that's too bad."

Hearing his name Smitty wagged his tail and smiled.

The sheriff laughed. "He's grinning at me. I think I've been had."

The End

Sadie's Palace
Linda Welker

The camel stood by the fence gazing at me with her enormous sad eyes. I held out an apple in the palm of my hand. Her rubbery lips closed around it; careful not to hurt my fingers, she picked it up, turned her head and began to crunch with strong teeth.

Sadie was part of the family. She came as my birthday present with a purple bow stuck on her head when I was ten years old. As far as camels go she was a short one, only six foot two inches tall. At twenty-two I reached her height. I grew up with Sadie on Grandpa's ranch in Texas. Now I am leaving and somehow she knew.

My grandfather supported my desire to be a veterinarian by giving me Sadie. He said a vet had to learn to love all animals. My mom thought camels were ugly.

"You aren't ugly. Your beautiful, aren't you Sadie?" I said remembering the day Sadie came. Grandpa backed the truck up to the corral and unloaded the camel with that silly bow on her head."

"What are we going to do with that?" Mom asked with her hands on her hips.

"It's a birthday present for Herby." Grandpa held the camel's halter in one hand while patting her neck with the other. "Her name is Sadie, isn't she a beauty? Because she has one hump, she's called a Dromedary camel."

I straddled the top rail of the corral, torn between wanting to touch the beast and fear. "Does she bite?"

"No, but if you make her mad she'll spit at you."

"Wonderful," Mom said, rolling her eyes.

"Cool," I said.

We witnessed this skill a few minutes later, after grandpa put the camel in the corral. The three horses in the next corral went crazy like an alien creature from another planet landed in their midst. They neighed and reared up. Sadie trotted to the side of the fence and spit a sloppy glob over the rail. It flew across five feet of air before falling to the ground. This made the horses more agitated; they reared, kicked and ran in circles. Sadie sent a second jet stream in their direction, a loud bellow coming from her throat.

"Dad, I don't think horses and camels like each other." Mom said as if she had just learned a new fact of life.

"I think you're right, Girlie," Grandpa said. He always called my mom Girlie. He jumped into the corral, grabbed the halter, and led Sadie out. She followed him without protest. Mom and I trailed behind. Grandpa took her to the dog pen behind the barn out of sight of the horses. The dog pen was only a twelve-foot square inside a four-foot high chain link fence.

Sadie's rear bumped the fence when she turned around, but she didn't seem to mind. She kept staring at me through super long eyelashes. I finally gathered up my courage and touched her on the nose. A low rumbling sound like a cat purring was her response. .

"She likes you," Grandpa said. "Happy Birthday, Herby."

"Dad," Mom said, "why couldn't you just get him a puppy for his birthday?"

"Girlie, this is going to be fun."

Mom and I watched him walk away. Grandpa had a powerful determined stride in spite of an extreme bow in his skinny legs from years on horseback. He was the man in charge of his large ranch and ran it with a humorous twinkle in his eye. He loved a good joke and springing surprises on people like my mom and me.

After my father died in an auto accident when I was a baby, grandpa stepped in to take his place. I never met my grandmother. The story goes she didn't take to ranch life. She moved away to New York City, leaving Grandpa and three children. My mom was the youngest and the only girl.

The next week we built a stable and corral for the camel away from the horses. Grandpa painted a sign in red paint and hung it above the door. *Sadie's Palace.*

Grandpa was right, Sadie was fun. She liked everybody and adored me. It took a while for the ranch hands to warm up to her. When they discovered her ability to haul heavy loads, long distances, over rough terrain, they put Sadie to work. As the sun came up and activities started on the ranch, Sadie howled like a lovesick coon dog with a sore throat until someone came and let her out of the palace. She followed me around like a shadow. If I went too long without petting her or talking to her, she'd nudge me with her nose, as if to say, "don't ignore me."

After a couple of months, Grandpa decided we should go camel riding. He tweaked a horse saddle to fit her.

"I'll go first, in case she gives us a problem." Sadie obediently knelt and grandpa climbed on. He gently kicked her with his heels. She didn't move. "Pull the halter to get her started," he told to me.

I pulled and pulled. Sadie was a rock. She'd haul anything we put on her back all over the ranch, but now she wouldn't budge.

Mom sat down on a plastic lawn chair. "This may take a while," she said.

Grandpa kneed and kicked Sadie's belly with no results. "Push," he shouted to a couple of the ranch hands gawking in fascination at the sight of the boss on a camel. They pushed on her rump like they did to get a horse in a horse trailer. Sadie dug her huge feet in the dirt, straightened her legs, turned her head and spit at grandpa on her back. Grandpa jerked to the side to avoid the spray and started slipping off. The men caught him, before he hit the ground.

Mom laughed so hard she cried and had to wipe the tears off her face with the back of her hand.

"Herby she's your girlfriend, you try." Grandpa said. He picked me up and sat me on her back. I kicked, Grandpa pulled, the ranch hands pushed, Mom giggled, and Sadie didn't take a step. Grandpa picked up Sadie's front leg and moved it ahead; as soon as he let go she put it back where it was.

Mom's laughter escalated, she leaned back and the chair fell over. She lay on her back, feet waving in the air, her stomach convulsing with giggles.

Grandpa mumbled something as he rammed his hat on his head and walked away, with the ranch hands following him. Mom picked herself up and skipped into the house. I perched on Sadie like a bird on a fence for an hour while she refused to move. I pleaded, I begged, and since Mom couldn't hear, I cussed. Still nothing happened until I said, "Sadie kneel." She did and I climbed off. Sadie trotted over to the palace corral and waited for me to open the gate to let her in.

"So what, if we can't ride the camel," Grandpa said. "Riding is what horses are for."

"She's a pasture decoration. That's all she's good for," Mom complained.

I didn't care. I loved Sadie anyway. She made me popular with the other kids in high school. Lots of them had horses; none of them possessed a camel. The school bus stop was a half a mile from the house. When Sadie saw me coming home, she'd gallop down the road to meet me.

Grandpa delighted in her as much as I did. One time he caught one of the hands hitting her with a stick. Within an hour, that guy found himself looking for new employment.

After high school I commuted to college while still living at home, now I was on my way to vet school in California. Mom, Grandpa, and Sadie stood by the road and watched me drive away.

I was only gone two days before the phone calls started coming.

8:00 PM, Tuesday, first week at vet school.

"Hi Mom. How's Sadie?"

"She is driving us crazy. Wandering around looking for you and bellowing all the time."

5:30 PM, Friday, second week at vet school.

"Hi Grandpa. How's Sadie?"

"Your girlfriend's driving us crazy. Won't co-operate with anyone. She's stopped eating."

"Don't worry; Grandpa, camels can live a long time without food. They live off the fat in their humps."

"Well, anyway, I had the vet out. He gave her a vitamin shot."

3:30 PM, Wednesday, third week.

"Hi Grandpa. How's Sadie?"

"Your girlfriend's still bellowing for you. I think I need to find a camel shrink."

1:30 PM, Saturday, fourth week.

"Hi Mom, How's Sadie?"

"She ran off. Dad stopped work on the ranch and has all the hands out looking for her."

6:00 PM, Thursday, fifth week.

"Hi Mom, find Sadie yet?"

"No, Dad had to put the hands back to work, but he's still out looking, the stubborn old fool. He's seventy-one and his cataracts are worse. He wouldn't be able to see her if he did find her. I told him to take the jeep but he insisted on going by horseback."

1:00 AM, Friday, fifth week.

"Hi Mom, what's wrong?"

"Dad fell off his horse and broke his leg. I'm at the hospital and they're operating right now. Putting pins in his leg."

"I'll get a plane out in the morning, Mom. I'll call and let you know what flight."

"Wait, I haven't told you the whole story. He was out looking for Sadie, when his horse spooked and threw him. He hit his head and was knocked out. When he came too the horse was gone, but lying beside him was Sadie. He crawled up on her back and she brought him right to the front door of the house."

"Well, I'll be damned! No one was ever been able to ride Sadie before. Is Grandpa going to be okay?"

"The doctor said his horseback riding days are done. He'll probably have to walk with a cane. The broken leg will be weak. I think his pride is hurt worse than the leg. He's mortified that he fell off a horse."

"How's Sadie?"

"She seems to be okay. I had them lock her up in the palace and told them under no circumstances are they to let her out until you get there."

By the time I arrived in Texas, visited Grandpa in the hospital, and drove to the ranch it was almost dark. I opened the palace door and Sadie charged out. She stopped with a skid of her feet, turned her head and glared at me. A glint of recognition flicked in her eyes. She rubbed her nose across my face and hair. A soft rumbling came from her throat. I put my arms around her neck.

"Sadie, you've got to behave yourself. You're driving everyone crazy." I fed her and we took a long walk, as I told her about vet school.

The End

A Small Dream
Don Kafrissen

As dreams go, this one wasn't a big one, but it was recurring. It didn't come every night, just once in a while for about a month. Now to me, this was unusual because I seldom dream, and when I do it dissipates like smoke in the morning. The more I try to grab it, the thinner and more transparent it becomes until seconds later it's gone, and I've forgotten it was ever there. But this dream hung on, clear and detailed. I kind of liked it. It was worth thinking about, rolling around in my head, toying with, remembering.

Let me tell you about my dream. Every morning, as is my habit, I go out my rear porch door and walk to my workshop. From the top step I can look over at the property next door and there is a small clearing. Some mornings, when it is a bit misty, I see the sun streaming down and illuminating that clearing, and it is lovely. I have seen deer and raccoons and armadillos there. Each morning I glance over at that little clearing and smile. It's a nice way to start the day.

Anyway, in this dream I'm doing what I usually do in the morning, but this time, out of the mist, I see a figure, a woman. She is slim, blonde, and nude. She walks daintily into the clearing, but partway across pauses and looks right at me. And smiles. I am struck. An image of Mary Travers from the '60s folk group, Peter, Paul and Mary immediately comes to mind. I guess it's the hair. Her hair was straight and long with evenly cut bangs. I've always been in love with Mary Travers, even now, 50 years later.

So it was a nice dream – a pretty girl I didn't know who smiled at me and walked through my favorite clearing. Like I said, just a small dream that was nice. No endlessly falling, no being chased by monsters, no drowning. Not a life changer or scare-the-shit-out-of-me.

But I got to wondering about the girl. I don't remember ever having a dream about someone I'd never met.

I am in the tool business. Part of my business is picking up and delivering to various customers. Several months after my dream, I received a call from a local sheet metal shop. I'd heard that a brother and sister had bought the place. One of the owners, Andy, said he'd been trying to find somebody to fix a particular tool and two people had recommended me. Would I come and get it, and quote a price to fix it? I did so the next morning, and returned the tool four days later repaired and for less money than I'd quoted, a ruse I often used with new customers. But since he was a new customer, I asked about getting paid up front.

"Just go in the office and see my sister, Sally." He waved me toward the front of the building.

As I knocked and stepped into the office, I was dumbstruck. There she was, my "dream girl."

After the paperwork was completed, we asked simultaneously, "Don't I know you from someplace?" We both laughed and that broke the tension.

Over the next several months, we did a lot of business and I became friends with both Andy and especially Sally. It became easy for me to joke with her, and we even met a couple of times outside of work, purely by accident, of course. One day I asked if she'd like to grab a coffee and a donut. She would, and as we sat there talking, I told her about the dream. I told her all the details, the streaming sun, the soft grass, the moss draped trees, everything. After I'd finally run down, she sat back in the booth and just looked at me, neither smiling nor frowning. The minutes stretched on and I began to feel uncomfortable. I hoped I hadn't offended her. I had expected her to be shocked or angry or even uncomfortable.

Finally she grinned and asked, "Where do you live?"

The End

Sparrow on Whole Wheat

Jill V. Svoboda

My name is Fern Girard, and I've lived in this co-op apartment building for so many years that I've seen my neighborhood go from posh to rundown and back to up-and-coming. I've been here longer than anyone else in the building. I think that should earn me some special consideration, don't you?

Today when I went out to the front hallway to get my mail, my next-door neighbor's copy of newspaper was still lying in front of her door. It was almost noon, and if she'd wanted her paper, she'd have picked it up hours ago. So I swiped it.

I sat down at my kitchen table and opened the paper to the comics section, taking an occasional sip of vodka from the bottle so I wouldn't have to wash a glass. I was feeling nice and mellow. But then I decided to crack open the kitchen window, the one that looks out onto the courtyard, to get some fresh air.

Wouldn't you know, the first thing I saw was Shadrach, the evil black tomcat that belongs to my neighbors, the Morleys. He'd caught a sparrow, and I watched him toss the bird into the air with one clever paw. The bird flapped down to the winter-killed grass, ran a few steps and tried to lift off. Before it could escape, Shadrach swatted it down with his other paw and began chewing on a mangled wing.

That was the last straw. I'd put up with the cat's bird-killing far too long. I heaved myself out of my chair, bumping the table and knocking over my vodka bottle in the process. Most of the contents spilled onto the kitchen floor. It was cheap booze, but it was all I had left, and that made me even angrier.

So I grabbed my broom and limped out of my kitchen door as fast as I could. Maybe I could still rescue the terrified sparrow from the cat-without-a-conscience.

Shadrach was crouched over his dying prey, looking up as if he dared me to do anything about it. I swung my broom at him. I wanted to kill him, I really did, so I brought the broom down with all the strength my old shoulders could muster, but Shadrach scooted out unharmed, the sparrow clenched in his teeth. The broom hit the frozen ground so hard it sent a jolt of pain right up through my wrists, all the way up my arms and into my head. I almost passed out.

Shadrach knew he'd won. He waltzed up to me, dropped the bleeding sparrow at my feet and ran off. I swear that cat was laughing at me.

I hated Shadrach, but right at that moment I hated his owners even more. Holier-than-thou S. Maxwell Morley and his long, skinny wife, Marcella Osborne Morley, let their several cats run free, even though I've complained time and time again that cats are filthy bird-murderers and should always be imprisoned indoors. But no. That bleeding liberal Max–as Mr. Morley prefers to be known–insists that cats have the God-given right to prowl. The God-given rights of birds don't cut any ice with him.

It's not like that black-hearted Shadrach kills because he's hungry. The only kind of bird he ever eats is processed chicken from a can.

Now all my vodka's gone, and I don't have the money to buy more. It's the Morleys' fault. They're as much to blame as their cat Shadrach.

Then I got a really bright idea that would stop Mister Max Morley and his foul feline in their self-righteous tracks. I picked up the dead sparrow by one foot and carried it into my apartment, where I set it on the kitchen counter. I had some nice china plates I'd found at a yard sale, and I picked one that had a rim decorated with sweet little violets.

I hadn't bought food in a while. The Social Security check was later than usual this month. But I still a loaf of whole wheat bread in the fridge. I took out a couple of slices and put one on the plate. I spooned mayonnaise on it until it oozed over the side of the bread, and I cut some lettuce leaves to fit precisely on top. Then I picked up the deceased sparrow and opened out its torn little wings so I could position it in the center of the lettuce. Its body was still warm, and a drop of its blood landed on the plate. I thought it made an appetizing splash of color. I topped it all with a second slice of bread and sliced a carrot into curls for garnish. Never let it be said that I didn't know how to make a good sandwich.

All that work was making me thirsty. I wanted some vodka. I picked up the fallen bottle and discovered that only a swallow remained. The rest had spilled onto the floor. Maybe it's a good thing my arthritis hurts so much that I can't get down on my knees. I needed a drink so bad I might have lapped it up off the linoleum. But I knew if I got down there I couldn't stand up again.

I found a pencil and printed a note on the back of an unpaid electric bill. The note said, "Dear Max and Marcella, since your cat Shadrach caught this bird, he must have meant it for your lunch. So here is your bird sandwich. Bon appetít." See, I'd been to college for a year, oh, a long time ago, and I knew a little French. Then I signed it, "Your friend, Fern Girard." Only I think I forgot the "r" in "friend."

Anyway, I took the plate over to the Morleys' back door–it's just a few steps away from mine in the apartment building–and set the plate down at their doorstep. Then I rang their doorbell and scooted back into my place to await the outcome of my plan.

It wasn't long in coming. I heard a door open, and then a little shriek. That had to be the proper Marcella–a good loud scream wouldn't suit her. Just a little shriek. Then her composure deserted her, and she couldn't keep herself from yelling, "Max! Max!" I peered out of my window and saw him come running. Who'd have thought an 80-year old drunk could move so fast?

I heard Max ask, "What's all this about?" Marcella turned to him and showed him the plate. He poked at the bird with his index finger. "It's still warm." Every line in his face said disgust.

"Fern did this!" Marcella held up my note and waved it under Max's red nose. "How could she? Aren't we her friends?"

I laughed out loud. I hope she heard me.

Then Marcella complained, at the top of her lungs, I might add, "Don't we get her groceries for her? Don't we buy her vodka? Isn't that enough? Why this–abomination? What does she want?"

Just as Marcella said that, that black devil Shadrach streaked across the courtyard. I grabbed for my broom again, but the tomcat darted between Marcella's scrawny legs and ran into the Morleys' apartment. Good thing he did. I'd have been after him if he'd given me half a chance.

Alerted by the shouting, the nearest neighbors came out to see what was going on. That's one of the entertaining things about living in a cooperative apartment building. Everyone knows everyone else's business. There are no secrets. That busybody Ruth Jo Kramer who lives upstairs from me leaned out of her kitchen window. "Stop all this yelling! You woke me up from a nice nap!"

Well, I didn't feel sorry for her, not at all, that nosy old witch. I giggled.

Benjamin and Josh, the two queens who live next to Ruth Jo, pranced out onto their balcony and looked down at the scene. Josh pointed to the plate in Marcella's hand. "What is that?"

Benjamin peered nearsightedly over the railing. "Why, I do believe it's a bird sandwich."

By now I was giggling uncontrollably. Guess the vodka was still working.

Eduardo, whose apartment fronted on the opposite side of the courtyard, appeared in his doorway. "Who'd make a sandwich for a bird?"

"Not a sandwich for a bird," Josh corrected Eduardo. "A sandwich with bird filling. A sparrow sandwich, in fact." Eduardo didn't know what to say to that. He just stood there with his mouth open. A bird could have flown right into it.

Marcella was still standing frozen in her doorway, my lovely plate in her hand. Max patted her shoulder. "Well, my dear, what shall we do with this item?"

"Just wait until I get my hands on that Fern!" Marcella raised her arm as if to throw the plate down and smash it, but Max stopped her before major damage was done. Then she sat down on the threshold, put the plate on her knees and burst into tears. "This is all so cruel. I need a drink."

Well, so do I, lady, I thought. If your blasted cat hadn't killed that bird and made me knock over my bottle, I'd have one too. That *was* a crying matter. So I did just that–I sat back down at my kitchen table, put my face in my hands and bawled. My bird sandwich wouldn't bring back the bird. It wouldn't change Shadrach. Max and Marcella would have the last laugh. Now who would get my vodka for me?

I must have fallen asleep, because when I heard the doorbell ring, the kitchen was dark and only the electronic

clock on the stove shed any light on the scene. The clock
read 7:10. Morning or night? No idea. This time of year, it's
dark at seven. Either seven.

I got up, slow, no other way I can get up considering
how much my back aches and my knees hurt. It really gets to
me. I used to be a dancer, good enough to get me a regular
job in the chorus line at the old Rivoli Theatre. Sometimes I
dream I'm dancing, kicking just as high as I always did.
When I wake up from that dream, I go straight for the bottle.
I don't like remembering how it used to be.

The doorbell rang again. "C'mon, Fern, I know you're
in there sulking."

It was S. Maxwell Morley.

"Go away, you bird murderer."

"Marcella made some chili and a batch of coconut
cookies. How about coming over for a bite to eat?"

I was hungry, but it wasn't just the food that sucked me
in. The Morleys have vodka. They *always* have vodka. The
two of them were the biggest lushes in the building. I knew I
could get a drink there.

"Just a minute, please, I'm coming." I opened the door
and there stood Max, as unrepentant as you please.

"Food's getting cold," said Max.

A few flakes of snow were falling. I took my coat from
the hook by the door and wrapped it around my shoulders.
At my age, one can't be too careful. If I catch a cold, it lasts
for weeks.

Marcella greeted us at the kitchen door, just as
sickeningly sweet as she could be. "Hi, Fern, glad to see
you," she simpered, as if the gift of a dead-sparrow-on-
whole-wheat sandwich was a fine thing, exactly what she
might expect from a friend. "Come on in and get warm.
Maybe you'd like a bowl of chili? And a drink before
dinner?"

I hadn't eaten all day, and the chili smelled good, even
if I had to kowtow to bird killers to get some of it. I sat down
across the table from Marcella and Max, and Max put some

ice cubes in a glass and poured in a whole lot of vodka. I grabbed it with both hands because my hands were shaking and took a big gulp.

Shadrach swaggered past me, tail high in the air, and stood expectantly at the kitchen door. Max reached over and pulled it open, and the black cat walked out, turning back to look at me with a smirk on his whiskered face.

When we'd polished off our chili, Marcella poured us all some more vodka and brought out the coconut cookies. They were neatly stacked on my flowered plate, the same one I'd served the sparrow sandwich on.

Marcella caught me staring at it. "Don't worry. Max buried the bird in the courtyard, and I washed the plate in very hot water."

Marcella was lying. Max hadn't buried that bird. The ground was still frozen, and besides I saw some feathers plastered with mayonnaise sticking out of the kitchen wastebasket. Probably she did wash the plate, though.

Well, I thought, I may have lost this battle, but I still haven't lost the war. I'll get that Shadrach yet. I held out my glass. "A little more vodka, please."

We were all feeling pretty good about each other again when it got to be time for me to go home. Marcella spooned some leftover chili into an old margarine container and put some more cookies on my flowered plate, covering them with foil. Then she capped the half-finished quart bottle of vodka we'd been working on. Bottle and all went into a bag for me to take home. "Fern, you and I'll go grocery shopping at the supermarket tomorrow," she promised, slurring most of her words. Marcella just can't hold her liquor.

By this time half an inch of snow had fallen. and I could see cat tracks leading toward my door. Shadrach stood right in my path, growling. I aimed a hard kick right at him. He leaped clear at the last second, and I whacked my toe on the garbage can behind him, knocking it over. It hit the pavement with a bang.

I wished I'd worn something sturdier than my house slippers when I went out. My toes smarted something fierce from the impact. Best to get inside and numb them with some vodka.

I'll get that cat tomorrow, I swear.

The End

The Sweetest of All

Johanna M. Bolton

I never doubted my husband loved me, and especially not now as he sat across the table, holding my hands tenderly in both of his. Candlelight glittered off my diamond ring and the gold band behind it worn thin by years. A hushed murmur of restaurant conversation faded into the background, muted by the private booths. Somewhere soft music created a mood of romance. My husband grinned at me, a silly grin that still melted my heart.

"You know I love you," he was saying. "I'll never love another woman as much." He took his eyes from mine and focused on the diamond ring instead, a full carat stone he had given me two years ago on our anniversary. "This is so hard," he murmured.

What a curious thing to say. I could feel a frown wrinkle my forehead, but I waited patiently.

"There's something I have to tell you," he continued and I knew that tone. This was something serious.

The warmth inside me faded replaced by a small coil of dread. Oh my God, what now? I thought to myself. He's dying? We're bankrupt? Something happened to one of the kids? "What?" I demanded. "What is it?"

He drew a deep breath and plunged. "Judith, I want a divorce."

My mouth dropped open. If I expected anything it wasn't this. I forced myself to speak softly. "A divorce? You want a divorce?"

"Yes," he answered quickly.

I yanked my hands from his and sat back in the booth, my wonderful dinner now a sickening lump in my stomach.

"But before you get mad, please listen to me," he begged speaking faster.

"Why should I listen," I hissed. "I think I've heard enough." I threw my napkin on the table, grabbed my purse, and scooted to the end of the banquette.

"Judith. No, wait!' Kyle said quickly as I rose to my feet on the uncomfortable, but sexy open-toed sling-backs I had bought just for this night. Despite myself, I hesitated and he pressed on. "Judith, I'm gay."

This second bombshell knocked the air from my lungs and I dropped back onto the padded bench, trying to breathe despite the shock.

"I'm gay," he repeated. "And I've been seeing another man."

I was speechless. My husband, the father of my children, the man who slept beside me every night for the past 21 years, was just now telling me he's a homosexual? I could only stare at him, my mind full of disjointed thoughts.

"Oh, God, Judith, don't condemn me," he wailed softly, and a tear actually appeared, threading its way down his cheek. "I need your help and understanding."

I dug a Kleenex from my purse and silently handed it across the table, the automatic response of a mother.

"I fought it for years, but I can't fight anymore. I know this isn't fair to you, but Judy, you'll find someone else," he added, his voice throbbing with sincerity. "I know it. You're too wonderful and you deserve much more then I can give. You don't need to be tied for the rest of your life to an... an aging fairy."

When I didn't say anything he continued. "I didn't want to tell you before. I forced myself to wait until the kids were in college." He looked at me, gauging my reaction. "Judy, say something," he begged.

What could I say? My husband was gay. "This... this other man. How long has it been going on?"

"A year and a half," he sighed.

A year and a half of little or no sex -- for me, that is. A year and a half of working late, the weekend *business* trips, the phone calls... Now it all started making sense. "And you love him?" I asked, keeping calm when all I wanted to do was scream.

"Yes," he replied in a small trembling voice. "I love him very much. I want to be with him."

My world was in pieces, shattered all around me. "So what happens now?" I had to know.

"You don't have to worry about anything. I've started the paperwork. They'll let you know when the divorce is final. All you have to do is sign this." He pulled a document from inside his suit jacket and set it in front of me on the damask tablecloth.

I stared stupidly at the words for a moment before fumbling a pair of reading glasses from my purse.

Divorce, I read. And the grounds were incompatibility. Well, that was certainly right. And Kyle had it all so well planned. How like him, I thought sarcastically. I sighed. What should I do? Get a lawyer? Fight? Fight what? The man was gay and I certainly didn't need that complication in my life. No, Kyle was right. It would be best to get it over with as quickly and easily as possible.

I picked up the pen and signed.

"I made sure you're provided for," he was saying. "You get the house and all the money from our joint savings."

"Our savings?"

"And the minivan. That's always been yours anyway. My car, though..."

Oh, yes. The car. That damned car! The testosterone machine, I called it. He bought it about a year ago as part of some midlife crisis. "It's still in the shop."

"I think we ought to sell it," Kyle was saying. "It's practically new. It will bring a good price and we can split the money."

Generous to the last, I thought bitterly. That damned car!

"But since I'm leaving in the morning, could you take care of it for me? You can send me half the money."

I finally focused on what he was saying. "What do you mean you're leaving in the morning?"

"Pat's family has a business in San Diego. We're going to run it for them."

Pat. His name is Patrick, I thought irrationally. He's Irish? "San Diego?" I spoke out loud. "That's clear across the continent."

"I know. But this way you won't have to answer awkward questions about Pat and me."

"When are you moving?"

"I've already packed. We're leaving in the morning."

I gasped. "So soon?"

"I thought it would be best," he explained. "A fast clean break."

"Kyle, you're just walking out of my life? After 21 years? Just like that?"

"Oh, God, Judith! Do you know how hard this is for me! I'm so torn. Part of me really wants to stay with you. All I can think of is the good life we had together. Our family. But I can't. I just can't!" Tears came, and I fished out another Kleenex.

"Alright, I see your point," I soothed, playing along. "A clean break. You're right."

"I'll drive you home," he told me, solicitous to the last.

"No. I want to be alone. I'll drive myself."

"Are you sure?"

"Yes."

He looked into my eyes and a tremulous smile stretched his lips. "I love you, Judith. I love you so very much. You know that don't you?"

❋

I drove home in a daze. I would have to get used to being alone again, but maybe some good could come from it. I was still relatively young -- I mean, 41 wasn't so old. I had a lot of life ahead of me. And I had my health. And my figure. I really wasn't that bad looking for an old broad who'd had two kids. Now I could do some of the things I wanted to do, like go back to college myself. Maybe start writing again.

I eased the van into the garage and turned off the engine. Spike started barking in the house. I should go and let him out. I sighed. I was glad he left me the dog.

The dog... That thought finally broke me. I put my head down on the steering wheel and started crying. My heart was broken.

Kyle! Kyle, my love, I wept.

You bastard! How could you do this to me? I gave you twenty-one years! I gave you two wonderful children! I cleaned your house, washed your underwear. I cooked. I even went to all those boring office parties.

Anger and pain expressed themselves as the tears flowed. And finally slowed. I dug out the last Kleenex, wiped my face and blew my nose. All right, Judith, it's just another disaster. Get over it.

Right.

I climbed stiffly from the van, looking at the empty place in the garage where Kyle's car usually sat. That damned car! And it was just like him to leave it to me to sell it. I started thinking how I could word the ad as I climbed the steps and unlocked the door to the house. Spike greeted me with a wagging tail and then dashed out into the dark backyard.

I wandered through the downstairs feeling sorry for myself, sniffing, my nose still running from the tears. I paused at the door to Kyle's home office and then switched on the light. I rarely came in here and so I didn't realize he'd been moving things. The room had an abandoned feel. Echoing. However, the computer was still there. The screen was dark, but when I touched the mouse, it lit showing one of those annoying message boxes superimposed over a program. Kyle had been in the middle of something when the computer locked up.

I dropped into the chair and looked more closely at the screen. Kyle had been reformatting the hard drive, I realized. Why would he want to do that, I wondered? Hummm... Maybe he was hiding something? I never used the home computer since I had one at work, but I had a sudden strong urge to see what Kyle had been up to. My fingers found the keys that would abort the reformatting.

There was no sound for a while except a clicking keyboard. Kyle's online password was stored, a convenience for him and now for me. All his emails were filed -- love letters from Pat, and Kyle's replies.

I gasped when I opened the first one and saw what it contained. I made myself read them all, becoming more and more angry as a story of deception and lies unfolded through the emails. Pat and Kyle had planned this whole thing, and there was nothing the "old lady" as they called me, could do about it now. Or was there? I hunted further and found something really interesting.

Kyle had said I could have the entire savings account. According to online banking, however, our joint savings had been a lot more than a paltry twenty-two hundred dollars.

I sat back in the chair, tapping my fingernail against my teeth. Should I do it? Why not, another part of my mind argued? Until the papers were filed in the morning, I was still Kyle's wife. I had all the right in the world to do it. And, he did say I could have *all* the savings.

I love online banking. So convenient! I felt myself smiling as I transferred the more than two hundred thousand dollars he had just removed back into our savings account. That would definitely pay my college tuition!

It was well after midnight when I finally shut the computer down, mentally grateful for Microsoft's irritating habit of locking up programs without warning. If the reformatting had continued, I would never have learned the truth.

I let Spike back in before pouring myself a glass of Chablis. As I stood in the kitchen ... my kitchen, I took a deep breath. I had faced disaster and come out on top. I was a new woman. A free woman. I smiled and took a drink of wine and went peacefully to bed.

Behind me the computer monitor shone in the dark study. On the screen was the ad I had so carefully written. Too bad Kyle would never see it, although maybe I'd better send him -- and Patricia -- a copy along with their half of the money.

Divorce Forces Sale: 2011 metallic Carmon Red Porsche 911 GT2 (6 cylinders), black leather, bucket seats, power everything, keyless entry, anti-lock brakes, custom wheels, new Michelin tires, CD/AM/FM, air, like new, just back from scheduled maintenance; $1.00
813-555-2000.

The End

To Tombouctou & Back
Don Kafrissen

Keith slowed the battered British Jeep and stopped. The sudden silence woke Peter and Don who were dozing fitfully in the hot open vehicle. Don reached for his water bottle and just let a small dribble trickle into his parched lips.

"What are we stopping for, mate?" asked Peter.

"Dunno. Thought I saw something up on the dune." He gestured about two o'clock to our right. He'd shut the small Rolls-Royce diesel engine down as he slowed, as was our custom. Fuel was precious and we'd gone through nearly half. We'd expected to get more in Maurice Cortier as we'd been told but they were out and another delivery wasn't expected for a week. We'd pushed on. Our goal was the mythical city of Timbuktu, or as it was pronounced in this corner of the world, Tombouctou.

A week ago we'd been sitting around a campfire in a small campground just outside Marrakech, high in the Atlas Mountains of Morocco. Peter and Keith were Brits from Yorkshire just taking a leisurely drive in the country, as they called it. I was with my wife and two small children traveling in a VW camper around Europe and North Africa. Keith Houser had mustered out of the British SAS the year before after a brutal year long posting in Aden, had purchased a surplus Austin Commers jeep and along with longtime friend Peter Bridgeton had wandered aimlessly around Spain, Portugal and now Morocco.

The talk had turned to faraway places with strange sounding names and, of course, Timbuktu had come up. Peter dug out a well-worn map of North Africa and had informed us that we'll never be closer. "It's only about 1600 miles from here, you know lads."

I looked at my wife, "No, my VW would never make it. Besides I want to be in Pamplona next month." My wife wanted to watch the running of the bulls – or as we put it, the trampling of the idiots.

Keith laughed and in his slow and steady Yorkshireman's way said, "No, Don, we'll take the Commer. It gets good mileage, has room for three and lots of petrol containers." He looked at Peter's map. We can sprint down in about a week." He looked up with a studious look on his well-tanned and stubbled face, "Ten days at the outside. Right Peter?"

Peter nodded vigorously and replied, "Righto. We can get petrol in Abada in Algeria, then in Adrar and finally in Maurice Cortier before the long run down to Timbuktu. That's about 900 K or so." He whipped out his pocket calculator and punched the buttons. "We'll only need 140 liters of petrol." He jumped up and started walking toward other campsites yelling, "Hello chaps, we need to borrow some petrol containers for a couple of weeks. What have you got?"

I talked it over with my wife that night and, though doubtful, she agreed that we would never be closer and she felt quite safe in the campground. There were more than fifty campers there and several had volunteered to stay with her until I returned. So the die was cast. The next morning, we filled the tank, stored 8-5 gal. Jerry cans in the back and left, taking as little kit as we could. Many people who'd heard of the plan had given us postcards to mail from Timbuktu when we arrived.

The morning's drive took us east to Ksar es Souk, a small trading town on the backside of the mountains. What had started out as a chilly morning had turned oppressively hot as we came out onto the pan of the great Western Sahara desert. We crossed the border into Algeria with no problems, only declaring the obligatory bottle of cheap whiskey for the border guards to confiscate. With a crash of the stamp into our passports and a wave, we were off on the great adventure. If we only knew.

South to Adrar where fuel was plentiful and cheap, then the long monotonous run south across sweeping dunes, a road that was only delineated by rounded cone shaped markers, which we tried to keep to our right. Sometimes the road was covered with drifted sand. Once three motorcyclists heading north passed us. A wave, a hum and the dots before us were now dots behind us. We saw nary a camel. The road we were on was part of the old north/south trade route, which brought trade goods, which didn't get shipped by sea from equatorial Africa north by the Bedouins. The sun beat down and we all wore dark sunglasses and kepis, hats with neck covers. Keith had insisted and now I knew why. The high kepis allowed the scalp room to breathe and the drapes hanging down, of course, kept the neck from burning. I felt like I was in the French Foreign Legion.

We waited, climbing out and stretching our legs. We'd been running for hours, only stopping to pour precious diesel fuel into our trusty jeep and an occasional drink into thirsty us. The dots on the dune ridge grew larger, then into a line.

As it poured over the ridge, it looked like an invading army, but it was a Bedouin band headed west toward Mauritania and the coast, we suspected. A thousand miles of nothing but sand and an occasional well, which the leaders knew all too well. As they got closer, we noted camels as pack animals, a few donkeys, also with packs and people walking, many with staffs. The women were with the flocks of goats which trailed along behind. This particular area of the desert was parched and barren but many areas along their route had oases and scrub plants. Goats and camels were the only beasts that would eat almost everything.

The headman strode up to us like some biblical figure, touching his chest and forehead and greeting us in Arabic. Keith, who spoke a brand of Arabic returned the Muslim greeting and asked if all was well with him. He grinned a toothless grin and shouted that he had a new son. We all smiled and Keith wished him a thousand happiness's and many more sons. On instinct, Keith asked Peter for a small present for the headman. Peter thought for a moment and pulled out a small cardboard kaleidoscope from his backpack. He handed it to the headman with a small bow. Peter said that it was a present from all of us to his new son. The man frowned and looked at the small, brightly colored cardboard cylinder. Peter put it to his eye and turned the end, pointing it at the sun. The man gasped and nearly dropped it. In a flurry of Arabic, he called to several men who stood silently behind him, perched on one leg, leaning on their staffs. They came forward and each looked through the cylinder. They were astounded. One by one they bowed low to us. The headman recited something to Keith then, stuffing the cylinder in a fold of his robe, strode off.

"What did he say?" I asked.

"Well," Keith drawled, "it seems that we are now members of his tribe. He asked the other chaps, sub-headmen, I presume, to memorize our faces." We turned and watched the rapidly retreating small army disappear into the distance. "Well, mount up, lads, still a frightful distance to go to the village of T." He started the jeep as we climbed in and hollered over the engine, "We'll make camp tonight in Aquerakom. There's a well there and we can fill our water jugs."

The night was unusually cool and I huddled in my sleeping bag, shivering most of the night. I didn't think I would be glad for the heat but I was. It got hot fast and after breakfast, we bathed in one of the pools at the oasis, our first bath since leaving Marrakech. Today would be our last on the road. Tonight we would wine and dine in Timbuktu! I don't know what I expected but anything was better than being on the road.

According to our map, we'd crossed into Mali just before night. There had been nothing to mark the border, no guards, and no roadblock, not even a line in the sand. I guess we'll have to get our passports stamped in Timbuktu or Taudenni, the only town showing before Timbuktu.

Just before noon, we sighted Taudenni, a small mud or block town. Peter drove up slowly. Usually a group of children would swarm over us in the little towns and villages. Nothing this time. No one in sight. We drove on through the main street noting a police station, a gas station and a small marketplace. But no people. Peter stopped at the petrol station and we climbed out uneasily. Keith reached under the seat and pulled out a pistol, a Walther PPK, and slid it into his pocket. He pushed open the door to the station office and went inside. Peter and I waited by the jeep. In a moment he was out shaking his head and wiping his hand on his trouser leg.

"Fill up and lets go," he ordered. "Fast."

Peter frowned, "Why? What is it, Keith?"

Keith was squirting petrol from the pump on his hand and shaking it vigorously to dry it. "Not sure. I saw it in Aden. Its either smallpox or plague. Open pustules on his skin." He gestured with his hand, "Bloke's dead two, maybe three days. I thought it was odd those motorcyclists not stopping to chat."

We hurriedly filled the tank and the jerry cans and drove off fast, not bothering to check any of the other buildings. The silence was oppressive. I thought we should have done something, maybe seen if any others were still alive. But what could we have done? We only had a small first aid kit and obviously others had been there before us. My cheerful mood at finally coming to one of my life's dreams was ashes in my mouth. I knew Peter felt the same. Keith was a hardened warrior, not long from a poorly managed guerilla war so the death didn't penetrate him like it did us. Hours later we saw the first indications of the approach to Timbuktu. The road grew imperceptibly wider; the scrub bushes grew more frequent as we got closer to the Niger River. We dropped over a crusted ridge and there was the city before us on the south side of the river. An ancient bridge crossed into the city.

I wish I could tell you that it gleamed with golden minaret's, that domes of marble poked out of freshly whitewashed castles and that brocaded warriors of Allah rode white steeds down streets lined with fountains. But it was not to be. Timbuktu was a city of mud and dirt and dun colored stone. Few streets were paved and rubble lay everywhere.

It did shimmer in the late afternoon sun however, and the stench wafted over the river to us. You see, we never did make it into that fabled city. The local police had a barrier up on our side of the bridge. No one from the north who had passed through Taoudenni was allowed to approach. The fear of the plague was evident in their eyes and the menacing way they held their AK-47's. I noted that they were cheap copies which might misfire at any moment but only one had to work.

There was a small camp off to the west side of the road where we swapped stories and news with the others who'd been turned away. Two South Africans in an American Jeep coming from the south agreed to return with us to Taoudenni and on to Morocco. The police even refused to take our postcards, though they insisted on us leaving some money on a rock nearby.

A week later we were back in the campground in Marrakech, tired, finally clean again and no closer to our dream than before. Maybe it is better sometimes to dream the dream than actually achieve it.

The End

Triangle

John Boyle

An eleven year-old girl looks out of place standing on New York's seediest East River dock. Especially after midnight. Not that the flickering yellow lights casting distorted shadows revealed all that much about my small, scrawny body. Still, the thick black Russian hair dangling all the way to my backside labeled me as a female. And considering the time and the place, it wouldn't be too long before some pedophilic asshole came slithering over.

Eleven years old. *Chyort voz'mi!* Even after ninety-seven years as a sexless vampire, getting reset to my death-age grossed me out. No way would I follow the rules on this one. The second any *zhopa's* hand touched my panties, he'd feel my fangs in his neck. Let the master rage all he wanted, turning my glamour childlike went over the line even for a *dolboeb* like him.

Besides, he'd never really convinced me with his, 'they need to know why they're arrived in hell' line. Maybe my dead flesh can't feel anything, but I think the master just enjoys my embarrassment as my backside is ground into some dirty alley pavement as I lie there waiting for the *zhopa* to seal his fate. Getting the crap and blood out of my hair out afterwards! *Blei*! The things I endure for a good meal.

Burning red eyes stared from the ground behind a broken drainpipe. It saw me looking and crawled out. Its basketball-like body consisted of little besides tiny eyes and a huge mouth that held rows and rows of razor-sharp teeth. From the thing's bottom protruded a dozen five-inch-long tentacles so it could move. A cleaner. A fresh one. No scars.

"Lev? Is that you? Lover, you always promised me you'd take the other option."

The thing on the ground squirmed, its teeth chattering in a parody of a buzz saw. I realized I'd never asked a cleaner its pre-hell name before. Probably that was something the master forbade them to utter.

The cleaner squeaked almost understandable words through its huge distorted mouth. "I deal with master. Wait for you I can. Only one hundred years as cleaners then both of us together. One meal." Lev paused, probably wondering how I'd take his offhand confirmation of the end awaiting me.

I nodded, after all it wasn't a secret. Perhaps the only benefit of being one of the master's minions was that after our time on Earth we earned a one-time offer to go to the head of the line. No long wait for us. I'd heard hell's real pain was watching that, slow, unavoidable feast. Gruesome as it sounds, as far as I know, every dammed soul scrambles onto that plate when given the chance. After all, for those of us who've cut our ties with the one who exists beyond time, the master's teeth provide our only exit. No one is stupid enough to spend forever trapped with the master in the cold bubble of an empty and forgotten universe. When I thought about the enormity of the master's fate, I knew when the time came for me to lie down on that plate and put the requisite apple in my mouth, a small part of me would actually feel sorry for creation's biggest loser.

"Not to full moon you have," squeaked Lev. "Tonight. New partner tonight. By sunup all must be done. Or..." The thing's teeth began chattering uncontrollably, but I guessed what it was trying to say. If I didn't replace Lev with a new partner before the sun came up, I would start my hundred years as a cleaner.

Mudak! Now I understood why the asshole had screwed with my glamour. The master wanted me partnered with the kind of lowlife sleezeball that would rape an eleven-year old. I screamed in frustration and tried to kick poor Lev. Those tentacles do let the little walking mouths move fast. It was even quick enough to doge the foot of an angry vampire.

I sat down on the roadway and would have cried if it were possible. The cleaner, keeping its distance, eyed me carefully. After a minute, I looked at its glowing red eyes.

"I'm sorry Lev, it's just too much," I whispered. "Too much pain, too much darkness, too much evil." I held out my hand to him. "If you could see my glamour, you'd understand. I'm showing my death-age. I look like I did when you turned me."

Lev's tentacles contracted and his round body slummed to the pavement. That was as close as he could come to expressing sympathy.

Fifty or sixty years ago, I'd finally forgiven Lev for turning me into a vampire. It's not like he didn't have to feed too, and for male vamps, finding meals is decidedly harder. And well, it's not like I hadn't agreed.

Even though dead flesh can't remember, if we feed enough, from some otherworld realm a few human-qualities are returned to us. I do shit like this so I can remember my few short years of life. And, of course, the day when it ended.

The Triangle Shirtwaist Company liked Russian immigrants. They especially liked young females who worked hard and never protested. While most of their workers were between twelve and sixteen, my cousin Natasha and I were scrawny even for eleven and some half-forgotten humanity had caused the fat overseer to offer us jobs. Almost no pay, but even a small pittance would help keep our starving families fed.

The only condition involved a willingness to hide at the bottom of boxes of waste cloth should any city inspector enter the building. Not a problem until the twenty-fifth of March, nineteen eleven. The day of the great fire.

The noise, shouting, and people running around like crazy sent Natasha and me diving to the bottom of the closest rag-box. The opportunity to hide had only happened once before, so we jumped at the chance to get an easy hour instead of our heavy end-of-shift clean-up chores. Snuggled, giggling, at the bottom of that smelly box we didn't even notice the smoke until it was as thick as the darkest Russian fog.

Hiding may have saved our lives. By the time we emerged, the several hundred other girls trapped on the ninth floor had tried and failed at all the other means of escape. With the main stairwell ablaze and discovering the only other exit firmly locked, the workers had charged to the fire escape. Dozens died after the few small screws, holding the flimsy thing to the wall, pulled out.

We'd missed last elevator trip to safety. I saw a young woman jump into the shaft and try to grab the rusted elevator cable. She screamed when her weight caused the jagged, frayed cable to rip her hands to shreds. She fell, still howling, to join the broken bodies piled on the elevator roof. Years later, after I'd learned to read English, I saw a newspaper account saying they'd found more than two dozen broken bodies on top of that elevator. Those lucky few crammed inside the cab for the last trip to survival had endured a rain of blood all the way to the ground floor.

Flames and smoke were everywhere. Familiar surroundings became disorienting as nothing looked like what I remembered. Perhaps that was how we got pushed to the back of the panicking girls around the open window. Zhanna, standing behind us, strayed too close to a burning box of rags. Suddenly her dress roared into flames. She began screaming and running toward the open window. The others dove out of her way and let her pass. Despite the unbearable pain, her hair now a mass of back char, she paused before jumping. Nine stories to the sidewalk.

As the flames grew larger and the smoke thickened, the wailing increased as each girl grasped the terrible choice she now faced. Two girls, holding hands, suddenly ran for the window. Then they were gone. Natasha pressed herself against me and began sobbing. I pulled her away from the nearest flames, their heat already blistering my arms and making my hair frizzle so much I could smell it even over the smoke.

"The window," I said. "It won't hurt like the flames. I'll hold your hand. I'll not let go until we're in heaven."

"But it's a sin," Natasha gasped between coughs. "The priest says suicides don't go to heaven." I started to argue religion, but a huge flame shot out of the wall and we both dove to the floor. I saw a less dangerous place about five yards away and pulled my terrified cousin toward it. The corner of her dress began burning. I slapped out the flames, amazed at how much pain even lightly scorched fingers could produce.

"Do you wish to live!"

I spun and saw Lev for the first time. Tall, dark and dressed like a Russian prince, he stood against the wall and for some reason the air around us was no longer hazy. I coughed a couple more times before finding my voice.

"Please sir," I begged while nursing my hand. "Please help us."

"I can save but one of you," he pointed at me. "Only one." He pointed at Natasha. "If you want to be the one, you must condemn her to the flames. Your life for hers."

A wall cracked open, years of accumulated cotton lint inside the wood partition burned so fast it exploded. Sparkling flames shot toward us like a giant multi-fingered hand poised to grab.

Time stopped.

The great fist of flame hovered inches from me. Natasha, who stood to the side and would miss that deadly fireball, had her mouth open in a frozen scream of absolute terror.

"Choose," said the man. "You or her." I stood quivering, until one trembling finger pointed at my cousin. As in one of those slow-motion scenes from one of the countless movies that I've watched while waiting for some filthy creep to spot the small and defenseless woman sitting alone, I watched the burning embers swerve and engulf Natasha's dress. The thin cotton flared, sparkling like a perverted Christmas tree. I screamed "No, no. I take it back." But the flames had found their prey.

I know I tried to hide my face, but the man's strong arms forced me to watch. Natasha's worn-thin dress exploded like oil-soaked kindling. My cousin screamed and danced in a futile effort to put out the flames. I wailed in sympathy as that iron grip held my shoulder.

Her screams. Her screams were so loud. They told of a pain I could never endure. I saw her skin turning black. I refuse to remember anything beyond that point.

After Natasha stopped moving, my new partner, Lev, picked me up and carried me on a complicated path through smoke-filled corridors and stairways. Then we were on the building's roof. Dozens of other workers surrounded around us and I saw that some people in the taller building alongside ours had lowered a ladder down. In a fairly orderly fashion, we lucky ones climbed to safety. I suppose I was in shock and remember little else until midnight when Lev woke me up.

"We made a deal," was all he said before sinking his fangs into my neck. I discovered being drained of blood is a painless death. The pain only started after his fangs began pumping our mixed blood back into me.

But that pain was as nothing compared to the horror awaiting me after my first meal as a vampire. Once my fate was sealed, the master drew my soul into his dark realm and I found myself looking up at his hundred-foot tall, naked body. Sexless. Anger shot though me, all those lectures about sex and lust being the greatest tool of evil, and the devil doesn't even have the apparatus!

"My new little vampire," boomed the master in my Russian dialect. "Come, watch me eat. All my anger turned to pure terror as his giant hand swept me up and placed me on top of a towering mound made from millions of human skulls. In the center of the mound lay a huge blood-stained plate. No other utensils. "This is where sins become my food," he said. Then he reached down and snatched something near his foot and dropped it beside me. It was a middle-aged woman, naked, and in her hand she held an apple. She looked at me; her eyes flashed anger and she spat at my feet.

"Lev must have been really desperate to replace me with a scrawny little *manda* like you," she said in Russian. "You think being a vampire is going to make you big and powerful? Stupid *shloocha*, you've become the lowest of the low. Then she looked down and shook her head.

"Yet another poor stupid doomed girl," I heard her mutter. "Won't even last a year." Then she shoved the apple into her mouth and ran to the plate. She turned to me, gave a wave and lay down. The master picked her up and popped her into his mouth. She grunted more than howled, and for several minutes the only sound in hell was the crunching of her bones. Then, with blood still dripping down his chin, he pried her skull from between his teeth and added it to the mound.

"Nice," the master said after a loud burp. "Old vampires are always especially flavorful. "Little Valentina, I do hope you survive long enough to become as tasty." I screamed, went to my knees and sobbed. Then, while I cried, the master told me of the rules I'd be following in my new life as one of his minions. Evil likes rules; there were a lot of them.

Sometime later, when the master felt sure I'd abandoned all hope, he returned me to the land of the living. And a new vampire roamed the streets of New York.

I patted the hairless skin of what had once been Lev's head and forced myself not to let the anger return. Since that terrible initiation, we'd been together for almost a hundred years. I'd watched his unfed hunger drive him to the edge of final death a dozen times before the night he'd gotten too weak to find shelter from the sun. The yuck factor might be a lot higher, but girl vamps don't struggle to find victims like the guys do.

There was a noise behind me and I guessed the master had sent dinner. Lev disappeared with the speed only another cleaner could match. I turned. A little luck. Not one pedophilic asshole, but three. Maybe one of them wasn't quite the scumbag as his buddies. Maybe one was just some *perhot' podzalupnaya* afraid to say no. Not the best choice for someone who'd share my existence until one of us was caught by the sun, but hopefully not as bad as their bottom-feeding leader. I'd drag things out so I could figure out the pecking order.

We went through all the usual, "what do have we here," and "aren't you a little young to be out all alone," bullshit. I acted weak and pathetic as they surrounded me. Even whimpering when one ran his hand through my long hair. I labeled them; Tattoo, Red Jacket and Mustache. Mustache seemed to be the weakest. Red Jacket might be the instigator, but it wasn't clear. I resigned myself to gritting my teeth and doing it the master's way. Probably the guy who went last would be the least offensive asshole.

The conversation followed its dreary formula until Tattoo and Mustache each grabbed one of my arms and forced me down onto the roadway. Tattoo yanked my dress up and made the expected crude remarks. Red Jacket knelt between my legs. Yep, the leader gets the first shot. Have fun *zhopa*, fifteen minutes tops and you'll be learning the rules of hell. I started the little mantra I used at times like this--I'm dead. I can't feel it. It means nothing.

The screech of a car's breaks was followed by the crunch of a crumbling fender. Red Jacket spun around, but Tattoo and Mustache continued keeping me pinned.

"What the...." Red Jacket jumped to his feet then took a step backward, almost tripping over one of my legs.

Ok. I was every bit as surprised as Red Jacket. There, running toward us and waving an aluminum cane over his head while repeatedly shouting, "Stop. Stop," was a small, doubled-up old man wearing one of those hospital gowns that flap open to reveal the patient's ass. This guy was old. Ninety, a hundred, when they're that far gone who can tell? The stupid old fart tried to hit Red Jacket on the top of his head with his cane. The young man blocked the blow, and then shoved his fist into the man's nose. The old guy collapsed.

Red Jacket massaged his fist and cursed repeatedly. Then, quite casually, he took out a knife, bent over, and shoved it into my would-be rescuer's stomach. The old guy grunted, but was too weak to make much noise. With a wide grin that showed all of his decayed front teeth, Red Jacket walked back to me. "Sorry for the delay, missy. I'll make it up to you by giving you something special." Tattoo laughed.

"Leave the little girl alone." The old guy had raised himself up on one elbow. I had to admire his spunk. Besides the blood running from his nose, the knife stuck out of his belly surrounded by a growing red stain. Moving had to hurt like hell.

"Shit," said Red Jacket. "Bruce, go shut the old fart up. I got better things to do." He pointed at Mustache. There followed a short delay as Tattoo maneuvered to grab both of my arms so Mustache could scramble to his feet.

"Please," gasped the old guy. "Don't hurt the little girl."

I lost it. Perhaps it was seeing what poor Lev had turned into. Perhaps it was remembering the Triangle fire. Perhaps it was watching a stupid old fart rush into certain death just to save a child he didn't know. Or maybe some remnant of my forgotten womanhood had finally had enough.

Tattoo's head flew across the road. Before he could scream at the red spray that showered him, Mustache felt a hand ram into his chest, grasp his heart, and then continue out his back. Red Jacket wasn't their leader for nothing. He took off running much faster than I expected. Why, he must have cleared thirty--maybe forty feet before I shook Mustache's body off my arm and caught up with him. I shoved Red Jacket forward, my hand riding the back of his head all the way to the roadway. I heard the satisfying crack of a skull shattering against concrete. A couple of spasms and my last attacker stopped moving.

I turned back to see hundreds of starving cleaners swarming over Tattoo and Mustache. It made me realize that now all three fools were dead, I'd not be feeding tonight. Cleaners worked fast. In a few minutes my attacker's bodies, clothes, shoes and even their pocket change would be gone. There wouldn't even be a red stain on the sidewalk. I walked past the buffet and over to my fallen rescuer. Tough old fart, he was still breathing.

Lev nudged against my calf. "Master says this man's soul has almost left his body, so feeding from him won't hurt too much. If you feed now, you'll live. You can find a new partner later."

"His life thread connects to the other. He's a good person."

"He's almost dead, and his thread weakens. Painful, but you can handle it. The master will grant you a week to find another partner. Otherwise...." He stopped. We both knew what 'otherwise' would mean.

Once, Lev had confessed to me that he'd been desperate enough to feed on the blood of one who hadn't cut their ties to the other. He admitted it hurt almost beyond endurance, but normally a male vamp's meals only came after he'd enticed some fool into performing an evil that would make him the master's rightful property. Males lived on the edge of starvation.

I'd never done it. I didn't have much pride left, but I felt that feeding on only those who'd condemned themselves was the one thing that separated me from the master. I guessed the evil bastard had set up this situation to change that. It would explain the unexpected arrival of this old fool who lay at my feet clinging to life by the slimmest thread.

I knelt by the old man. A decent man who hadn't hesitated to put his life on the line to save a child. That's the kind of stupid thing a human would do.

I'd been a human once.

"I can't," I whispered to Lev. "I just can't do it." I thought the little cleaner would run around and scream in protest. But he just moved close and pressed against my leg.

"The sun will be up in a few hours," I said. "Do you want to stay? I've seen far too much for even a dammed soul to endure. I'm ready to watch the sunrise one more time." Lev crawled between my knees and settled onto the roadway. The old man opened his eyes.

"Why, its little Valentina," the man said. "You haven't changed a bit." I screamed and threw myself backward. Lev scurried across the road and did that blendy-disappear thing that was a cleaner's best trick.

"How," I gasped. "How could you know my name?"

The man shook his head and stared at me for almost a minute. "I'm not sure. Maybe it's because I'm just about dead. Why yes, now I understand--the walls are fading away.

It's all coming back to me. Once, long ago, I was your cousin Natasha." He put his hand to his head and his eyes seemed unfocused. "Well, what do you know, dying's kinda fun?" He sat still for what seemed like an eternity. "Poor Betty, she'll catch such hell for leaving my bed-rail down." He laughed and slapped his thigh. Yep, just minutes from death and he laughed.

"You're a man," I said forcefully. "My cousin Natasha was a girl. She died ninety-seven years ago."

"Died rather horribly as I recall," the man said and nodded. "And after a short, brutal life as an exploited child-laborer. You get lots and lots of good karma for something like that. My next family was the greatest. I was born to loving, caring, middle-class folk who were always supportive. I want you to know, Valentina, that I've just finished living a great life and have you to thank for it. It could just as easily have gone the other way, you know. If those embers had hit your dress instead of mine..." His voice faded. Then he blinked. "Why, I never would have married Alice. Pete and Samantha...God, they never would have been born. Oh, my poor little Val. The price you paid to bring happiness to so many people."

I sat there on the street not knowing if I believed him.

"Want to see pictures of my grandkids?" he said and smiled. "Oh shit, they're back in the nursing home. Well, take my word for it, all six are the greatest. I brought the first little girl into the world myself--oh, did I tell you that I'm a retired gynecologist?" He stopped. "Sorry, that didn't make much sense did it? Too many memories, too much information, coming at me all at once. It all gets a bit confusing."

"You're really serious aren't you?" I managed to say.

"Valentina, Val, it can't be a coincidence that I drove a car in a half-stupor all the way across town to end up here with you--and now I can remember my life as Natasha. No doubt someone up there wants you back."

"There is no back," I said. "I'm one of the dammed."

"Who says so? The prince of evil and the father of lies? Val, you might look young, but you're not eleven any more. Despite what your stupid master claims, he's not really in control. There's far more forgiveness in the universe than he wants you to know about. Did you ever wonder why he burps after every meal? You think maybe a human soul contains something he can't digest?"

"I'm a vampire. I kill. There's not enough forgiveness in all of creation for something like me."

Lev scurried across the roadway to my side. His little round head began nudging my arm. "Forgive me, you did." He slowly squeaked.

"I'm not--"

Lev screeched and moved so fast it looked as if he'd disappeared. I turned and saw he'd sunk his teeth to Red Jacket's leg. I gasped, the guy's forehead remained caved in from where I'd driven his head into the street. Yet there he was, standing--moving. While I watched, Red Jacket reached down and, with one hand, ripped Lev, and most of the flesh, from his leg. He tossed the cleaner so far away the small creature disappeared into the darkness. I knew it took super-human strength to dislodge those terrible teeth once they'd entered flesh.

Zombie. One of the master's denizens Lev had warned me to avoid at any price. While human flesh would keep them alive, all of them sought their true prey--Vampires. The one creature whose blood would return their bodies to a pre-death condition. It saw me and instinctively knew what it needed.

I was on my feet and luring the thing away from the old man. A smart zombie would pause and grab a mouthful of brains before fighting a vampire. But this freshly-turned fiend hadn't learned all the tricks. It focused on me and charged. Those stupid movies have it wrong when they portray zombies as slow, uncoordinated creatures. Undead creatures don't actually use their life-muscles, so a zombie can move just as fast as a vampire. I got in a good kick before retreating, but Red Jacket was more than twice my weight so it didn't slow him any.

As he turned to follow me, I saw, in his stumble, one small advantage. Red Jacket still thought he was alive and hadn't yet caught on to his increased speed and strength. I put every ounce of my being into a low rush that slammed into Red Jacket's leg. I hit the spot Lev had stripped with his oversized mouth. Red Jacket heard the crack as both the exposed tibia and fibula shattered. The zombie, still believing he needed that leg, went down.

I knew of only one way to kill a zombie. And there was only one suitable weapon in the vicinity. I ran to the old man and yanked the protruding knife out of his stomach. I didn't dare stop moving to see his reaction. Somehow, I had to get the zombie's head off his shoulders. And do it before he grabbed me and started chowing down.

He was getting smarter. The broken leg bones realigned themselves, and after a few tentative tries, he unsteadily struggled to his feet. By that time, I'd circled behind him and launched a leap which ended with me smacking into his back where I clung like a leech. He grunted and stumbled forward before trying to buck me off.

For once, my small size worked in my favor. With my arms and legs wrapped around him, he could shake, buck and gyrate all he wanted, but I wasn't going anyplace. I took my time lining up the little knife--I'd only get one chance. Finally I rammed the blade into the thing's neck and felt it grind against vertebrae. The zombie screeched, grabbed my arm and yanked.

I'd angled the blade just right. When the zombie pulled my arm forward, the blade was hooked behind its neck bones. My arm as a lever, and Red Jacket's own strength, did the rest. The knife sliced through his bones, his windpipe, voice box and all the odd ligaments and muscles holding his head onto his shoulders. He couldn't say, "opps!" so I said it for him. Yeah, suddenly becoming ten times stronger can be a real bugger.

I kicked the head into the gutter. Before it'd rolled to a stop, the cleaners swarmed out of the shadows. "Next time, do your job when you're supposed to," I shouted. "Then we wouldn't have these kinds of problems." Still, it wasn't their fault. When I'd turned my back on Red Jacket, the master must have seized the opportunity. It took an especially vile and evil soul to re-animate as a zombie, so I guessed New York would be a lot better off without Red Jacket prowling its streets.

I walked over to the old man. Pulling the knife out of his stomach had let the blood begin flowing in earnest. A good-sized puddle had formed beneath him so I was surprised to discover he remained conscious.

"I don't have long, Val," gasped the old man, "so let me say this quickly. I'm sure I was sent here to assure you that you've been forgiven. It's time for you to end this stupid half-life."

I knelt on the roadway beside him--Natasha. "No," I whispered. "I can't be forgiven. But maybe it's enough to admit that I condemned you die in my place. Every night, before I start to move, I shout your name into the darkness and say how sorry I am. But some sins...well, sometimes we get what we deserve."

I inched forward so I could rest his head on my knees. "This time I'll hold you until the end."

"I sure lived an eventful life," the old man whispered. "Saw much good and more bad than I want to remember. In World War Two, I was with the Ninth Armored Infantry when they entered Buchenwald. I was only one of those battle-hardened American soldiers who lost their lunch that day. Val, I've seen what those who've given themselves to real evil are capable of doing. Little cousin, I can assure you that you've never come close."

"I condemned you to die instead of me," I whispered. "How can anyone forgive a vampire?"

"A vampire uh? Well, they've a thing of the past. Your master doesn't need to waste his power on such petty creatures anymore. That's why people are now writing books and making movies about romantic and heroic vampires. Human imagination has stolen them away from evil. I bet you're the last real one."

The long speech left him exhausted, so we sat in silence. Lev returned and pressed against my side. I patted his hairless head and he settled onto the roadway. Natasha's breathing became more and more shallow. I doubted she would have the energy to speak again. "I've never stopped loving you cousin," I said quietly. "You are my only good memory in a long pathetic lifetime of pain and darkness." Something trickled down my nose. For the first time in a hundred years, I'd shed a tear. It landed on Natasha's cheek and the old man opened her eyes.

"Forgiveness," he whispered. "That's the one thing your master can never digest. Now forgive yourself, Valentina, for I have forgiven you." His eyes closed. I wanted to pretend I could see some trace of Natasha in that wrinkled face, but after a minute I admitted it only looked like an old dead guy.

Still, I sat there and held his cold hand as the eastern sky brightened. Lev pressed against my side and tried not to shake too badly. Or maybe I was the one shaking. But my mind kept repeating Natasha had forgiven me. Trust, love, or just the plain weariness of evil gave me the strength to remain seated. Whether Natasha's forgiveness was enough or not, the master had just lost his last vampire.

A few wispy clouds began to turn from gray to orange.

It was going to be a glorious sunrise.

❀

On March 25th 1911, just before the shift end, a fire began in the piles of cotton lint and rags littering the eighth floor of the Asch Building where the Triangle Shirtwaist Company operated. Many garment workers, mostly those on the ninth floor, were trapped when the fire engulfed the stairway. With the collapse of the flimsy fire escape, they found the only other escape route locked shut. That day, either 147 or 148 workers died. 62 chose to jump to their deaths from an open window rather than suffer the agony of the flames.

The company owners were acquitted of any wrongdoing.

The End

It All Happened Before

The bookstore holds the ticket to memories
New books crack open to World War II
tanks, generals, Nazis and GIs
Vietnam approaches on the bookshelves
preserved in picture books

Somehow it seems all wrong
I don't remember it that way
Everything in order, organized
Complete with maps and letters
Sanitized suffering

My memories are all messed up
Scattered snapshots of times past
Uncle Duffy and Aunt Ginny
smiling in front of their new house
He looks great in his army suit

Ginny crying at the kitchen table
"He's never coming back
I hate the Germans.
I hate the VC.
I hate the US."
Aunt Ginny stayed with us
assembled telephones at Western Electric
and voted for Eisenhower, Nixon, and Reagan

Will anybody buy the book
About the widows and widowers
Left in the wake of war?
WWII, Korea, Vietnam, Iraq, Afghanistan
What are these survivors doing now?

Lying down beside their husbands
for the first time in fifty years?
Nursing home? Remarried?
Teacher? Bus driver?
Are the kids OK?

What's it like to see the vase
He gave her flowers in
Used to save spare change that
blooms into a Christmas bicycle?

Tattoos and Skin

Before I die I'll cover myself in tattoos
Eye in the back of my head
Garden of roses on my feet
Proper nouns, active verbs, mysterious scenes

When I die, a taxidermist will cure my skin
And make a set of tattoo cards
Family and friends will have a souvenir
A commemorative deck of life

A relic of an illustrated person
Seventy-year-old U-Tube video
A rose garden
Illustrated on top of my right foot
Kicking a beach ball
Dancing barefoot
A beautiful card amid
Anonymous ashes

My memory living long
Maybe famous, sold on E-Bay
Immortality in a slipcase

Smooth Jazz

Mama, I love you, but I gotta get out.
Away from yelling and screaming, hitting and lies,
Name calling and tears,
Smoke and crack and booze.

The street's a lot calmer. At least there's more space.
Nobody knows me out here.
I can erase my face.

"Hey, kid!"
A sharp dressed dude with a flashy smile calls to me.
He's got gold chains around his neck,
Shoes with box toes,
A cool tailor-made suit,
A wide-brimmed hat.

"C'mere son. You cool. Yeh, you."
I come to him.
He's surrounded by guys in hip-hop pants,
Girls in tight shorts.
"Hey, baby bro, how old are you?"
"Ten," I reply.
"You brave, com'in up just like that."

I feel good.
He called me brave.
Nobody ever called me brave.
Everyone's smiling and so friendly.
I could use a good friend.

"'Cause you so brave I'm gonna give you
this five dollar bill.
Go on, take it.
You earned it.
It's from me,
Your pal, Smooth Jazz.
My friends call me Jazz.

Now come around tomorrow.
I might have some work for you to do."

I look at the bill in my hand,
The tight shorts,
The hip-hop pants,
The wonderful gold-chained man.
"Thank you, Sm--"

"Jazz!" they all shout and laugh.
"Jazz," I say.
I learn quick.

Now I'm walking down the street,
With five dollars in my hand,
I stop and buy some chocolate candy bars.
I've got change in my pocket
For the first time in my life.

My sister gets some chocolate,
Li'l brother too.
Everybody's happy.
And Jazz is my big man.

Jazz, day one: "Stand across the street, baby bro,
In front of the grocery store.
When we wave, you wave.
It's just a game."
"Jazz!" they all shout and wave.
He gives me a ten dollar bill.

Jazz, day two: "Stand on the corner, baby bro,
When a cop car comes by, wave."
"Jazz!" they all shout and wave.
Another ten dollars.

Jazz, week one: "Take this bag to the man across the
street,
He'll give you money. Bring it here, little cool man."

He gives me twenty dollars,
I learn quick.

I buy my sister a pretty dress.
Thank you, Jazz.
I've got a real job.
You are God.

Jazz, year two: "We got trouble.
Pimps tryin' to move into my territory.
Gotta show them who's boss,
You, cool man."
He gives me a thousand dollars and a pistol.
I learn quick.

I rent Mama a new crib.
She so skinny,
Can hardly walk,
Too much crack and too much booze.

I don't know the guy,
In the fancy car with the cool rims.
When he pulls up,
I shoot him in the head.
I learn quick.

I kill a man,
Shed a tattoo tear.
It's just business.
I'm a businessman.
I'm Jazz's best man.

Jazz, year nine: "You the best man I got."
He turns and smiles.
I shoot him in the face,
I learn quick.

Year ten: Mama died of crack cocaine,
I'm daddy now.

O.D. cocktail her best way out.

Baby sister's in college,
Li'l brother gonna be a doctor.
How many dead men does it take to make a doctor?
I learn quick.

*Smooth Jazz first appeared in the May, 2010 issue of Steam
Ticket, a literary journal published by the University of
Wisconsin at LaCrosse.*

Young Man's Tune

Deathdog's piercing howl in the heart
passion in the gut
Easy, breezy, crackpot smile
Purgatory's lungs breathing in
filled with sorrows of failed relationships

You'll still be here tomorrow, Antwan
At least you know when your time's up
Your appeal, a measuring stick
Live longer on appeal than on the street

Would you fight so hard the dark, silent panic
wearing a quadriplegic body disguise?
Is the mystery in drug and alcohol soaked days
worth the sober walk to the room,
where an audience prays to see you die?

My last meal: a corned beef sandwich, a dark beer
From a pub that lost its allure years ago
In what rooms did agents of time conspire
to turn the brewery's copper kettles
into tightly wound electrodes?

A full and honest voice of innocent youth
stopped by brutal abuse, sings again
Pure virtuous voice resounds
Lives on in hip-hop fragments—
dead before age twenty-five.

White Collar Crime

I'm the man they can't do without
These company walls are where I live
I have five patents to my name
The company makes millions off my brain
The CEO was my best friend

What have you done for me lately?
That's why I have to sell or go bankrupt
I know you understand
Here's some money
Thanks for your dedication
Thanks for your lifetime

Keep in touch
I'm 55 years old, my hands shake

Al Svoboda

UNUS SPATUS TERRIBULUS

Jerryus Cowlingus

Unus femaleus species teen-agerum brattus ambulatum outum porticus at decius o'clockus, et pater oratum,"Wherus tu thinkus tu goest thisus timus of nightus?"

"Oh daddicus, tu est fuddicus-duddicus. Est goingus tous particus toga."

"Tu meanest unus fuckus-ruckus?"

"Daddicus!"

Mater rushum intoum solarium. "Whatus going onus herem?"

"Mommicus, daddicus hast mouthus potticus!"

"Yourus femaleus species teen-agerum brattus est goingum to a particus toga!"

"So whattus?" Mater respondum.

"Thatus toga est wayum too shortus!" Pater screamus.

"Est stylus," Mater saidum.

"Est vulgar," Pater saidum.

"Allus girlus wearam togas shortum."

"Tu est non allus girlus."

"Oh, daddicus!"

"Who est meetingum at particus toga?"

"Brutus Juniorum."

"Senatorum Brutus maleus species teen-agerum brattus?"

"Veritatus, Daddicus."

"Non est trustus hisus daddicus."

"Why notus?"

"Brutus est stabbus tu in the backus ifus he hadus the chanceus."

"Oh, Daddicus!"

"Giveus a breakus," Mater saidum.

"Be homus beforeus the roosterus crowum."

"Oh, Daddicus, tu est so schoolus oldus."

"Et comest straightest homus ifus Cleopatra showsus upus atus particus toga."

"Whatus is wrongus with Cleopatra?"

"Non likus herus aspus."

"Herus whatus?" Mater screamum.

"Aspus! Aspus!"

"Oh," mater saidum. "Neverum mindum."

"Onum lastest thingum," pater saidum to femaleum species teen-agerum brattus."

"Whatus nowum?" femaleum saidum with a sighum.

"Don'tus rideus in chariotus of that maleum species teen-agerum brattus!"

"Oh, Daddicus!"

Endicus

War Dogs

Judy G. Burford

Margaret Winters is perched on a stool, in the den, a picture in one hand, military dog tags in the other. She's not sure why she got the urge to go through this box today, of all days. Thirty-eight years ago, today, her husband Phillip died of a massive heart attack.

She recalls two uniformed officers coming to the door, that Tuesday afternoon, just before dinner. Margaret remembers the day because she taught a class on Tuesday evenings, which she had to cancel. Just minutes after the officers left, Phillip pressed his palm against the center of his chest and gasped. He dropped to the floor and Margaret knelt beside him, trying her best to beat down the panic threatening to burst from her any second. Remembering her CPR training, she went through the ABC process: airway, breathing and circulation. Phillip was still breathing. Margaret ran to the phone, in the kitchen, and dialed the number for an ambulance. She was so glad she'd typed out the emergency numbers and taped them to the wall beside the phone. The ambulance arrived and the attendants assessed Phillip's condition before bundling him onto a stretcher and wheeling him to their vehicle.

A tear runs down her face as she recalls the words of the emergency room doctor, "I'm very sorry, your husband didn't make it. It was a massive heart attack."

No, thinks Margaret, *it was a broken heart.*

The clock, in the den, chimes the quarter hour, bringing Margaret back to the moment. She looks down at the picture in her left hand. "Charlie, my sweet, sweet son." He looks happy, if one can look happy in a war zone. To her, he's handsome, like his father, although his high forehead hints that he may be bald one day. His wire-rimmed glasses and long nose are not unlike those you see in a costume store. Margaret smiles. *Charlie would tease me about where he inherited those features, if he could read my mind.* He's wearing a camouflage jacket over an army-issue shirt. He has his army issue pants rolled up at the bottom with his boots showing below. *My Charlie, always a trend-setter when it comes to his wardrobe.*

Charlie is kneeling, in the picture, holding the collar of what Margaret assumes is a 'war dog'. The dog, with typical husky markings, has its tail held tall, as if it appreciates the soldier's visit. There are three makeshift sheds, in the background of the picture, each with an opening, but no door. Their size makes it obvious they were made for dogs. Margaret is grateful Charlie had a companion to ease the stress of being there.

A single burned tree trunk stands tall, behind them, as if to defy the battle that ensued around it. By the look of the new trees growing behind it, Margaret determines the battle must have been a few years earlier. It's hard to believe Charlie served nearly ten years over there.

"Stupid, damn government. Can't keep their noses out of everybody else's business."

Margaret recalls when the U.S. entered the Vietnam war, in 1965. They claimed they had to fill the spot the French vacated and keep South Vietnam from becoming a communist nation.

"Maybe you should have done your homework better and looked into why the French pulled out. Maybe they saw what it took you ten years to see. That North Vietnam was not to be defeated. Ten years, and so many lives lost, and for what? After our soldiers pulled out, South Vietnam surrendered. They are a communist nation. And I've lost my son and my husband."

Margaret can't bear to hold it in any longer. She rests her face in her palms and sobs for several minutes. She is barely aware of the clock chiming the half hour. When she is able to compose herself, she brings the picture close to her face and kisses her son's lips. "I'll always love you Charlie."

The End

A Warrior's Story
Don Kafrissen

I am a warrior. That's the only label I can apply to myself. I am a sergeant in the U.S. Army. I am a grunt. I am not a Ranger or Special Forces. I am not a SEAL or a member of any of the other so-called elite units. In another time I might have been one of Hannibal's men or Saladin's. Nevertheless, I am still a warrior. I have no name any longer, just Sarge. I never used to think of myself as a warrior but since we have been fighting these wars for so long, I can think of myself as nothing else. I don't feel that I am a patriot or even that I know what my men and I are fighting for. We just fight and rest when we can.

I do not count the days or weeks left or how long I have been here. I don't care. It is what I do, maybe what I have been destined to do. I have only two jobs, kill the enemy and keep them from killing us. Do I care if we win? Not really, for I have no concept of what winning means in the greater picture. We grunts in the field rarely even hear about the greater picture. We live day to day. For all I know, we may be on the wrong side. I do not care anymore.

When I first came here I thought we had a mission, clearly defined, and that we were here to win. Win what, I found myself asking? I lead a platoon of ten men. I have been here forever. Some of the men who looked to me have been killed. They are replaced. And so it goes. For the last month we have been designated LURPS. That means Long Range Reconnaissance Patrol. I like this best. We have no officers to oversee us, to make us dress properly or to send in our reports.

Our radioman was wounded only a week after we started out. He stepped on a small mine. He died the next day and nobody picked up his damaged radio. I have his dog tags in my pocket. We have a mission. Our mission is to support a Special Forces team behind enemy lines, doing what, I don't know.

We have set up ambushes twice and twice we have defeated the enemy with no losses. I have no feelings left for the enemy warriors. I don't think I have any feelings left for anything anymore. When our radioman was shot, I looked at the wound and felt nothing. I knew he would die and so did he. We sat with him for that night and part of the next day. It would have been foolish to call in an evac chopper. Why waste more men on a dying man? We moved out after leaving his body for the animals.

The jungle is always wet and dripping. I have been wet so long that I don't remember what dry feels like. The sun rarely comes out and when it does, we still stick to the trees, for cover. We will meet up with the SF team tomorrow. I was not told how many men are in the SF team, just follow their orders. That's all we ever do. I was given their co-ordinates and my men and I will be there.

I think I have been here three years. Once I went back to the world and didn't like it. I came back and signed papers saying that I would stay for as long as I could, forever. In the world, there are rules – in the jungle, you make up the rules. We will stop to eat soon. We each pack our own food. I eat little, like my enemy. I pack some protein bars, rice and cornmeal. Anything else I can find in the jungle. My men feel the same way. We eat snake often. It is nourishing, easy to catch and tastes good; and what's more, they are plentiful here. Sometimes we find bird's eggs and often catch a monkey. We skirt villages and only sneak near after dark. We liberate the fruit on the cultivated trees like mangos, plantains and bananas. Once in a while we liberate a chicken or a small hog. Life goes on.

My platoon point man motions us to stop. We are quiet and squat in the shadows. A woman walks by on a nearby path. She has a basket on her head. We must be near a village. She is within six or seven feet of us but never sees or hears us. We have become very good at what we do. It has been a long time since I was with a woman. I feel no need any more. I never think about women; not my mother or sister or old girlfriends. I rarely even dream anymore.

That night we hole up against the trunk of a fallen tree. It was very big and we are hidden from most sides in a shallow depression. Tonight I permit a small fire. We cook some small rodents my first has shot with the crossbow he carries. We eat with our hands and knives. I am handed half of a protein bar and tuck it into my pocket while the rice boils. Later, I set my watches and we grab some sleep. I sleep lightly, my mind processing every jungle noise. It automatically hears then discards the snores and breathing of my men, the normal jungle noises and even evaluates the silences. Did something disturb a night bird? Was the distant growl of a tiger coming closer or fading away? My unconscious mind decides while my conscious mind sleeps. This keeps me alive. My men too.

Morning comes with the squawking of a macaw. I open an eye and can see my hand. It is just morning, gray and misty. I stood a two-hour watch from midnight to two. Nothing happened. No unusual noises disturbed the jungle sounds. The village must not be close. I nudge a nearby leg. Slowly we wake and stretch. I whistle softly and the two scouts come in silently. They are PFC's and have been with me for over a year. We eat some dried monkey jerky and rice balls from last night soundlessly. We clean our weapons and ammo.

I nod and we move out, checking our compasses. I glance at my map. About eight klicks to go. I sight a hill and signal our point man with a whistle. We have a whole set of whistles. It's funny, the more whistles we've developed, the less we talk. Short words, then grunts. We also use hand signals. Even when sitting around at meals, we use hand signals, grunts and whistles. It works for us. New men either learn fast or are gone.

We slip between the trees and ease over the hummocks. The ground is marshy. The hill is before us and in a few minutes I feel the rise. The marsh is behind and as we rise, the trees grow sparse. We stop at a signal from up forward. Though we are beside the trail, I see what the private is pointing toward. It is a string, maybe a wire, low and crossing the trail. He points again at a pile of leaves and branches. We carefully pull them away. It is a mortar shell connected to the trip wire. I slip up beside him. We can't cut the string. The Charlies would know we were there, but we can make it malfunction.

I grin and we carefully unscrew the primer. I pull it out and put a piece of bark on top of the cap, then screw it back to the shell and place the shell in its hole. We cover it with its blanket of leaves. My men grin at me. We have maybe saved a villager.

On the other side of the hill we spot a small clearing with a light colored rock. Our meeting point. I gesture left and right. We fan out and move down quietly. As we circle the clearing, we hunker down to wait. In a short time, I feel a touch on my shoulder. I look up at the camo-streaked face of an older man. He moves his lips close to my ear. "Your guys are good. I'm Hammer."

I nod. "Sarge."

"How many men?"

"Nine."

"Lose one?"

I nod. "You?"

He holds up three fingers.

"Plan?" I ask.

He pulls out a duplicate of my map and points to a place about 3 klicks west. "Tunnel. HQ. A general."

I nod again.

He holds up his three fingers and points down.

I whistle a series that sounds like a small sparrow from home. My men slip silently to me. They spot Hammer and raise their weapons. I hand signal them that its O.K.

He signals to follow him. After a few minutes another slips into our file, then a third. We keep moving. The mist has cleared so we stay in the shadows at a fast trot. After a while, Hammer signals us to stop, then gather around. He pulls out his map again and lays it on a log. He points, "Here is where our intel says there is a tunnel entrance. It is supposed to be a CP (Command Post) and a General is there. Our orders are to go in and get him and bring him back." He looks at me. "Sarge," he jabs at another point on the map about two klicks away, "this is our LZ (Landing Zone). An evac Huey will be landing there in about three hours," he looks at his watch, "at exactly 1400 hours. If anything happens to us, get your men there." He looks around at each of us, "In any case, that's where we're headed with the General. My men and I will go in and get him. You men will form a perimeter and make sure nobody goes in and only we come out, understand?"

I nod and a couple of my men also. These guys are tunnel rats, one of the worst jobs a man can have. Glad it isn't us that have to go down.

Hammer and the two men with him, wiry little guys, tie black bandanas around their heads and lay down their packs and peel off their already soaked shirts. They replace their boots with black sneakers and tuck their pant legs into black socks. Hammer reaches into his pack and pulls out three handguns, fairly small caliber and three tubes about six inches long. They screw them to the gun barrels. Silencers. He hands each man a gun and 4 clips. Everything is black. Finally each man pulls out a pair of goggles and a small flashlight. They push the buttons but no light shines. One man grins. "Nightlight," he says with an accent I can't place.

"Let's go," orders Hammer.

We slip down into the small valley, Hammer on point. We stop behind a clump of bushes. Hammer points to a flat spot with a tree to the right. I nod and gesture to my men. They fan out, five to the left, three to the right. Hammer touches my shoulder, nudging me. I look at him a moment and move right a few feet and find a comfortable position. I set my M-16 on full auto and wait. The three SF men crawl into the clearing. I scan for snipers with a small pair of binoculars. Nothing.

I watch the men disappear into a dip in the ground. Time crawls by. Suddenly I hear a shot. It is from one of our rifles. Again, another short burst this time, from my right. Then another and another from the men to my right.

One of my PFC's runs over. "Charlies, lots of them, Sarge. Just appeared. Must be another tunnel exit."

"Can we hold them?"

He shrugs, "Not for long. There's already a couple of dozen up and out. We're shooting, but they've got good cover in the trees." He glanced over my shoulder, "Company, Sarge."

Sure enough, Hammer was running our way, dragging a small, uniformed figure by tied hands. When he got to us, he said, "Let's go. My guys will be out in a second."

I whistled loudly with my fingers. It was to pull back. Hammer clocked the squirming Charlie over the head with the butt of his pistol then tossed him onto his shoulder. Without looking back he started for the LZ. I knew from the fire that my men were withdrawing toward me. I looked into the clearing and saw two figures come out of the fold. One was dragging a leg and being helped by the other. When they were only about 15 or 20 feet from the bare spot, it erupted; dirt clods flying everywhere, two trees toppled and the little clearing seemed to cave in. The two SF guys were just past it and heading our way. I waved to them and they came toward me at a broken run. The hurt one was grinning. I motioned them past me. They knew the way. My men were forming on me and we kept up a steady barrage at the shadows in the trees. I saw one of my men clutch his face and go down. I looked. A piece of his skull and an ear were missing. I wrapped a bandage around his head and got him to his feet. We walked backward while firing. Finally we started leapfrogging four men at a time. I gave the wounded man to my first and pointed. He nodded and slung his rifle, and then I helped him hoist the man onto his shoulders. He headed after the SF guys.

I whistled a sharp series of blasts. Now we were in full leapfrog retreat. Twenty feet, stop and position. A whistle then another. We kept this up for twenty minutes. The enemy fire grew in intensity. There were a lot more than a couple of dozen of them now. We took another hit. One man shot in the shoulder, then another in the gut. Bandage and keep moving, keep shooting. A shot pinged off my helmet, and then another tore at my collar. I ducked behind a tree. Another man shot in the calf. Bandage and keep moving. I called, "The LZ is close. Keep moving!"

I heard rotors, then a fusillade of shots. The Charlies had heard too. The chopper went up high. We were at the edge of the LZ. The SF guys were in the center. One had popped smoke. Hammer turned and waved to us. The chopper suddenly dropped like a stone and looked like it would land on top of Hammer and his guys, one who was lying on his back not moving.

I whistled shrilly. My men started coming out of the trees and running toward the chopper's open door, the door gunner firing over their heads as they crouched low. Two were limping and one was being helped. Suddenly a burst of fire and one went down. I laid a long burst of fire behind the remaining men. I ran for the chopper, firing behind my hip. Hammer was already inside, one of his men on a seat and it looked like the General on the floor. Three of my men were inside and helping the others.

The pilot screamed, "Too many! Too many! I can't take off!"

I looked at him and he held up his hands, "Nine," he screamed again and held up nine fingers.

I looked at Hammer. We were being peppered by small arms fire. One of my men caught a round in the back, which went right through and into the leg of another. Only one man too many now. Most hurt. I looked around at my men. The man who'd taken the round in the gut was unconscious, lying on top of the General, blood soaking his uniform. I quickly felt his throat. Thready. He wouldn't make it back. I hauled him out by a leg. As he fell on the ground, Hammer leaned out and shot him in the head. The pilot revved the engine and we leaped off the ground going straight up as fast as we could, the pilot looking down to keep his bearings through the small opening in the trees. The door gunner spraying the edge of the clearing back and forth, casings chattering and pinging on the metal floor. I brushed a pile out the door and sat back leaning against someone's legs. We were up and over the canopy, three hundred, four hundred, five hundred feet. Now out of range.

My man who'd been shot in the face half grinned from under his bandage. He said something I couldn't hear. I leaned toward him, "Glad you didn't pick me, Sarge." I patted his shoulder. One of the other men pricked his arm with a needle. Morphine, I guessed. I nudged the General. He moved a little, drawing up a leg. Well, at least he was alive, the bastard. Three good men for this little shit; four, if you count the tunnel rat. All of a sudden I wanted to throw his skinny ass out of the chopper. I moved a hand toward him and looked up at a loud click. Hammer was pointing the silenced pistol at me and shaking his head no. I sat back and sighed.

Mission accomplished.

The End

Water and Light

Living where the sun detonates its full glory
with a warrior's fierce abandon
there are many things

for which to offer thanks: massive live oaks rooted
centuries deep, whose sprawling limbs and beckoning

shadows hide our dirty Southern secrets while offering
birdsong,
crisp and sweet; and relief in pattering rain, shivered

off leaves in stirred breezes, and the creek, upon whose
banks
I kneel, praying that this cool water cupped in my palm
is clean

Enough an, and for uncontained radiance, spontaneous
and dappled,
Trailing slowly across a ground folio of last fall's twigs
and cones

That reminds us often our own leaf-littered darkness
Is pierced by sharp, faceted slivers of light.

Christine Cock

Wheels

Mary Cooper

"What the hell are you talking about, 'wheels'? What's that supposed to mean?"

"It's the answer to everything, Sally; the meaning of life." Dr. Plummer spoke as if it was an undisputed fact. "Every aspect of existence from the tiniest flagella to the orbits of the planets revolve in a circular motion—"

"Orbits are elliptical—"

"Which, as you know, are elongated spheres, circles, wheels." He held up a forestalling hand. "Now don't interrupt me…"

Sally saw the fanatical gleam in his eye, sighed, and eased back in her seat. There was no use trying to have a normal conversation when he got like this. May as well wait him out.

He continued without pause, "…the spinning of the earth gives rise to gravity, seasonal change, all the things that make life on this planet possible. Everything moves in cycles: the moon and tides, even the history of man. Just look at our own bodies, for pity's sake. The circulatory system is what keeps us going! Our very lives revolve around multiple cycles, our internal "wheels", if you will. You, being a woman, should know…"

"Stuart, I don't think…"

Dr. Plummer went on as though she hadn't spoken. "What made it possible for civilization to advance beyond the primitive cave? The invention of the wheel! What makes every part of this world work? The glorious wheel! Economy, ecology, every type of science and industry would be lost without it!"

Wow, he's really on a roll this time. Sally tamped down her irritation, watching the passion of his argument turn his cheeks ruddy. She took a deep breath and exhaled it slowly. He was escalating into a lecture worthy of a UNESCO address with no sign of winding down. She gazed at him over her glasses and mentally rehearsed the preamble to the constitution. We the people…

Twenty minutes later, in mid-sentence, Dr. Plummer looked at Sally and finally saw her. She knew the moment it happened, watched in horrid fascination as the color drained completely from his face and cast a greenish pall over his features. His words faltered and he stumbled back into a chair.

"Stu!" She jumped up, worried. He seemed about to cry, pass out, vomit…

Some people reacted to momentous news with a hug or a glass of champagne. She gets psychological disassociation and a half-hour lecture. She was going to have his baby for heaven's sake!

Why, oh, why had she fallen in love with a philosophy professor?

The End

Winter Woods

C. J. Goldman

Winter comes, marked by daylight growing shorter and leaves falling from the trees. Soon there is a quiet in the winter wood, a silence that the soul alone can hear. December winds blow, an icy chill that threatens all that lives there.

When the tips of the pines touch the twinkling stars on a cold crisp night in December, all the woods seem to slumber. The great bald eagle, living symbol of our freedom, sits stolidly on a jagged stump, feathers ruffled against the cold.

Wind whispers silent through skeletal branches. Within the forest shadows a bobcat rests, draped over time worn boulders. Awakened by the rising sun he greets the day with watchful eyes. He knows; somewhere there is food.

Shore birds with spindly legs and wave rippled bodies wade happily along the creek, searching the rocks for tasty tidbits. Their feet have to be cold, but they don't seem aware of it.

Among a flock of wild turkeys, grazing in the meadow, gobblers proudly display fanned-out tail feathers glistening in the sun. They strut with puffed chests while the hens hustle their half grown flock of babies along the grazing path. They're not impressed.

The big birds move along an old split-rail fence, scoured by wind and mellowed by time. The wooden fence rails were hand-hewn from majestic American chestnut trees. They have character etched in every natural imperfection, some more than a century ago.

The winter woods and all its creatures wait in anticipation for spring to release the icy grip of winter.

An old owl sits studiously plump on a high branch where he can see anything that moves. He is a master hunter; he can turn his head one hundred and eighty degrees scanning the forest floor for prey. Then, silent as soft falling snow, he swoops through the trees to capture his prize with razor sharp talons.

The winter forest seems enchanted. The conifers are bowed, their greenery burdened by puffs of powdery snow. The bright male cardinal wears a black mask over scarlet plumage and huddles next to his mate singing a sweet song. He screeches in protest as when his love song is interrupted by a herd of deer leaping through snow banks to the meadow.

The little red fox wears a chest of ruffled white fur. He listens with black tipped ears and sniffs the brisk air with his pointy nose, hoping to find a tasty morsel beneath the snow-covered leaves on the forest floor.

The bubbling brook is a glorious free fall of rivulets cascading from an icy spring. It flows, thousands of glistening droplets, over a waterfall into the pool of icy water where lazy trout are sleeping.

From the big icy pond comes the forlorn cry of the loons taking off for the sky. They circle and then return, webbed feet out in front of them as they ski along the top of the water. Settling in a group they begin grooming.

Upon the wooded hills above the river the naked dogwoods sway as the breeze twists among their branches. The flowering crab trees, pregnant with buds, are impatient for spring. Soon they will to riot, cascades of delicate white and deep pink blossoms in the warming sunshine. Wild honeysuckle also waits its turn, tangled beneath the trees, a dappled carpet of scarlet, orange and rose surrounded by snow and forest magic.

The End

Writer's Delirium

My head is like a balloon tied on by a string,
freely disconnected,
like the words that float from my mouth and
leak from my fingertips onto the smooth, white
page
of the computer screen.
I've heard that Writers' Block is the anathema,
the Boogeyman, the Curse,
for those
who communicate this way;
but I thought it couldn't happen to me.
And it hasn't really,
not technically speaking,
since there is no blockage or constipation,
no blank mind devoid of imagination,
just the opposite in fact—
a plethora of words, unrelated, unintelligible:
Cartwheels for Dixie inside Manitoba rains,
gelatinous Mumfries baking bread puddings
for expired sardines.
See what I mean?
Light and frothy concoctions floating up,
up, up.
Senseless acts of wording,
must be stopped.
Must be stopped, or corked, or popped
or gagged or draped or suffocated,
this delirium of sorts;
I've tried to hang on

but I can't stop now.
I've drifted beyond the furthest buoy
swaying in the night sky,
and into a cloud momentous.
I can't seem to find my way back.

                                        Mary Cooper

The Yard Sale Mystery

Judy G. Burford

While on my way to get coffee, an entourage of bikers wiz past me. Many of them have bearded faces and are wearing leathers with club symbols and names on them. The hair on my arms begins to stand up. What are they up to? Then it hits me, they're probably on their way to Port Dover for the Friday the 13th gathering. That's one place I'll avoid, over a 100,000 bikers crammed into a tiny village all drinking beer and using God knows what drugs.

As I'm about to pass the corner of Ponsford Place, I notice a Yard Sale sign pointing down that street. Now I'm not one to stop at Yard Sales. In fact, I like to call them garbage sales. I can't for the life of me think why I would want somebody else's garbage. After all, it's only been four years since I downsized to the condo and got rid of truckloads of my own junk.

Something seems to draw me to this sale, don't ask me what. I just have the notion to turn the wheel of my car and venture down the street. As I pull up in front of the house, with the lawn covered in "treasures," I feel butterflies in my stomach. What the heck, I must be getting soft. Well, they do say your brain turns to mush as you get older, don't they? I know it takes me and three friends to complete one sentence most days. Getting old sucks!

So I get out of the car and I mosey up the driveway, hoping not to be noticed. I start to weave my way in and out of the various tables strewn with what some would call trash and others would call treasures. Hmm, *that's interesting*, I think, *Blue Mountain Pottery. I thought that died with my mother's generation.* I browse through a box of paperbacks, now those I do categorize as treasures books being my passion. To my surprise, I come across a couple that I still don't possess. I tuck those under one arm and continue to browse.

"What's this?" I look around, hoping no one heard me speak aloud. *Get hold of yourself*, I think. *It's kind of hard to remain incognito when your mouth's flapping.*

The item that caught my eye is a box the size of my Houghton Mifflin Canadian Dictionary, about seven inches by ten inches by two inches. I pick it up, again looking around to see if anyone is watching me. The home owners are deep in conversation with another shopper who arrived shortly after me. I turn the box over. It has some indecipherable lettering etched on the bottom along with the year 1929. *Old*, I think. I try to open it, without success. Now my curiosity is peeked. There's a sticker on the box showing, $2.50. I'll bite. I wander over to the home owners with my books and the puzzling box. My total purchase comes to $3.00.

I think, *Start the car!* Like the Ikea commercial.

I decide to go through the drive-through to get my coffee as I'm anxious to get home and pry open the box to see what's inside. I pull into the garage and waste no time getting into the house. I fling my jacket over the kitchen chair, run downstairs to get a screw driver, and return breathless. With quivering hands, I try to pry open the lid. No luck. I try again. Still no luck. I put all my might behind the third thrust. As the lid opens, a puff of smoke rises from the box. I jump back, expecting the thing to blow up.

"You may have three wishes," says the image that appears when the smoke clears.

"Who are you?" I ask.

"I'm the genie from the box," the figure replies.

"What do you mean three wishes? This can't be happening," I retort.

"You opened the box, now I am your servant. Tell me what it is that you wish for?"

"Well, give me a minute," I reply.

"It's yours," replies my genie.

"What. No." I gasp. "I mean give me time to think."

"Your second wish is my command."

"No." I sigh in exasperation. "Give me a break!"

As fast as I get the words out, I feel and hear a crack. My left femur goes limp and I find myself in a puddle on the kitchen floor, writhing in pain. During the same instant, my genie disappears into a second puff of smoke.

I reach up for the wooden box and throw it across the room. It hits the glass door of the oven which shatters into millions of pieces across the kitchen floor. With that, the expletives start to fly.

Finally, I pull my dead weight over to the kitchen counter, reach for the phone, and dial 911. At least I've got two books to get me through my recovery.

The End

Group 4   by Al Svoboda

Earthquake

Here, take these eyes. See through eyelids
Worn from fear. Flesh abraded to shreds
by evaporated order. Heaps of nature
(smashed powerful poses) like trees
planted, virgin growth. Living on
woody flesh generations past, once reaching
to the sun. Water on vertical woody rivers
flowing to leaves and buds
Drawn to the sunlight

Poems and prose living on naked words
In all their arrangements, different from
What they feed on.
Pages reaching for the reader's eye
Bound sweat of dendrites growing
Palms over water
Daises in the field
Moss on the rock
Words enough to cover them all

Words fall off the edges of desolation
Emptiness between stars measures
Loneliness among the ruined

Communication

With the announcement, an answer
Approval and argument
Books cry data, discussion
Sometimes doubt, expression and feelings
Flowing information

Interviews of language made into letters
For mailing magazines
Memories of mistakes to name
A few newspaper opinion pages
Pronouncements that protest questions
Reactions to reason

What is the request?
A secret in a sentence
A sign in a speech

Incident

Old four-cylinder econo-box

                                        car signaled a left turn
 I slowed
        It turned left
           Neat as a phlebotomist's

                                          poke
dart of a red pick-up drove right into the fresh space instantly
left

                                              by the box
                        Right where I was aiming
              Perfect timed
tailgate vanished before I could slam on the brakes
                        Surprised
                              Speechless

I stepped on the gas

                        My wife came out of her doze:
                        What's going on?
                        But the show was over

                                          Al Svoboda

ABOUT THE WRITERS

Marlene A Becker is a retired ninja who writes when she's not training horses or working for the Citrus County Health Department. She lives in the woods with a bunch of parrots, several second-hand dogs, retired chickens, and three horses. She has written and illustrated comic books, worked on cartoon shows including "Ren & Stimpy" and "Back to the Future." She is working on her second novel featuring a Catholic deacon who is called to solve mysteries with the help of some ghosts and other unusual beings.

One time newspaper feature writer and college media liaison, **Johanna M Bolton** is the author of six published novels, as well as material for various textbooks including Barron's Educational Series. She writes mysteries and sometimes science fiction. Her short stories, poetry, and essays have appeared in a number of publications , and her books have won several awards including the Royal Palm for Literature and a Quill & Scroll. Her novels – *Alien Within, The City of Three Moons, Lady and the Pirate, Heirs to the Empire*, and *Tangled Tales* are available from amazon.com.

John Boyle is from England, born in the post-war baby boom years. His schooling fell behind as a result of many long hospital stays as a child, but when he was thirteen an aunt and uncle gave him a chance to immigrate to America. When he got here he had to play an extensive game of catch-up in school. Boyle became an American on America's very first "Law Day." He claims that "becoming an American remains one of the proudest events of my life." After he received his degree from the University of South Florida, he married the most perfect woman in the world "for me," he said. "We moved to Chicago to see snow and to live in a big city. I now look back on those few short years with great fondness. An accident that left my wife in a vegetative state drove us both back to Florida and family support. Being house-bound, I built an alternative energy device called a ferromagnetic generator and began writing novels—always a lifelong desire." His non-fiction title *Psionic Generator Pattern Book*, and his novel, *Daughter of a Fallen Angel,* are available from amazon.com.

Judy G. Burford is a Canadian Snowbird who winters in Florida with her husband, Ned. This retired Special Education Teacher enjoys golf, family, friends, and her two Yorkies, when she isn't reading or working on short stories, poetry, or her current novel, *Compelling Desire to Kill.* She is a member of the Canadian Authors Association, Crime Writers of Canada, and Sisters in Crime as well as two Florida and one on-line critique groups. Connect with her on Facebook, Linked-in, Pinterest, Twitter, or at www.judyburford.net.

All of **Christine Cock's** professional life has been focused on conservation. She worked on the curatorial staffs at both the Jacksonville Museum of Arts and Sciences and in Zoo Conservation at Busch Gardens, Tampa Bay. In 1993 she returned to school and received a BA in Creative Writing from Eckerd College. Her writing has been published in Calyx, A Journal of Art and Literature, The Eckerd Review, Appaloosa, The Nature Study Magazine and more. Her poetry has been displayed at Busch Gardens and at the Florida Museum of Natural History, Gainesville, Florida.

Mary Cooper is a retired flamenco dancer who moved to Florida to raise Ibizian hounds and Siamese fighting fish. She worked as the political reporter for a major newspaper until she decided that if she had to write fiction, she could create more believable stories on her own. Sometimes she is inspired to write poetry.

Jerry Cowling is a Brooksville free-lance writer and storyteller. He has written three books, *Lincoln in the*

Basement, Sins of the Family and *Davy Crockett's Butterfly*, and a play, *What in the Dickens Happened to Scrooge?* Two CDs feature his stories, *A Storyteller's Christmas* and *Out Standing in the Field of Storytelling.* Cowling has had guest columns published in the St. Petersburg Times and short stories in Cynic Online Magazine.

Joan Donohue has a BA degree in Theatre from Barry University in Miami. She has been a resident of Brooksville for over twenty years and has seen a lot of changes. She has a husband and three grown children, and her favorite pastimes are writing and painting. She writes short stories, poetry, and essays as well as fascinating memoirs both factual and fictional.

C.J. Goldman writes novels, novellas, and features for newspapers, magazines. She has also written a cookbook as well as articles for the master gardener class she attended. You'd never believe she's the mother of three, grandmother of seven and great-grandmother of two children! Goldman was a registered nurse for twenty years working in ER, ICU and specialized in hemodialysis. She also managed her own race horse stables, training horses professionally to race in Florida and Delaware. During that time she even sold horses to Arabian Sheiks and shipped them to Dubai, Arabia. Never one for the sedentary life, Goldman likes to be active. "My husband and I rode our motorcycles and went camping in to the Smokey Mountains," she said. "We went scuba diving in Key West for lobster and Queen Conch." She currently lives in Spring Hill with the same husband, a cat, a bird, and six black laying hens. "My life passions are reading, writing, animals and gardening."

Michael Goldman retired from his two businesses, swimming pools and real estate, to write a sequel to his first book. *Vision in the Forest* is a novel about the Vikings. Other than writing, his passion is scuba diving. Goldman says: "There are many stories I want to write and am working on them now while at the same time I attend a writing group to help further my skills. Stories of the Vikings and Native Americans are my special interest."

When **Don Kafrissen** isn't writing, he builds street rods (cars) from scratch. He likes to travel and once spent a couple years driving a VW camper around Europe and across North Africa, having many adventures. After that he and his wife lived for 10 years on a 40 ft sailboat in the Caribbean. Deciding they had enough of the water, they built a house in the woods where they live with the two dogs who found them and two cats, also volumteers. Don's novels include the critically acclaimed *Brothers Beyond Blood* and a mystery, *Missing Pieces.* He is currently at work on another book about the holocaust survivors.

Sam Kafrissen is a retired schoolteacher from Boston area who coaches wrestling and writes a weekly column for a local newspaper. When he's not in Boston he writes from his Cape Cod summer home and grills great ribs! His novel is available from amazon.com.

Dennis Pupello was born in the Einstein Dome on Mars where his parents worked as engineers with the terraforming project. He returned to Earth to attend MIT for his advanced degrees, and majored in Space Dynamics and Cosmology. He attained his PhD in the double major, but never made it back to Mars. Recently retired, he lives in Florida with an English Mastiff and two Abyssinian cats. He writes satire and science fiction as well as science texts and reviews for a number of publishers.

Mary H. Sheldon is a Vermonter transplanted in Florida and she loves both places. She has written 2 plays: *The Family Tree* and *Hot Coffee and Live Bait.* She now sells mobile homes in a 55+ community while working on the next play, or maybe it's a novel, *Is it Mehetabel?* Mary will write poems, too, if necessary for survival or sanity.

In Chicago **Jill V. Svoboda** enjoyed a long career as a magazine writer and editor, a marketing and public relations specialist, and an adjunct professor of English at Northeastern Illinois University. Her novella, "*Roses and Revenge*," was published in a Chicago-based magazine, "A Great Read." She has won two awards in the annual Writers' Digest Writing Competitions, one for a memoir, "*Of Mice and a Man*," and the second for a short story, "*The Mule Kicker*." Now at home in Florida, Svoboda often dodges the hard work of writing by playing clawhammer-style banjo.

After a long career as an artist working in many media, **Al Svoboda** turned to poetry as his preferred form of expression. He has published a poetry chapbook called *Openings*, for which he also created the cover art and illustrations, and has another chapbook in process. His narrative poem "Smooth Jazz" appeared in the May 2010 issue of *Steam Ticket*, a literary journal published by the University of Wisconsin-LaCrosse. Al's poem "Tattoos and Skin" was named Best Poem at Pasco Hernando Community College's semi-annual poetry event in December, 2010, where he also was honored with the Best Presentation award. When he can find a spare moment, Al plays jazz on the piano and Irish tunes on the concertina and penny whistle. He and his wife, Jill, live across the Withlacoochee River in Sumter County.

Linda Welker first started writing in college. The business of living and pressures of time interfered with creativity. Now in retirement she has revisited her desire to write. A hundred short stories and a novel rest in her computer. She lives in the woods with her dogs, cats, and trees. You will find her work in the following anthologies: *Mosaic* by the Brooksville Writers Group; *Windows*, the East Hernando Writers Group; *Unpolished, The Voyagers,* and *Gossamer Night* from the Belle Letters Writers; and *My Wheels* by the Florida Writers Association. Her novel *Fragile Clowns* and a story collection *Sadie's Palace* can be found on Amazon.com.

Karen Ann Wilson is an award-winning author, specializing in mystery fiction and animal and nature-related non-fiction. She has published four novels (Berkley Prime Crime.) Her latest book, entitled *Wrinkles in Time*, is about bloodhounds in law enforcement. She has spoken at several writers' and fan conferences, including Sleuthfest (Florida Chapter of Mystery Writers of America) and Malice Domestic. Her novels, *Beware Sleeping Dogs, Circle of Wolves, Eight Dogs Flying,* and *Copy Cat Crimes* are available from amazon.com.

Visit The Brooksville Writers' Group at
http://idbpi.wordpress.com

International Digital Book Publishing Industries was born eighteen years ago, long before Kindle or Nook , as an effort to create a small hand-held book reader with digitized content that included fiction, nonfiction, & textbooks. We created a prototype and took the idea to publishers, booksellers, and anyone else we could think of. Everyone was enthused, so much in fact that they all came out with their own versions of the digital reader.

Undaunted, IDBPI now publishes a variety of paper as well as digital books. The company has offices in Florida, Boston, and California.

Titles include:

The Brooksville Writers' Group
MOSAIC 2014
MOSAIC 2010

Don Kafrissen
Brothers Beyond Blood
Missing Pieces
White Emeralds

Jerry Cowling
Lincoln in the Basement
Dave Crocket's Butterfly
Sins of the Father
James Brown

Sam Kafrissen
Mill Town

Cassie Malloy
Experion

Johanna M Bolton
The Alien Within
The City of Three Moons
The Lady and the Pirate
Tangled Tales
Heirs to the Empire
Headstudies

Visit us at http://idbpi.wordpress.com

www.ingramcontent.com/pod-product-compliance
Lightning Source LLC
Chambersburg PA
CBHW061554170626
46811CB00001B/194